Playing Flirty

Playing Flirty

SHAMEEZ PATEL

FOREVER
New York Boston

Forever
Hachette Book Group
1290 Avenue of the Americas, New York, NY 10104
read-forever.com
@readforeverpub

First Edition: January 2025

Forever is an imprint of Grand Central Publishing. The Forever name and logo are registered trademarks of Hachette Book Group, Inc.

The publisher is not responsible for websites (or their content) that are not owned by the publisher.

Forever books may be purchased in bulk for business, educational, or promotional use. For information, please contact your local bookseller or the Hachette Book Group Special Markets Department at special.markets@hbgusa.com.

Print book interior design by Amnet ContentSource

Library of Congress Cataloging-in-Publication Data

Names: Patel, Shameez, author.
Title: Playing flirty / Shameez Patel.
Description: First edition. | New York : Forever, 2025.
Identifiers: LCCN 2024025461 | ISBN 9781538768389 (trade paperback) | ISBN 9781538768396 (ebook)
Subjects: LCGFT: Romance fiction. | Novels.
Classification: LCC PR9369.4.P39 P57 2025 | DDC 823/.92—dc23/eng/20240614
LC record available at https://lccn.loc.gov/2024025461

ISBNs: 9781538768389 (trade paperback), 9781538768396 (ebook)

Printed in the United States of America

CCR

10 9 8 7 6 5 4 3 2 1

For Yumna & Nuhaa:
I could not have done this without you.

Round 1

If life was a game, I'd made a wrong turn.

In my constant effort to achieve everything on my Life Goals spreadsheet, I ended up taking on too much work and enrolling in a postgraduate business course that I had very little interest in.

Which is why I was sitting in my office finishing up a mind-numbingly boring report while the sunset's orange glow smeared itself across my desk.

Shaun, my office mate, wheeled over to me from his desk, his backpack zipped up and balanced on his lap. "Come to game night."

If it weren't for this report I would, and he knew that. Game night was my favorite night of the week. The only time I could forget about work, forget about my goals, and play board games. And at least half the time, I'd win.

"You're not usually this persistent," I huffed out and tucked a strand of my wavy black hair behind my ear.

An email notification popped up. I navigated to my inbox. More promotional mail.

One day I would print out all these emails and bury myself under their weight as punishment for signing up to so many newsletters.

Shaun scrutinized my laptop screen. "You're not even working," he said and shuddered. "For someone who lives her life via spreadsheets, your inbox is a nightmare."

He was right, and sorting through it was one of the items on my growing to-do list. Once something was on the list, it had to be done. That was the rule I'd set for myself.

"Organized chaos." I closed the window before spinning around and studying him. "This is the third time you're asking, and the answer hasn't changed: I have deadlines to meet."

He met my gaze, and his golden brows jumped toward each other. After years of working together and playing games every Wednesday night, I knew all his tells.

"I'll help you with your deadlines," he said. "But you need to be there tonight."

"What's happening tonight?"

He broke eye contact and pushed himself back until his chair knocked against his desk. He hopped up and ran a hand through his blond hair, tugging as he reached the ends. "Rose Marie Jones," he said.

He only used my full name when he was scolding me or about to tell me something big. I took a deep breath as I anticipated his next words. "Shaun Henry Ashdern," I replied, mimicking his tone.

He nodded, gearing up for his big confession, but then shook his head. The bright fluorescent lights of the office threw a shadow along the lines of his forehead while he fumbled his words. "I'm proposing to Neema and you're our best friend and I need you there," he rambled off.

My ears perked at his words, and a number of squeals escaped me. I barreled into him.

He steadied us and chuckled. "I take it you approve? I know you had your engagement scheduled before ours, but . . . I can't wait. I love her. I just—"

"Of course, you fool." I pushed him away, trying to think of something better to say, but there weren't words to express my joy or the strange curdling sensation in my stomach that I chose to ignore. "I'm updating my Life Goals spreadsheet anyway. That deadline has come and gone." I offered him a smile, hoping it seemed as genuine as I wanted it to be. "I am so happy for you, but I wish you'd told me sooner. I could have helped you plan something."

"I ordered flowers?" he said as though it were a question. "And I couldn't rely on you keeping this a secret. Rose, you're terrible with secrets."

I shrugged, not bothering to deny it.

"But I am relying on you for everything else," he continued. "We have an hour and a half, so let's grab all the party supplies you keep in your desk drawer and get out of this place."

Shaun wasted no time dragging me out of the office. The sea breeze from the San Diego Bay was pleasant against my skin as we stepped outside, and I hurried to match his long stride.

Within fifteen minutes, we reached his upscale apartment.

He unlocked the door and skipped into the living room. His excitement was finally overriding his nerves. He spun around at the same time my phone pinged.

"I don't trust you," he said, extending his hand palm up and wiggling his fingers.

I narrowed my eyes and clawed my phone from the depths of chaos, also known as my backpack. Neema's name flashed across my notifications. Before I could consider replying, Shaun snatched my phone. He walked into the adjacent kitchen and placed it on top of the refrigerator. His cheeky smile mimicked mine.

The click of a door opening drew my attention. William, Shaun's half brother and my number one gaming nemesis, walked out of his bedroom and settled on the gray couch like a dark cloud. He stretched out his long pajama-clad legs and leaned back before lifting a controller and resuming the game that had been paused.

"Hobbit," he said, his voice gruff and rarely used except to antagonize me.

I trudged toward him and scowled in his direction even though he wasn't looking at me. I was sure he could feel it, based on the smirk threatening at the corner of his mouth.

While I was proud of my hobbit height, and even cosplayed as a hobbit not once but twice—despite having never seen a brown-skinned hobbit on-screen—I still didn't like the way he said it, which was every single time since Shaun first introduced us.

"William." I gave him a sickeningly sweet smile before stepping in front of him and blocking his view. "Could you please remove yourself and change into your formal pajama pants?"

Teasing William was one of the games I liked to play.

"My formal pajamas?" He hit pause and met my gaze. A familiar mask settled over his almost-black eyes, making him impossible to read. "What's the occasion? Is Gandalf coming for tea?"

Teasing me was one of *his*.

I crossed my arms and made a dramatic show of rolling my eyes. "Oh, stop being so bitter because I beat you last week."

"One time." One of his dark eyebrows cocked upward. "What of the three weeks before that? Need I remind you of that time you—"

A whoosh of air escaped me before he could retell my most embarrassing loss. "Don't start with that. You're picking a fight."

"Ah, babe, I'm a lover not a fighter." He winked at me and then returned his focus to his game despite me standing right in front of the TV.

Everything William said was measured to get the biggest reaction out of me.

And it always worked.

I stomped over to my backpack and grabbed the bunting before climbing onto the other couch. "Don't call me *babe*," I snapped, irritation still burning through my veins. William had a way of getting under my skin when he wanted to. Which was often.

My foot sank in between the cushions, and I wiggled it loose.

"Where is our Perfect Patrick this evening?" William's tone dripped sarcasm from directly behind me.

He leaned close and took the end of the bunting from my outstretched fingers before sticking it against the wall. I hadn't even heard him get up.

"He'll be here," I said, hoping my boyfriend would see my text and arrive in time.

I hopped off the couch and met Shaun in the kitchen, where he was messily—and frantically—icing cupcakes.

"Could you maybe make a pot of coffee? Or tea? She prefers coffee, right?"

It was clear Shaun needed reassurance.

"You know what she likes. Stop panicking." I pushed him aside and handed him a broom. "I'll take over here. Go be useful somewhere far away from the kitchen. Sweep the balcony."

His smile reappeared, and he bounced away, resembling an eager golden retriever. There was no one more cheerful and good-natured than him.

While he was out of sight, I climbed the counter and retrieved my phone from atop the refrigerator. Glancing at it, I sighed. No reply from Patrick. I dialed his number, and it rang a few times. No answer. He couldn't miss game night tonight—he couldn't miss my best friends' engagement.

"All this setting up would go much faster if we didn't have guests standing around playing on their phones." William's deep voice reached across the living room as he packed away his controllers. "Shaun should have placed it higher."

In the time I'd looked away, he'd also managed to hang the other banner.

I shoved my phone into my pocket. "I can climb anything."

William straightened, and his mouth kicked up on one side to reveal the mischievous smirk he wore far too easily. "Good to know."

Wicked man.

I grumbled and slid off the counter, landing on the floor at the same time William stepped into the kitchen carrying an empty glass. He stopped inches away from slamming into me. I craned my neck and looked up at him. His height always took me by surprise.

William was tall—like really tall. Thor-tall, except Shaun was the blue-eyed, blond-haired brother. William's eyes were dark, nearly as dark as his black hair and long eyelashes, and probably as dark as his soul.

"Where's Sexy Stacey?" I took a few steps back and picked up the almost-empty piping bag as Shaun came back inside.

William's eyebrows drew together, and the line dividing them deepened. There was a shadow cast across his irises, but I imagined them going a shade darker.

"We broke up." He gave a half shrug, placed the glass on the counter, and turned on his heel before walking across the living room to his bedroom.

"*Aaaah*," Shaun groaned, stumbling to lean against the kitchen island. "Forgot to tell you she's been hooking up with her manager, and when William called her out, she said some nasty things to him and blamed him for a bunch of stuff that wasn't his fault."

"Maybe it was true." As soon as I said the words, I regretted them.

Shaun raised an eyebrow in warning.

William reappeared holding a pair of jeans and a T-shirt, his eyes narrowed as they always did before he said something snarky. But Shaun raised a hand, silencing him, and gestured for him to join us.

"What now?" William asked.

Shaun released a long sigh. "Since the two of you can't communicate like adults unless it's a game, tonight's game is: Play nice and don't ruin my proposal or I am going to kill you both."

William was shaking his head at the same time I'd started nodding.

Play nice. I could do that. I could win that.

"Sure." I flashed William my nicest smile.

"Yeah, that's it," Shaun said, pointing at my face. "Now you." He looked over at his brother.

William only sighed. A quick eye roll let me know I'd won this round.

Round 2

My best friend and roommate had a habit of knowing everything—which is probably why Neema arrived carrying a two-tier cake.

She placed the vanilla-frosted cake on the table and straightened to her full height, only a couple inches shorter than Shaun. The dark brown skin of her legs contrasted beautifully with the hem of her yellow summer dress. Her short, black, curly hair bounced around her smiling face.

The second she reached me, she leaned in for a hug and whispered, "I'm going to say yes."

"Uh, duh," I whispered back.

I peeked over her shoulder at Shaun, who'd been scratching his blond hair every few seconds—a nervous tic I'd noticed during meetings. The poor man would be bald on one side by his midthirties.

"Wanted you to be the first one to know." She let go of me and threw herself into her soon-to-be fiancé's arms.

I pressed my lips together tightly to keep from grinning—until William interrupted it.

"She's going to say no," he whispered.

How did he get next to me without making any sound? Not a single creak. Maybe niceness was what weighed regular people down.

I closed my eyes—my patience-o-meter for William's nonsense had reached capacity. "You know they're happy. Why are you being such a wet blanket?"

"Love is temporary. Why would anyone pretend otherwise?"

I looked up at him, ready to hit him or curse, but he stared down at me with his shoulders slumped and his gaze dropping from mine to his feet. The smirk that usually resided on his mouth was nowhere to be seen.

Putting my daggers away, I managed a gentle, "Sorry about Stace."

He shrugged and ran his hands over his face while exhaling. "It's okay. Wasn't serious."

"Do I get a point for being nice?" I teased, and when his dimple reappeared, I counted it as a victory.

"Half a point, maybe."

He followed me to the door as Claire and Lincoln—a best-friend duo Neema and I had met during our university days—arrived.

Lincoln walked inside carrying two bags that I knew were filled with sweetmeats made especially for me by his mother. I could already taste my favorite cardamom-spiced shortbread cookie. As he passed me, he touched my shoulder gently in greeting, which was miles more than he used to do when we first met.

Unlike Claire, who I'd hit it off with within seconds of meeting. She stumbled in and wrapped her arms around me.

"A hug?" I exclaimed.

"Don't get used to it. I'm just excited." She released me, and her grin matched mine.

The sharp sound of Shaun's whistle officially started game night.

"Let's play," he said, swallowing hard and plastering a smile on his reddened face.

Each week, one of us picked a game. Then we'd signal the start of game night with our own personalized call. Shaun used a whistle. Neema whistled too, but used her fingers in her mouth, like an angry sports coach. Claire used one of her kid's old squeaky toys, and Lincoln's call was the *Super Mario Bros.* theme song.

I started every gaming session by beatboxing the first few seconds of the *Star Wars* opening song, much to everyone's displeasure.

William joined us most of the time but pretended he wasn't part of our group. He never picked a game or had a call, but I imagined he'd initialize game night by sighing about it.

We chose our tokens while Shaun set up the Monopoly board. He offered me a wink, knowing the game was one of my favorites. It took patience and planning—two of my strengths. Regardless of the theme or version, the rules were the same, and there were no surprises.

We settled in as if it were any other night with laughter filling the air.

I hopped up to my knees and extended my palm as William landed on one of my properties. "Money, please," I said to him with a wiggle of my eyebrows.

"It doesn't reflect well on you that you're good at this capitalism-inspired game," he grumbled and handed over his colorful paper money.

Shaun cleared his throat, interrupting the comeback I had lingering on my tongue. He cleared his throat again, louder now, until everyone turned their attention to him. If I hadn't known what was about to happen, I would have thought he was sick.

"Neema." Shaun scratched the side of his head again. "This is the . . . uhm . . . *Lord of the Rings*–themed Monopoly. *Lord of the Rings*. Or one ring. Like the one precious ring, like rings are important." Shaun's blue eyes darted back and forth between Neema and his own hands.

Up, down, up, down—watching the speed of his moving pupils made me dizzy.

"I love you," Neema said, stroking his bicep. "Come on, ask me. I've prepared my best way to say yes, and it doesn't involve discussing Gollum."

"Bit of a mean way to refer to Rose," William chimed in from across the board.

I bit down on my lip, barely suppressing the giggle trying to escape. He knew as well as anyone that I appreciated a good *Lord of the Rings* reference, but I wouldn't give him the satisfaction or ruin this moment for my two best friends.

Shaun hobbled down onto one knee in front of Neema and gulped. "Will you marry me?"

A beautiful smile spread across Neema's face before she leaned down and kissed him on the mouth. She slid off the couch and into his arms before whispering something in his ear that only he could hear.

Shaun's face burst into a smile.

The warmth of joy spread across every part of me. Pulling out my phone to take a photo of them, I couldn't help noticing Patrick hadn't replied to my text. He hadn't even read it. My chest tightened but I ignored it. My best friends were getting married, and that's all that mattered.

With shaking hands, Shaun slipped the princess-cut diamond onto Neema's slender finger. She turned to me, showing it off, and I pulled her in for a hug. Claire joined us, and I figured we had thirty to forty seconds before the three of us became blubbering messes. It didn't take much to make us cry, and when one of us cried, we all did.

After two generous slices of cake, I joined Shaun and Neema on the balcony and congratulated them once more.

"We couldn't have done it without you," Neema said, squeezing my arm. "Thank you."

My eyes prickled with tears.

"Patrick working late?" she asked, nudging her shoulder against mine.

I nodded.

She sighed in the way she did whenever Patrick didn't show up. "Do you want me to give you a ride home? I'd give you my car, but I have an early morning meeting I have to get to."

Neema and I usually drove home together, or Patrick would pick me up. But with Shaun's arm curled around her waist and his eyes glistening with adoration, I couldn't bear to pull her away from him.

"No." I blew out a sigh. "You stay. I'll take the bus or call a taxi. I'm a big girl."

"Based on the facts we are presented with," William said, walking onto the balcony and lifting his hand high, then lowering it until it was about level with the top of my head, "that is not true."

I shot him a death stare.

His brows popped up before he ran a hand through his dark, tousled hair. Permanent bedhead that was impossible to tame. "I could give you a ride. I'm on my way out," he said.

"Ten points to William!" Shaun cheered.

Neema giggled in his grip.

I groaned but William only grinned, exposing his deep dimple. "Come on, Rose, I don't have all night."

My name sounded foreign on his tongue, startling me. Grabbing my things, I gave Shaun and Neema one last hug and followed William downstairs to the parking garage. I looked for the latest GTI in crisp white and assumed it was his.

He climbed in and opened the passenger door from the inside. Then he stared at me while I reached for my seat belt like I was the strangest thing in existence. Not unusual for him.

"What?" I bit out, struggling with the belt.

"Why didn't you take your backpack off?"

Admittedly, I'd forgotten because I was thinking about how we'd barely ever been alone together. But now it was too late, and I had to commit to keeping the backpack on. I turned my attention to the problematic latch and struggled for a few seconds. It wasn't clicking in.

Leaning over, he took the buckle from me and snapped it into place. His pine and lavender scent washed over me before he pulled away.

"Thanks," I said with an internal curse. Bested by a seat belt in front of my nemesis.

He rubbed the back of his neck and blew out a short breath before starting the car. It came alive with a deep rumble that shook my bones. Pulling out of the garage, he took the corner faster than I'd anticipated, leaving part of my insides somewhere before the bend.

"This isn't *Need for Speed*!"

A breathy laugh escaped him, but his hands stayed flexed around the steering wheel and his eyes fixed on the road.

"Where are you off to?" I asked to fill the silence.

"Nowhere interesting," he replied, which was probably code for meeting a girl.

In all the time I'd known William, he was rarely short of a date.

With that thought, I took out my phone and scrolled to Patrick's name. There I found a text with a promise of dinner *and* a movie on Friday night. I gnawed on my lip, wanting to curb my enthusiasm.

William glanced over, his eyes falling on my lit-up phone. Disdain returned to his features, and he turned on the radio, surrounding us with smooth classic rock. The unread email notifications called for my attention, and I sifted through them with one subject heading standing out from all the rest:

```
Calling All Board Game Creators: Original
Board Game Submissions Now Open
```

My heart zoomed. My finger hovered over the bolded text, but before my thoughts could run to the dream hidden in the corner of my mind, the car stopped.

"We're here," William said.

Pulled out of my daze, I glanced down at the email and exited the app. *No way. I can't think about that.*

William hit the unlock button. "Out, out, out, loser. I've got places to be."

I released the seat belt—successfully—and glared at him. "Loser? I won at Monopoly."

"And I won at"—he curled his fingers into air quotes—"'Playing Nice.'"

A chuckle teased, and I stepped out of the car into the cold air. "That's not a real game."

"Oh, don't be a sore loser," he said with a wink.

"I'll win next time," I said and closed the door before he could reply.

But the window slid down.

Crossing my arms, I waited for whatever it was he wanted to say.

William leaned over, making eye contact with me before his signature smirk returned. "Game on."

Round 3

Dinner and a movie was revised to just dinner. Then, due to a marketing-related emergency—whatever that meant—our entire date was reduced to "I'll bring dessert. Love you."

In Patrick's defense, he arrived with backup in the form of chocolate chip cookies. He knew the way to my heart was through chocolate and sugar, and he got the expensive, buttery ones that melted on my tongue.

"How were your meetings?" I asked, popping an entire cookie into my mouth.

The second the words left my lips, Patrick launched into describing each moment in excruciating detail, as if leading up to the climax of his favorite movie.

"They loved the pitch. I could have stopped mid-presentation and we'd still have won the contract." His familiar green eyes lit up in a way they only did when he spoke about work. But, stopping suddenly, his cheeks reddened, and he cut himself off—something he did frequently when he was too excited. "How was your day? I'm sorry I missed the proposal and messed up our date again."

Sighing, he twirled his fingers through my long black hair.

"No, tell me more about the meeting. Marketing sounds more exciting than investment plans."

"Ah, babe, it is." He leaned back onto the couch and draped an arm around me.

I inhaled his fresh minty scent and blew out a quiet breath. "Sometimes I think it's time to switch careers, but what would I switch to? I'm an investment analyst, that's all I know. I'd just go and do it elsewhere." Anxiety and despondency settled in my stomach, and I reached for another cookie to replace that feeling with sugar.

"What are you passionate about? Except board games. Do not say board games."

And now that was all I could think about.

"There's actually a competition happening at the moment, and the winning game will be produced into an actual board game that gets sold in stores and played by real people everywhere." I was aware of my voice increasing in pitch, but I couldn't help it. "There's a decent cash prize too and—"

"Be serious." He shook his head with a small smile.

His tone pinched at my chest and clipped my sentence.

"You used to like board games," I reminded him.

"Yeah, but we were students. Everyone was playing Risk and Explosive Kittens and whatever."

Exploding Kittens. I didn't bother correcting him.

He lifted my chin and met my gaze. His eyes held an expression that said, *Please don't turn this into a thing*.

"Where do you picture yourself five years from now?" he asked.

Now, that was a question I had an answer to. I slipped out of his grasp and grabbed my laptop.

"Oh, here it comes." He laughed, rubbing his hands along his beige chinos. "Rose Marie Jones's infamous Life Goals spreadsheet."

I navigated to the spreadsheet and opened the tab for my five-year projection. "Oh." I breathed out a heavy sigh before clearing my throat. "I'd have finished this stupid MBA, and that would lead to the department head promotion—so that's cool, I suppose. Good news is, I'd already be married and have a kid. Or I'd be pregnant. I left some wiggle room."

A flush crept across my cheeks at having made these decisions without him. "And there's a whole bunch of other stuff, but you don't wanna know." I slammed my laptop shut before he could see that my Life Goals had me listed as "engaged" a few months ago—before Shaun and Neema.

Perhaps he was planning to propose or perhaps business proposals were the only ones on his mind.

"How about you?" I asked.

"I'd like to be the COO by then," he said without hesitating, as if the words had been sitting on the tip of his tongue. Like me, he had it all planned out.

Patrick leaned back, his eyelids drooping. I closed my own eyes, picturing my future. Department head at M&G Group. Married to Patrick. Kid on the way. We'd have a house, and we'd stay in that house and build a home. It wasn't a bad future. It was better than the unknown—or what I'd had.

His eyes fluttered open. "If I want to reach that goal, I better get going." Standing, he straightened his shirt before popping his phone and wallet into his pocket.

"You can stay the night. There's space on my bed." I rolled out my aching neck and pointed at my bedroom.

"In between the piles of board games and books?" He offered me half a smile. "I'm exhausted. I need a proper rest before tomorrow."

"Golf with the boys?" I walked to the door and opened it.

"It's like your board games, except I network while doing it."

I searched for an appropriate response, but before I could think of anything, he kissed me on the top of my head.

"See you soon, babe," he said as he turned and left me standing in the doorway.

"Well, good luck," I whispered to his back.

It occurred to me that I hadn't told him I loved him. But I was frustrated—frustrated that I hated my job, frustrated that I had already paid the full fees for a degree program I was not enjoying that would further push me toward a corporate lifestyle, and ... well ... I was frustrated with him too. But I didn't like to think about that. Mostly, I was frustrated that, even with all this frustration, I was too scared to change any of it.

Walking back to my bedroom, I did what any mature adult would do: I video-called my mom. She answered on the first ring. I loved that about her.

"Hi, Rosie."

Her smiling face melted away my unease. Most people told me I resembled my mom—same full lips, light brown eyes, and pitch-black hair and what my mom called her "winter skin tone"—but I had my dad's straight nose.

"Mom." I beamed, enjoying the weight lifting from my chest. I had changed into my ugliest, most comfortable pajamas since no one would see them anyway. "How are you? Where are you?"

"Baby, we are in the most beautiful place in the world—Grand Baie in Mauritius. This morning, I fancied myself a taste of coconut and a man climbed the tree and hacked one off for me." She scrambled around, searching for something.

Finding her glasses, she slid them onto her face. I grinned at the missing arm, but it didn't seem to bother her. My parents were unconventional, for lack of a better term. Apparently, I was conceived during their honeymoon next to the

Victoria Falls. My parents copulated beside this landmark because they were overwhelmed with its beauty. Thankfully, my dad had the foresight to put up their tent before they went sightseeing.

And I've always wished she didn't feel the need to tell me that.

I crawled onto the corner of my bed. "That sounds amazing. How's Dad enjoying it?"

"He loves it. I think we may never leave. He's found his calling and joined a group of local fishermen." Her Indian accent made an appearance. It had mostly faded by the time I was a kid. My grandmother blamed it on spending too much time with "the whites" (i.e., my father, whom she did not approve of).

"Oh, please don't say that. You have to come back eventually. It's been six months without a visit." I let out a nervous laugh and looked away. I didn't want her to know that I still needed them.

"Why don't you come to us? You've been working long enough to have some savings for a bit of adventure. You used to love it. I have proof!"

My mother showed family photographs to anyone willing to look at them. Most of them were of me as a baby—on trains and planes and sleeping while strapped to my mother's back, a trick she learned in South Africa.

The photos became fewer as traveling became more expensive and I started costing a full ticket. My dad started flipping houses, and my mother did whatever she felt like doing— everything from knitting hats for homeless people to hosting "baked bake sales." (I learned my lesson the hard way with those as I had my first and last unsober experience. Surprisingly, it was a hit among the housewives.)

Once they had enough money, I was pulled from school for a monthlong adventure and then pushed back into whichever school would accept me afterward.

I blew out a long breath. "I don't know, Mom. I spent most of my savings on my MBA fees, and my next goal is to buy my own car."

"Oh, you and those Life Goals. Baby, let loose a little bit. How's Patrick? We haven't seen him in a while."

"How could you? You haven't been home in six months."

Mom cackled. "Do you still love him, Rosie?"

She asked this every time, and every time I nodded automatically before she finished the question.

"It's the least you can do for yourself," she continued. "Since you've decided to hate your job for the foreseeable future, you need to love the person you spend the rest of your time with. Talking about love, look who's arrived, smelling like fish and covered in sand!"

The camera swung around the room, and Dad's face filled the screen. His almost-white eyebrows popped up. "Hey, baby girl. How's your board game coming along? Can we buy it yet?"

My parents sat side by side, looking at me with wide eyes and even wider smiles as they awaited the news of my success based on absolutely nothing.

"Next question," I said, my eyes darting to where my Board-Game-in-Progress sat waiting for me.

"Still dating Shaun?" he asked, scratching his gray beard.

"Patrick, Dad. Shaun is my colleague. He's dating Neema. Remember? Actually, they're engaged!" A fresh wave of joy flooded over me.

My mom squealed. "Oh, wonderful. They're a lovely couple. So much passion in their eyes when they look at each other."

She was interrupted by my dad staring at her with their noses almost touching.

"Can you see the passion in my eyes, love?" he finally asked.

My mom howled with laughter and pulled him closer for a kiss. I truly wished the camera was positioned farther away.

"Gosh, get a room!" I begged.

"All right, my little hobbit. I think we have to go get that room. Can't delay matters of the heart. Chat soon. Love you forever and wherever," she called out.

The call ended, and I was thankful that this time she remembered to end it before dealing with "matters of the heart."

Perhaps it was the conversation with my parents, but my fingers found their way to the edge of my board game's box as I thought back to when I was eighteen years old and attended San Diego Comic-Con for the first time.

I had arrived in my best homemade hobbit costume. My hair was cropped short and naturally curly, much like Frodo's, but pitch-black. My little fangirl heart could not handle being around anime characters and superheroes, and neither could my phone's battery. It died before midafternoon, and I ended up sitting in the parking lot by myself, in costume, waiting for my mom to come and find me.

Aside from the general activities, I was there for two reasons. One, to find the board-gamers, and two, to introduce my board game to them.

The gaming area was much less crowded than the rest of the convention. Everyone was either playing or discussing games, and for the first time in my life, I wished I could break myself into multiple pieces and take part in everything.

Standing on the sidelines, I watched as a Gandalf annihilated a Hulk at a Yu-Gi-Oh! duel. I was frozen in place with my own deck of cards burning a hole through my backpack. I wouldn't have dared challenge Gandalf; maybe the fourteen-year-old Percy Jackson was more on my level.

When Gandalf won the next round, an accidental cheer escaped me. His gaze shot upward, and I burst into a fit of giggles—which he joined in.

"Thanks for being my very own hobbit cheerleader," he said, approaching me during an intermission.

I chuckled and looked up at him for what felt like miles. "Well, I mean, I'm Frodo, so it made sense."

He smiled, and my insides fluttered. Even with the beard and wig, he was very cute, and I wished I was wearing something that didn't involve covering my feet in fake hair.

We spent the next few hours discussing our favorite games, and I mustered up the courage to show him my board game. He listened to the rules, and as it was my first time explaining it to someone that wasn't my mom or dad, I discovered all the loopholes.

"While these rules don't entirely make sense, I'm ready to play," he announced with a grin far too cheeky for Gandalf.

"But it doesn't make sense," I said, embarrassed for wasting his time by thinking I had something. "I'm sorry. We don't have to play it. We can play—"

"Can I kiss you?" he said, interrupting me. The exposed parts of his cheeks flushed before he snapped his mouth shut.

I could still remember his quick, short breaths and the way I'd nodded. Before I could find any words, he leaned forward and pressed his mouth against mine. I had been kissed before, but no one had ever done it like that. His lips were soft, and I was unbothered by his long gray synthetic beard rubbing against my chin—I was too focused on how electricity seemed to be flowing through my body. The mere memory of that kiss made my heartbeat erratic.

He pulled away and smiled. "Let's try the game. I already know half the rules."

He said it so casually—as if I wouldn't be obsessing about that kiss for the rest of the day. But then he started playing the game—my game—and it evolved in each round.

I jumped out of my mind and lifted the lid of the box to stare at this version of the Board-Game-in-Progress—born through our playing and his suggestions. And with college and work, it was still exactly as it was back then.

What could have been, if I'd been braver—if I'd approached the group of gamers and asked them to play my game?

I didn't need the distraction or the reminder. There were deadlines I needed to meet, and a less-than-slim chance I'd win that competition, anyway.

I shoved the box underneath my desk.

Opening my laptop, I started on my assignment. In six months, I'd get my MBA and probably get promoted—which meant more money and more stability, both of which I wanted.

Right?

Second-guessing myself was becoming tiring.

Round 4

After a few sleepless nights and a mostly completed assignment, the absolute last thing I wanted was to attend this week's strategy meeting.

My boss, Jeffrey Markham, the M of M&G, stopped me after the meeting and smiled—the kind of smile that made the food in my stomach want to revisit my mouth.

"Could we have a quick chat in my office?"

I nodded, running through all the reasons he could possibly need to talk to me alone.

Shaun met my gaze, his eyebrows drawn together much like mine were, as I followed Mr. Markham.

A large wooden desk, about three times the size of mine, sat in the center of the room.

"So," Mr. Markham said and gestured to the two red velvet chairs, "you're a really great worker, and I am glad to see you on our team. You're not just a diversity hire."

I smiled awkwardly, very awkwardly, while taking my seat. "Uh, thank you?"

He turned on his coffee machine and then faced me, leaning forward onto the elbows of his gray jacket, which matched his pressed gray pants. He was above average in height and width, with broad shoulders and a puffed-out chest. "The thing is, you are incredibly distracting." He stared at my chest, and unease settled in my belly.

I was relieved I had thrown a scarf around my neck that morning to hide the somewhat revealing neckline of my blouse.

"Excuse me?" My heart pounded louder than the purr of his coffee machine.

His lingering gaze snapped up. "I mean, chatty. You're incredibly chatty, and it's distracting. I'm going to need you to rein it in."

I rubbed my clammy palms against my skirt and cleared my throat with the intention of telling him I didn't appreciate his comments. Or telling him I worked more than anyone else in this office. I should have pointed out I was the only one who had almost finished the degree they encouraged us to do. I should have mentioned I arrived in the dark and left hours after it turned dark once again. I should have said all of this, but instead I nodded, ignoring the thickness in my throat.

"I understand," I said. "Is that all?"

He sat back, and the leather squeaked underneath him. "You're an attractive young woman. If you keep your head down and work hard, there's a promotion in your future."

I was certain my awkward smile had turned into a grimace. I had lost the ability to talk and continued nodding, much to my dismay, until eventually the conversation ended.

When I left his office, I went straight to my desk. My stomach still roiled as I tried to make sense of what'd happened.

Shaun rolled his chair toward me. "What was that about?"

Without responding, I kicked his chair, sending him wheeling back to his desk.

I opened the office messaging service.

Rose Jones: Got a warning for being too
chatty.

Shaun Ashdern: What do you mean?

Rose Jones: What do you mean what do I
mean? He said I was too chatty and I was
distracting . . . So, stop talking to me.
YOU never get into any trouble. Golden boy.

Shaun Ashdern: Ouch.

Shaun Ashdern: But fair.

Shaun Ashdern: Coming to game night?

Rose Jones: It's my turn. I'd never miss it.

Shaun Ashdern: What are we playing?

Rose Jones: Do some work before I get
blamed for distracting you.

Shaun Ashdern: Fine.

When I arrived at Shaun's place, I was—as usual—greeted by
William, by not being greeted at all.

Apparently, gaining social skills on *The Sims* was more
important than in real life. I grabbed a chair and sat next to him.

He looked at me with a deep frown and adjusted the glasses
he rarely wore. "Pippin."

I ignored that, eager to win this round of Playing Nice
while finding a way to irritate him at the same time. "What's
your Sim's name?"

"Go away." He nudged me with his elbow.

I tried to make eye contact, which was how I gauged how
much longer I could tease him before he exploded. "What's
your Sim's wife's name?" I pointed at *The Sims* lady walking
around the house he'd built.

He ignored me.

I lowered my finger toward the power button. "Oh, what does this button do?"

He broke his focus and took off his spectacles. "Rose, I'm working."

Oops. His gaze was darker than I'd expected, and he used my real name.

Retreat. Retreat.

I stepped away from his computer. "You have a really cool job."

The easiest way to decompress William was by talking to him about the games he designed and reviewed for a living. It was every geeky teenager's dream.

"What do you want?" he asked, slipping the spectacles back on and turning his focus back to his game. "Are you still trying to win Shaun's stupid game?"

"No," I lied.

He smiled at his screen, his dimple coming out to play. He didn't buy that at all.

"Claire and Lincoln aren't coming. We need a fourth player for the ultimate gaming experience." I widened my eyes in what I hoped would be an irresistible manner, although I can't say I had a high success rate.

He pressed his pouty lips together and rolled his eyes. "Fine." His gaze slipped to my chest where my scarf had shifted, but it zapped back to his screen a microsecond later. He blew out a short breath. "Hold off on beatboxing for another twenty minutes or so."

Then Shaun pulled me away while bitching about our boss until Neema arrived with Bananagrams.

William trudged over and sat down on the large gray couch. He leaned back, stretching out his long legs in his sweatpants. "Let's get this over with," he said. "I'm about to teach Rose a lesson."

"You wish," I snapped, spreading out the lettered tiles, face down.

As soon as the game started, I flipped my tiles, and my brain went into overdrive, connecting the letters. Word games were my strength, and the only person who ever challenged me was William.

But William was distracted by the silly words Shaun made, and I claimed victory.

"Rematch," William said, taking all the tiles and flipping them face down.

Of course he'd want a rematch. And I'd win again. Except this time William was focused, and I was beginning to learn that, when William focused, there was little that could stand in his way. It shouldn't have come as a surprise when he won.

I groaned and double-checked his words to make sure he hadn't cheated. Damn him. He hadn't.

I challenged him to another match.

Which I shouldn't have.

After winning the last round, the dimple in his left cheek deepened at the corner of a smug grin. He walked back to his laptop. "Maybe next time you won't ask me to join, and you'll have a higher chance at winning."

So annoying.

Ignoring him, I made my way to the kitchen and turned on the kettle, which William had specifically bought after he'd heard me complain about the lack thereof one too many times. The gurgling noise of boiling water blocked out Patrick's entrance and his clipped footsteps. I looked up as he set a brown paper bag on the kitchen island between us.

"Hey, babe." He took out a pack of caramel popcorn and tossed it at Neema. "It's been a long day."

For Patrick, a long day was twelve hours or more at the office. Yet somehow, every light brown strand of hair was in place, and there wasn't a single crease in his black shirt. My days looked much different. After two hours in the office, I had usually managed to lose a hair tie and an earring, and accidentally sipped someone else's coffee.

"Hey, you," I replied.

He removed a maple syrup pie, and Shaun swiped it before it even hit the counter.

"And for you." He handed me half a dozen chocolate croissants.

Apparently, forgiveness had a price. And it was half a dozen chocolate croissants.

He leaned across the counter and kissed my cheek. "I missed you, babe, but I won't be staying long. I have—"

"Work," I interrupted, harsher than I intended. "I figured."

His leaf-green eyes were filled with apologies I was tired of hearing, and he was tired of making. "I need to talk to you about something."

My breath hitched in the second that passed.

"My dad is promoting me to national sales manager." He walked around the kitchen island toward me.

"That's amazing!"

His frown lines deepened.

I narrowed my eyes. "You're saying something good, but your face is saying something else."

"It means I have to leave town every now and again and take care of clients around the country." The corners of his mouth resisted the urge to break into a smile.

I was consumed by the familiar pang of guilt for making him hate how much he loved his job. Slapping on a smile, I gave him what I hoped were what Neema called *heart eyes*. "We should celebrate."

"We will, babe. We will when I get back. I found out today, but I have to fly off tomorrow morning. I'll be gone for about five or six days, one week max." He paused, waiting for my reaction.

"That's really exciting." I almost choked out the words. "Can't wait to hear all about it."

His face relaxed into a comfortable smile. "I should get home. I still have to practice my presentation a couple times before tomorrow's meeting." He took a pained breath and tried not to smile at the mention of his presentation. "I'm sorry."

"It's okay." Hoping to reassure him, I stood on tiptoes and kissed him on his lips—something he often shied away from in public.

His body stiffened, and not in a good way. He pulled away, his widened eyes searching the room to see if anyone had noticed my unacceptable public display of affection, but Shaun and Neema were watching TV and William's focus hadn't veered from his game.

Quickly, he made his escape, as if to avoid another surprise kiss.

As soon as I closed the door behind him, William turned toward me, a curve playing on his lips. "You must be a terrible kisser."

"Oh, wouldn't you like to know."

His smile fell, and for a second, another expression crossed his face. Before I could place the look, he glanced back at his screen and cursed out loud.

Again. And again. And again. He had been attacked by a screaming witch.

I would be lying if I said I didn't enjoy that.

Round 5

For the next few days, I third-wheeled Shaun and Neema more than usual to avoid my incessant overthinking. However, watching them adore each other was counterproductive, fueling the thoughts I'd been denying.

And when I wasn't thinking about Patrick, I was thinking about my Board-Game-in-Progress.

Which wasn't necessarily a good thing either.

I rubbed the growing ache between my brows.

"How are you holding up?" Neema asked, taking the other end of the couch and curling her legs underneath her.

"It's only a week." I shrugged, breaking eye contact.

"I miss Neema after a day." Shaun walked by and patted my head as if I were a dog. "Remember when I went on that hike and you had to deal with her?" He sat on the other couch and turned on the TV.

"Oh, I'll never forget." I laughed. "For three weeks, she practically followed me into the bathroom." It was the summer when Neema bought us matching vibrators. I returned mine—in the packaging. "You were so horny, it was ridiculous!"

Neema stretched out her leg and poked me with her toe. "Three weeks of no sex is nothing to joke about."

I chuckled, though I wasn't sure she was joking. Was three weeks really that long? I had no idea what was normal because I'd only ever been with Patrick. Before I could stop myself, I asked, "What's the longest you've gone without . . ." I hesitated and glanced toward William and Shaun.

William was in his corner and was scolding into his headset with a game of *DoTA* across his screen. And Shaun was scrolling through his drum and bass collection.

" . . . without being intimate?" I whispered the last words. My cheeks flushed at saying it out loud.

Neema, my sex-positive best friend, teased me. "Dear girl, I am a virgin flower, only to be plucked on the eve that I have been wed."

Shaun spun toward us. "What now?"

"Never mind. I hate both of you." I dropped my heated face into my hands.

"It was those three weeks," Neema said, looking at Shaun.

He nodded and pinched his mouth up on one end. "So, how long's it been?"

I covered my face and curled over the cushion I held, embarrassed about discussing it and embarrassed at my answer.

"Out with it. A month? Six months? Are you still a virgin?" Neema gasped. "Have you been lying about sex all this time? I could believe it. No one who is having sex hides behind their hands while talking about it." She pried my fingers away from my eyes.

"Three months," I blurted louder than intended. "And it will be three months and one week by the time he gets back."

William, who'd finished his game without my noticing, spun around in his chair and faced us. As he crossed his arms over his wide chest, his lips tipped up in an amused smile. "So Perfect Patrick isn't that perfect after all."

"No one invited you into this conversation, William," I snapped, wanting the couch to swallow me. I'd live inside it with the lost coins and other things that didn't have a place in the world.

Dramatic? Maybe a little.

He ignored me. "But what about hand stuff . . . or foot stuff, if you're into that—no judgment."

His smug grin and deep dimple gnawed at my insides. I threw the cushion at him and with the familiar urge to one-up him said, "You're not even in a relationship."

He caught it and smiled wider. "I'm actually off to pick up my date."

He stood and grabbed his keys, spinning the ring around his middle finger. Until this point, I hadn't noticed that, instead of his usual oversized hoodie and pajama pants, he wore black jeans with a fitted T-shirt that—and here's the shocker—was ironed. His tan, sculpted arms took me by surprise.

Noticing my eyes on his biceps, he flexed. He ran a hand through his black hair, but it did nothing in the way of taming it.

"Poor woman," I sniped.

"Oh, don't pity her. She'll be having a really, really good night."

I scrunched my face in disgust, and he replied with a cocky wink before leaving.

He was the most insufferable person who had ever existed.

The next game night took forever to come around. It was Claire's turn, and she chose one of my favorites: Balderdash.

Apparently, William's date had bailed on him so we had the pleasure of having him rain on our parade by "reluctantly" joining our game. One day he'd admit he enjoyed it, but today was not that day.

"What is the definition of the word 'spifflicated'?" Lincoln asked, scratching the dark stubble on his cheek while he waited for us to write down our made-up definitions.

Lincoln was a genius, and playing this game with him was always ultraembarrassing because, nine times out of ten, he knew the actual answer.

We scribbled our meanings, and something weird in my peripheral vision caught my attention—William's dimple was on show. He was smiling, and I couldn't figure out why.

I slid my sheet toward Lincoln. He stuck it into the pile and handed me one of his mother's homemade nankhatai cookies before shuffling the answer sheets.

Pushing his glasses up his straight nose, his expression in a perfect poker face, Lincoln read the first card. "Spifflicated: When you're caught in the act of pretending to be wealthier than you actually are."

That was my answer. And I was proud of it.

He continued. "Spifflicated: Being drunk."

Probably Shaun's.

Lincoln pulled the next paper and pressed his lips together. The corners of his mouth twitched as he held back an obvious grin. "Spifflicated: When a woman is deprived of satisfaction and becomes crankier than usual."

If looks could kill, William and anyone in his immediate proximity would explode into smithereens. Since that conversation, William had teased me about my love life, or the lack thereof, whenever he found an opening. It didn't help that I knew he had a line of women always waiting on him.

Shaun gave William a shake of his head.

Claire narrowed her eyes at him. "Why are you like this?"

I'd told Claire about the conversation she'd missed, and sadly, she could relate. She'd reassured me that plenty of people go through dry spells—even after marriage.

"Fine, fine, fine." William raised his hands in surrender.

But I only huffed in his direction.

For the rest of the game he managed to identify my answers and send all his points my way. And I think he did it on purpose.

I didn't care. I took the win, and as soon as the game ended, I escaped to their large balcony, hoping the familiar city lights could put me at ease. It was weird having a place be familiar after the upbringing I'd had, but San Diego had wiggled itself into my heart after just one Comic-Con.

Behind me, the door opened, and William's footsteps approached. I didn't need to confirm it was him—his pine and lavender scent reached me before he did.

"You still mad about the joke?" he asked, fidgeting with the strings of his gray joggers. "I didn't mean to upset you."

"Don't you have somewhere to be? On one of your dates?"

"Jealous?"

I glanced upward to catch his smirk. His eyes were light. He wanted to *play*. Everything was a game with him. Everything was a joke.

"I'm not in the mood, William. Go away."

"Go where? I live here." He leaned his hip on the balcony rail.

I pinched the bridge of my nose. "Fine. I'll go."

He jumped in front of me. "Don't go. I'm sorry." His eyes searched for mine, but I avoided his gaze. "Come on, admit it. You're crankier than usual. You don't laugh at any of my jokes anymore."

"Maybe it's because you're not funny."

"Hobbit," he said, and I knew he was trying to get my attention. "I'm really sorry. I didn't think it would actually upset you. We do this thing, and . . . I . . . " He hesitated, scrunching up his face. "I took it too far, and I won't do it again."

He wasn't wrong. I'd have teased him had the roles been reversed. William and I were usually doing one of two things, making fun of each other or having fun together. Although we'd never admit the latter.

I spun toward the railing once more and wrapped my hands around the cold metal. "Hobbits aren't very sexy." I breathed out, my eyes prickling.

"What?" he asked, his voice thick and distorted as if he needed to clear a bug from his windpipe.

I wasn't mad at him. I was just . . .

"Nothing." I brushed off the thought before I could dissect my withering self-esteem with William Ashdern. Making my way to the door once more, I paused and retreated into the safety of the game I knew how to play with him. "Perhaps when Perfect Patrick returns, I'll start feeling *Merry* again."

I stepped into the apartment and waited for his laugh—a hobbit reference should do the trick. But a quick glance over my shoulder showed me nothing but frown lines where I expected his ridiculous smile.

That night, I read and reread my assignment, typed a couple of paragraphs, read it once more, opened my browser, got distracted, checked my emails, added items to my wish list, closed the browser, and read my assignment—again. Rinse and repeat to infinity and beyond until my vision was blurry.

My chair rolled backward, and a loud crack echoed through the air. My heart froze—without looking, I knew. I knew what I'd crushed, and exactly what I'd find shattered on the floor.

A glance down proved me right, as sand from the Board-Game-in-Progress sunk into the soft carpet. Even though I hadn't worked on it in years, I dropped to my knees hoping I could salvage it. It was only one piece—the timer, easily replaceable, but my mom and I had made it together. Now all the broken bits of me were scattered all over the rug.

Cutting my finger on the sharp glass, I snapped upward. The bright red blood made my head spin. I hurried to the bathroom and rinsed my finger under cold water before assessing the damage. A Band-Aid should do the trick. I walked into the lounge where Shaun and Neema were going through her wedding Pinterest board. Catching a look at my hand, Neema stopped me and investigated.

"So, what time are you seeing Patrick tomorrow?" She studied the cut and then walked over to the kitchen where we kept the first-aid kit.

"Uhm, I don't know." I shrugged. "He said he'd let me know."

She noted the lack of enthusiasm in my voice with a deep inhale. But was it worth being excited? Would Patrick come over or go straight to work?

Neema returned and wrapped up my finger. "I know!" She clapped her hands together, her eyes wide with mischief. "Seduce him! You've been together for years. Maybe it's time to spice things up."

"Seduction? Have you met me?" I gestured to the Chewbacca onesie I wore. "Not a strong point. Bad idea. Bad friend."

Neema ran to her room and returned with a beige Burberry trench coat. "Okay, hear me out. He's tired, he's stressed, but you love each other. So make it easy for him." She put the coat on me as if I were a doll and tightened the belt. Staring down her long, straight nose, she lifted her brow. "You have a great waist and an excellent rack. Show up at his office wearing this, minus the onesie, and those shoes that I got you for your birthday that you haven't worn."

I shook my head. "I can barely walk in those."

"But it gives you that lift and makes your calves look amazing."

I shook my head again. "I don't understand."

Neema walked over to Shaun, who was now rummaging through our kitchen cabinets in search of some Earl Grey.

Splaying herself across the counter, she spoke in a low, sultry tone. "Good evening, Patrick. I have a delivery for you." Pretending to open her nonexistent coat, she turned to me and beamed. "You're the delivery!"

"No. No. No. Absolutely not." I was dizzy with the rate my head swung from side to side.

The goofiest smile appeared on Shaun's face, but there was something in his gaze that struck me.

Desire.

A gnawing ache clawed at my chest. *I wanted someone who looked at me like that. I needed it.*

Shaun bit his lip, and Neema leaned in, nearly kissing him before spinning to face me. "You see? Now he'd do anything I want."

"Anything," Shaun echoed.

"It'll be great," she promised. "I'll pick up some lingerie for you. I know you don't have any."

I was not going to argue about that.

Leaving Neema and Shaun to complete the fantasy they had started, I went to bed. In the safety of my duvet cocoon, I stared at the coat strewn across the back of my chair. My cheeks heated at the mere idea of it.

But that *desire*.

I was going to do this.

It was going to work.

Round 6

My hands fiddled with the belt for a few seconds while I tried to convince myself that this would all be okay. But when that didn't work, I tightened it around my "great waist" and squeezed the remaining air from my lungs. I had to trust Neema. She was a fashion stylist and dressed people for a living. If she had her way, she'd throw out every item in my closet. Finding my style was one of her career goals.

Neema coated my lips in ruby red and stepped back before spinning me around toward the mirror. My thick, wavy hair cascaded down to the center of my back, framing my curvy figure and round face. My lashes looked longer, my cheeks rosier, but the scatter of freckles on my nose was still there. The small mole on the underside of my jaw was also still there.

I was still me. The same person Patrick didn't seem too interested in. Bitter disappointment started in my stomach and shot out to my extremities.

Neema squeezed my shoulders. "You look hot."

"I can do this," I said with a nod, summoning confidence, and when it failed, my nod turned to a headshake. "Can I do this?"

"Damn right, baby girl. I'll drop you off on my way to Shaun. I don't think you should be getting into a taxi looking like this."

By the time I stepped out of Neema's car, my legs were wobbling and not because of the high-heeled shoes, although I couldn't say they helped my stability. Patrick's office loomed ahead of me. The lights were out on most floors, proving almost everyone understood work-life balance. But not Patrick.

The doorman lifted his hand and waved. "Miss Jones, it's lovely to see you."

Blood flooded my cheeks, and I hoped it wasn't obvious I was wearing nothing but skimpy lingerie beneath my coat.

I held up the brown paper bags of takeout, as if trying to prove I was here for something other than surprise office sex. He tapped his key chain against the scanner, and the door opened.

Scurrying ahead, I was overly aware of the click of my heels on the tiles and how they seemed to be in time with my ever-increasing heart rate.

Patrick's office was on the seventh floor and had a beautiful view of the city. When he started working here, we'd buy food from two local takeaways—he'd get butter chicken curry and I'd get ramen—and we'd picnic on the rooftop. I inhaled the mixed scents coming from the paper bags and remembered those moments.

My nerves were soon joined by excitement as I reached his office and peeked through the slightly opened door. Inside, Patrick frowned at his laptop screen, his brown hair messier than usual and his top two shirt buttons unfastened. I'd never seen him disheveled.

I knocked once. His head shot up. Confusion, joy, terror—those were the three emotions that flashed across his face.

"Hey, babe." He stood and walked toward me, offering me a peck on the lips. "What's, uh, going on?"

I had rehearsed this. I released a shaky breath and swallowed hard, summoning my sexiest voice. "I have a delivery for you."

He pointed at the paper bags. "Is it butter chicken? Babe, I've eaten. I sent you a text saying I'd bring dessert." He shook his head. "I know I have a lot to make up for, and I will. I just—"

"No more talking," I interrupted, thinking only of the picnics we used to have—of the history we shared.

I set the food on his desk and undid the belt of my coat, revealing the sexy black lace corset, held together by a bright red ribbon. The icy air in his always-cold office covered my bare skin, leaving goose bumps behind.

Before he could respond, I pulled him toward me for a kiss. And he flinched.

My hands dropped to my sides, taking my heart along with them to the depths of my stomach, lower even, to the floor where I stood.

"What are you doing?" he asked, his tone less soft than before. "And what are you wearing?"

Oxygen was unavailable to me as my shaking fingers tried to make sense of the belt. I wished for another coat, a pair of pants, a blanket, and on top of that, an aluminum blanket.

"What do you think I'm doing?" I struggled to get the words out through my thick throat. "I'm trying to seduce you at work, after hours, to make it as easy for you as possible."

He sighed and shook his head. "This isn't you. This is one of Neema's crazy ideas, isn't it?" He rubbed his face and dropped into the chair behind his desk. "I have a deadline before midnight. I can't do this with you. I'm not going to have this fight. Please, please can we talk tomorrow?"

The only thing more embarrassing than this situation was experiencing this situation while crying about it. I turned away in a poor attempt at hiding my wet cheeks. "We can, but we won't, because you'll be too busy."

"That's not fair."

Behind me, the wheels of his chair rolled against the protective plastic he kept on top of his carpet. Standing, he approached and pulled me into his arms. I swiped at my tears, and for a moment I thought things would be okay.

"I have to meet this deadline," he said. "I love you."

I nodded, not trusting myself to say anything else.

He released me and puffed out his chest on a deep inhale. Then, picking up the bags of food, he handed them to me. "I'll call you later. You should still eat this. It shouldn't go to waste. I'm quite stuffed . . . I obviously wasn't expecting this."

"I'm sorry." I swallowed down a fresh wave of tears as shame joined the hurricane of emotions swirling through me. "Anyway, I'm gonna go. Chat later."

He leaned down, and before his lips could meet mine, I turned my face, and his mouth landed on my cheek. He didn't say anything, and neither did I.

I raced back to the elevator, all the while struggling with the lump in my throat and the ache across my chest. I stared at the mirrored walls and took in my running makeup—the Joker had nothing on me.

Without making eye contact with the doorman, I lifted my hand in greeting and walked out. I fumbled with my phone and dialed Neema. It rang and rang.

No answer.

I tried Shaun. Same thing. They were probably too busy being in love—something I should have been doing.

Running through my options, I considered hailing a taxi but there was no way I was getting into a stranger's car dressed like this, and no driver needed the distraction of me crying in their backseat.

I walked without thinking, as if my legs knew where they were going. It was a familiar route. Blowing out a breath, I wiped my face and marched on while deeply regretting my choice of shoes.

Shaun's apartment was only a fifteen-minute walk, and I hoped we'd laugh about this whole thing when I got there.

His building grew larger as I neared, and I replayed everything Patrick had said, remembering every facial expression and even the lilt in his voice. I swiped at my tears again and nodded at someone who let me into the building.

Perhaps I was overreacting. Patrick was working. I suppose I wouldn't want him arriving half-naked while I was chasing a deadline.

I took the stairs as fast as I could, desperate to change my clothing. As I reached the second floor, my knees wobbled, and I lost my footing. A lightning bolt of pain traveled up my right leg, shooting up my side and screaming at my ankle.

Stupid, awful heels.

Falling forward, my hands hit the stone tiles, shielding my face from impact. Pain thumped through me. I lifted my arm to the railing and pulled myself up, afraid to put pressure on my foot. Shaun's apartment door was almost near enough to touch.

"Shaun?" I called.

Nothing.

I shifted my weight onto my right side, and agony shook through my nerves, almost blinding me.

The physical pain was only slightly better than the emotional one.

Round 7

Using the wall for support, I dragged myself to Shaun's front door. If *The Walking Dead* needed more cast members, this would make for an excellent audition.

Reaching the door, I curled my hand into a fist and banged. If they were having sex, it should be done by now. I hoped.

But my bad luck continued. And instead of my two best friends, William opened the door. His dark eyes widened, and his lips parted.

But today was the one day I couldn't handle his sarcastic nongreeting greeting, so I limped past him and dropped my bags on the ground before looking around. The living room and kitchen were empty, and the bathroom and Shaun's bedroom door stood open.

"They're not here," he said.

I held back the fresh wave of tears that threatened.

William's eyes traveled from my face down to my evil shoes. His eyebrows drew close as though trying to make sense of my clothing.

"Where are they?" My tone was desperate. "Both their cars are parked downstairs."

"Out—they walked. Went to get dinner." Still standing in the doorway, William's gaze lingered on mine.

A traitorous tear escaped, and I wobbled toward the doorway. Of all the people to witness my breakdown, did it have to be William frikken Ashdern? I would never stop hearing about this.

He stepped aside, and I ground my teeth to block the pain.

"Are you okay?" he asked, his voice quiet. If he wasn't the only person in the room, I would not have believed it was him talking.

"I'm fine." I placed my weight onto my injured ankle and winced.

Reaching for the wall, I threw myself against it and inhaled a deep breath, then pushed myself forward. Before I could take another step, two large hands gripped both sides of my waist. With one quick flip, William threw me over his shoulder as if I weighed nothing.

"What are you doing?" I choked out as he carried me inside the apartment. "Put me down, you Neanderthal." I'd never been stuck on someone's shoulder before, so I banged my fists against his firm back, but it made no difference.

Once more, my body twirled around as he carefully placed me on the couch. It wrapped around me like a hug—one I desperately wanted. Before I could say anything, William kneeled in front of me and unstrapped my sandal with a light touch I didn't know he was capable of.

A deep line divided his brows as he rotated my foot. "Does this hurt?"

"N-no," I stammered, noting his hot palms before a shock of pain raced through me. I pulled my leg back. "Ow!"

Straightening to his full height, he went to the kitchen and returned with a bag of frozen peas, a glass of water, and a bottle of ibuprofen. "This should help with the pain. I don't think it's broken."

"I know that." I moved my feet to the floor, and my ankle throbbed. "That's why I was leaving."

"Don't get up." He walked back to the kitchen and dug around in a cupboard above the stove. "You shouldn't put pressure on it. Plus, they'll probably be back soon if you want to wait."

I stared at his back and narrowed my eyes before downing the pills. "Why are you being nice to me?"

He returned with a bandage and wrapped it tightly around my ankle. "Shaun's game continues, and I declare myself the winner of this round." He shrugged, the corners of his mouth tilting upward.

Mine did too.

For a moment, I was confused by how carefully he cradled my foot. How was this the same person who communicated in grunts and groans? He looked like William, but he didn't act like him. He wasn't wearing pajama pants, either. Instead, he wore another pair of black jeans and a *Star Trek* T-shirt.

At no point did he look up at me. When he finished, he picked up his gaming controller and gestured to the TV. "You could join me. I don't bite—unless requested."

Ha. That was William, all right.

"What are you playing?" I asked.

"It's a new *Bloodbathers* scheduled for next year. They want me to check it out and recommend some changes," he said casually, as if that wasn't the coolest thing ever.

"How did you get this job? It's awesome."

His dimple made a deep divot in his cheek. "After *Walk of Death* got some attention, Thunderstruck Games offered me a job. Apparently, I'd managed to do what they couldn't." His smug smile appeared.

It made sense, since *Walk of Death* had been the number one most-played game for ages.

I'd been a bit starstruck when I first met William, the creator of a video game I'd played over and over—though I'd never tell him that.

"Now I test and tweak their games while I toy around with my next idea," he said, perching on the couch armrest.

"Is it *Walk of Death Two*? There's been rumors."

His gaze snapped toward me, turning playful. "How would those rumors have reached you?"

"It's one of my favorites," I admitted. But that was only half-true. It wasn't *one of* my favorites, it *was* my favorite, and I was sure nothing would ever top it. Unless there was a sequel.

The widest grin spread across his face, showing me a side of him he rarely revealed. It wasn't lost on me that his cheeks were tinged pink too. "Favorite, huh? Makes sense why you're so good at it."

"Can't believe I beat you at your own game, literally."

He bit his bottom lip. "I let you win."

I pulled a face.

He chuckled and, rubbing his neck, turned to face the screen. "I'm not working on a sequel. *Walk of Death* is exactly what I want it to be. There's another idea that's been plaguing me for years. I need to think it through a bit more. You'd love it."

"Oh yeah? Tell me more."

"Nah. Maybe I'd rather design a game impossible for you to win."

An uncharacteristic cackle escaped me. "You're so mean."

He laughed too, a light, playful laugh that tickled my skin. It lifted the mystery that often clouded around him.

"I wish I could design games for a living," I said, using one hand to ensure my coat was still completely closed.

Maybe that would have been my future if I'd given my Board-Game-in-Progress the time of day or entered that competition. Or maybe my game was terrible, and I'd end up exactly where I was now, except with more shame and rejection.

William looked at me, a spark of something I couldn't name in his eyes. "I could check if there are any openings at Thunderstruck." His gaze turned wicked, and the left side of his lips twitched up in a half smirk. "You'd make a great assistant."

I lifted one leg to kick him, and he caught it. Sliding down to the couch, he lifted both of my legs with his free hand, placed a pillow on his lap, and then lowered my feet on top of it.

My heartbeat skipped, and I nearly retracted, but William adjusted the frozen peas and passed me a controller. "You should keep your foot raised."

"Thank you." I took the controller, trying not to think about my feet on William's lap. Or on a pillow. But the pillow was on William's lap.

From the corner of my eye, I spotted his dangerous smirk, and his eyes dipping down to his lap for a split second. "What?" I asked, ready for the attack, preparing for the real William to reappear.

He turned his attention to the game and mumbled, "Your feet aren't quite as hairy as I imagined they'd be."

The loudest guffaw poured out of me. Even at my own expense, I enjoyed the hobbit reference, but mostly I enjoyed how, in this moment where everything felt upside down, that one comment made me feel normal.

A sense of calmness washed over me, and I almost forgot everything that had happened less than an hour ago.

After a few minutes of playing in comfortable silence—and William's gaze still focused on the screen—he sniffed the air. "Why am I smelling curry?"

"That's racist," I deadpanned.

"What?" He stopped the game and stared at me through wide, dark eyes. "No, I literally meant that I was smelling curry. I'm not trying to—"

A peal of laughter broke through the seriousness I had tried to feign.

His face relaxed, and he shook his head. "Not funny."

I was surprised by my own laughter. Gaming was all the distraction I'd needed. "There's butter chicken—oh, and ramen—in the bag I dropped over there. It's unwanted and untouched, much like I am. You're welcome to it."

"I want it." He dropped his controller and shifted my feet off his lap before standing. "Do you?"

Now that my stomach had released the tension, it grumbled. "Maybe a little ramen."

While he heated the food, my phone rang, but it was too far away and getting up was not an option.

William picked it up and smiled at the screen. "It's 'Dearest Mummy.'"

My cheeks burned. "She saved it that way!"

"You know," he said, ignoring my outstretched hand, "I've always wondered what kind of person raised you."

"Go ahead." I shrugged.

My mother would love this.

He slid his finger across the screen of my phone, which looked like a toy in his large hands.

"Hello, Rose's dearest mummy." He smiled, his dimple making an appearance again.

"Hello, young man. You have beautiful black eyes," my mother responded, unconcerned with the stranger answering my phone.

William giggled. He actually giggled.

When he was close enough, I snatched my phone from his hand. "Hi, Mom."

"Who was that?" Her eyebrows raised. Her hair stood in all directions, and I assumed the blanketed lump next to her was my sleeping father.

"William, Shaun's brother," I said. "What's up, Mom? You usually give me a warning before calling. Is everything okay?"

"Ah, William—the mean one," she responded.

From across the room, William's eyes widened as he mouthed the word "mean." I narrowed my eyes in his direction, and he failed to suppress a smile.

"Anyway," she continued, "I had a dream about you. You had blue hair, and it looked amazing. You should absolutely dye it. You'd have to strip your majestic black hair within an inch of its life, but I think it would be worth it."

"I'll consider it," I said with a smile, and when she was quiet, I added, "Mom, is that it?" My mother's dreams were often lengthy and descriptive. I'd read novels shorter than them.

"Oh yes, the dream—you were sad. Something told me to call, so I'm calling. Are you okay?" She leaned so close that her soft brown eyes took up most of the screen.

It wasn't the first time she'd done this, and most times she was right too. I nodded and whispered that I'd call her soon. While I could read from the lines on her face that she didn't believe me, she also knew not to push. Instead, she shouted, "Bye, William."

"Bye, Rosie's mummy!" he called back as the microwave pinged.

I ended the call and a notification popped up—a text from Patrick.

> **Patrick:** I'm sorry. I'm so sorry. I'm drowning at the moment.
> I'll come over on Saturday morning and make it up to you. It'll
> be amazing ;)

The awful feeling of twisted anxiety returned to my body in full force.

"Your mom seems cool." William walked back into the living room.

I shoved my phone face down. He didn't need to see that message. He'd never let it go.

"What did you expect? She raised me," I said.

A smile played on his lips. "That's why I didn't expect it."

"What's your mom like?" I asked as he handed me a bowl of ramen.

"Don't know." He lifted my feet and the pillow and then sat down before lowering them back to his lap. "She died when I was little, but my grandma showed me photos, and I look a lot like her." His eyes glazed over. "And she had a wonderful singing voice . . . That's all I know." He shook his head, the focus returning to his eyes.

"I'm sorry." I squeezed my eyes shut. I'd always known Shaun and William had different mothers—it was clear from their physical appearance alone—but I'd never questioned it.

I opened my mouth to say something more, but the pain coming off him in waves stopped me.

"Eat up before it gets cold and I have to reheat it for you." He smiled. No dimple.

I wanted the dimple back.

"What's your favorite game?" I asked.

He narrowed his eyes and swallowed his food before speaking. "I don't think I have a favorite. My favorite is always the next one I'm working on. You?" An eyebrow cocked upward. "Other than *Walk of Death*, obviously."

And the smile returned. With the dimple.

"Depends if we're talking about Xbox, PlayStation, or PC gaming. I suppose I play *Stardew Valley* the most, but I have been enjoying *Lady of War*—and, of course, always *DoTA*."

His eyes widened, and his jaw dropped. "You play *DoTA*? How come you've never mentioned it? I play it around you all the time."

The shock was so satisfying that I couldn't help grinning. Did he always have such an infectious smile? I blamed the dimple. Definitely. Maybe that was why he rarely smiled. It was too powerful.

William was frustratingly handsome. So much more handsome than I'd ever noticed. Well, maybe I *had* noticed. Anyone with eyes would have noticed. With his messy black hair, dark eyes, strong jawline, and wide shoulders, it was hard not to—but I didn't care.

Although this was the first time I had his full attention, and it knocked the air out of me. He was usually distracted. Usually playing a game. Usually wanting to be anywhere but near me unless he was competing with me.

I shook my head, trying to clear those thoughts. "I didn't want you to know how cool I actually am."

Then, in a classy Rose move, I spilled broth down my chin. It ran down my neck and onto my chest, nearing the coat.

William grabbed a napkin from the bag and leaned forward, wiping it up. He was so close that I could smell him—butter chicken, pine, and lavender.

While I was caught up in his scent, he shifted closer and adjusted my legs until I was almost on his lap. He tossed the napkin aside, his fingers grazing my calf as he did it.

My breath hitched as I watched his finger slide up to my thigh and then back down. His touch was light and barely there, his chest rising and falling against my legs. *Was I imagining it?* But when I looked into his eyes, they were darker than I'd ever seen them. My heart thundered in my chest as he froze. The spell breaking.

We sprung apart at the same time. I cleared my throat while he grabbed his controller and resumed the game.

With shaking hands, I lifted the controller, but my mind raced and my heart hadn't slowed.

What just happened?

Did I imagine that?

My body buzzed. What was this feeling? Why was electricity flowing through my veins and pumping my heart at an alarming rate?

No—I begged my mind to slow down. I had a boyfriend. And I was going to marry that boyfriend. William was simply a handsome distraction using his evil powers of seduction on me.

Before I could spiral, the door opened, and Neema and Shaun walked inside. I looked up and caught the surprise on their faces as they watched us playing in silence.

"Finally, Mom and Dad are home, and I don't need to babysit any longer." William turned off his game and grabbed his Nintendo Switch on his way to the balcony.

"Did his date get canceled?" Shaun asked me as he sat down. "He looks cranky."

"He didn't mention a date," I said.

Now William's clothing made sense.

"What happened to you?" Shaun pointed at my wrapped ankle.

"Tripped on the way up here." I clutched the controller even though the screen was black.

Neema sat next to me, in the same position William had been minutes before. She wrapped an arm around me. "What happened?"

"It didn't work," I croaked out. "He sent me away, knowing I was basically naked and there to throw myself at him. Well, at least now I know to never try to seduce a man. I'm obviously a hideous little hobbit."

Neema pulled me into a tight embrace. "Rosie, I think it's time you and Patrick have the talk. You deserve better."

"Better than Patrick?" I snuggled into Neema's tight grip. "Have you seen him? He's handsome, educated, and driven, and nice—well, mostly nice—and we've been together forever. I think he wants to marry me, which is kind of on schedule with my Life Goals, and I think this is a rough patch." I wiped my tears before taking a deep, shaky breath. "Plus, look—he sent me this apology text!"

"Fine. Let's go home. I'm driving." Neema squinted her eyes at me and sighed. "But if he ever, ever makes you cry again, I will claw out those pretty little green eyes of his."

She pulled me up from the couch, and I put all my pressure on my left foot, nearly tumbling.

Shaun hurried into William's room and returned with a crutch. "Use this." He held it toward me. "Luckily for you, William's had a broken ankle."

William.

"Uh—give me a second. I want to say bye to William."

Neema quirked a brow. "Okay, well . . . I'll pull the car around so it's closer."

Using the crutch, I wobbled onto their balcony and found William lying on a deck chair, his long legs dangling off the end. His gaze fixed on his console; Pokémon flashed on the screen.

"I wanted to say thank you for earlier, for everything," I managed, fighting back the urge to say something sarcastic and the opposing urge to let my mind wander back to that moment on the couch.

"Sure, no problem." He didn't look up.

"It was nice having a safe space to lick my wounds in this awful outfit." I was hoping to lighten the mood, but against my will, my voice cracked.

"With an *awful* outfit like that, there should have been licking involved." He looked up, and his eyes flashed in a way I now recognized. He returned his focus to the game as if he'd said nothing outrageous. "Good night, Rose."

With a mouth as dry as the desert, I managed a weak, "Good night, William."

I walked back into the living room, where Shaun helped me out of his apartment and downstairs. But I couldn't think of anything except the way William had looked at me. It wasn't his usual disdain, not even his occasional playfulness.

Desire. There was no other word for it.

I begged my brain to let it go—to stop showing me his eyes. Stop making my skin tingle where his fingers had stroked my legs. Stop hearing him say my name as if it were the first time my name had ever been spoken out loud.

I begged my brain to stop questioning my relationship with Patrick.

Round 8

On Saturday morning, I was bundled on the couch when Patrick arrived holding two cups of coffee and a brown paper bag. He walked in wearing a pair of fitted blue jeans and the whitest, brightest T-shirt I had ever seen—I couldn't look directly at it without squinting.

He slipped into the kitchen and turned the oven on before making his way to me.

"I missed you," he said.

"I would hope so," I replied, searching for the urge to be close to him and coming up empty.

He leaned down and kissed me, pulling away only long enough to mumble his apologies. Over and over. It was something we'd rehearsed before.

I'm sorry, he'd say.

I know, I'd reply.

He walked back to the kitchen and put the croissants in the oven.

"It says to bake them for ten minutes." He smiled, his eyes glinting as he neared me. "We could do a lot in ten minutes."

Strange panic built in my core, and I let out a nervous giggle. But there wasn't enough time to dissect those feelings before his mouth crashed against mine and he nudged me backward, lowering himself onto me.

This is fine. It's okay. This is what I wanted.

He unwrapped the blanket I held around myself and slid his hand beneath my shirt. I closed my eyes, waiting for euphoria to envelop me, for my skin to tingle, but it didn't.

I tried focusing on his warm body, on his fresh smell. I focused on the feeling of his skin against mine, but it didn't help. All I felt was the pain in my ankle.

And he knew.

I pushed my mouth against his, and it didn't fit. Had the shape of his lips changed in the time away?

"Stop," I said, before we started.

"Are you okay?" Patrick recoiled, pushing himself up and blowing out a long breath. Before he could say anything else, the smell of burning croissants called his attention, and he rushed to the kitchen, curse words following him.

I scrambled upright, and a pinch whirred up from my ankle to my knee.

"I'll order some breakfast," he said from the kitchen, his hands covering his face.

"It's okay. I'm not hungry."

Walking back toward the couch, he sat beside me in silence. A silence that used to be comfortable was now tense with unasked questions, holding answers neither of us wanted.

"I've ruined this, haven't I?" His soft green eyes pleaded for reassurance.

"I'm just stressed." I gestured to my foot. "And in a bit of pain."

He kissed me again, and I melted into the memories of our kisses—but not this one. This one made it hard to believe my body had ever wanted his touch. This one had me wondering whether my stomach still knew how to flutter.

Maybe there was something wrong with me.

"I'm gonna fix this." He pulled away from the kiss. "You come first, work is second."

"Let's not get ahead of ourselves. I'd be happy with being tied for first place."

A laugh escaped him. His hand slipped into mine, and he made a promise for each of my fingers. Promises I knew he'd try to keep, one of which included attending game nights—as an observer, of course.

"You've already got our entire lives planned out. It'll be okay," he said.

"I know," I replied, but even I didn't believe me.

As soon as Patrick left, I grabbed my phone and called the only person who might understand. Claire answered on the second attempt and agreed to meet me at the Arcade Café downtown.

By the time the bright neon lights of the café came into view, the painkillers had kicked in and my ankle was barely bothering me. I took the corner table because it had a full view of the five arcade machines they'd become known for: Pac-Man, Snow Bros, Donkey Kong, Space Invaders, and my personal favorite, Puzzle Bobble, which was currently occupied by a couple of kids.

Claire stepped inside and adjusted the pink scarf around her neck. Her beige knitted cardigan swung open, revealing a white blouse. Spotting me, her face burst into a soft smile, and knowing how much I enjoyed her rare hugs, she pulled me in for a tight squeeze.

"This place hasn't changed in years." She glanced around before scooching into the corner seat.

"Why fix something that isn't broken?" Mac, the café owner, said as he approached us to take our orders, even though he already knew what they'd be.

Mac opened this café years ago. He never put a sign on the front door, so it had become known as the Arcade Café with the absolute best croissants and coffee in town.

"Hi," Claire and I greeted him together.

With Mac's tan skin, floofy hair, and inviting smile, every person that stepped into this place stared at him, unsure whether they were attracted to him or wanted to be him. And he had the most wonderful personality to complement it.

"What are we here for today, ladies?" he asked.

"Cappuccinos, please," I said.

As soon as he was out of sight, Claire sighed. "I don't have much time. Dean's at work so I called my mom, and she's watching Hannah while she naps, and that'll probably last around two hours or so. And the longer I keep my mom at my place, the more she'll clean and discover the frumpled-up clothing I shoved into the closet before she arrived." Her face cracked into a smile.

I couldn't help but mimic her. "Your mom reminds me of Rinnia," I said, referring to the busybody mother in the Haunted Thrones series we were both obsessed with. Claire was to blame for the five never-ending fantasy series I was hooked on.

She burst out laughing, much as I'd hoped.

"Have you finished reading the latest one?" Her brown eyes were wide, and her fingers drummed excitedly on the table.

I shook my head and slammed my ears shut. "Don't say a word!"

Our cappuccinos arrived, and Claire pursed her lips up on one side, her brown eyes soft. "So, would you rather have coffee or tell me what's going on?"

I lifted my mug to my lips, attempting to stall what was going to come next.

"You don't have to," she added, blowing over her own cup. "We could enjoy our drinks, order dessert, and I'll watch you play Puzzle Bobble."

The tension across my shoulders lifted with her words, and for the next few minutes, that was what we did with a series of silly Would You Rather questions. When the two people at the table next to us left, they dragged their kids along with them, and my game was free. I sprinted toward the Puzzle Bobble machine with Claire on my heels.

I dropped a coin into the slot, and with my attention on the colorful balls, a moment of confidence surfaced. "The other day you mentioned going through a, uhm . . . dry spell."

"Mm-hmm," was all she said.

"How did you, uhh . . . fix it?" I swallowed hard, releasing a blue ball against another. "You don't have to answer that. I'm sorry. I've been going through . . . something." Everything that had happened—and hadn't—spilled out of my mouth, all while I progressed four rounds.

When I finally stopped talking, Claire pulled me in for a side hug, her head only a few inches higher than mine. "I hate that you're going through this."

I blew out a long breath and turned my attention back to the game. "I don't know what to do. He kissed me but I felt . . . I don't know. Maybe I didn't try hard enough."

"Speaking from experience here . . . you can't force it."

The heartache in her voice tore through me. When our friendship began, Dean was everywhere she was, but over the last couple years I had barely seen him.

"Oh," I breathed, aware that it took a lot out of her to open up. "I didn't realize it was that bad."

"I guarantee it's worse than you think. Between having Hannah in our bed and the hospital needing him all the time, it's almost impossible." She blew out a long breath. "But it's not that strange. I've spoken to other people. Unfortunately for you, Shaun and Neema are terrible examples. They're like rabbits."

This got a loud squawk of laughter out of me, and a few people turned to look at us. I covered my mouth with my hand.

"I know for a fact that Lincoln hasn't been with anyone in forever," she whispered.

"What about the girl he games with online?" I said, turning my focus back to the screen.

"They haven't met."

"It's been years!" I said, my jaw dropping.

Claire only shrugged. "You know Lincoln. He's . . . shy." A small smile crept onto her face. "He let you call him Link for four months before you found out that wasn't his name."

"He should have corrected me," I said, mortified at how I'd misheard him when we'd first met. Between the volume and depth of his voice, it was sometimes hard to hear him.

"It's nice to be able to talk about this," Claire said, looking up at the exposed trusses. "Marriage isn't always easy, and I didn't want to be a bummer when Neema and Shaun are so excited about their wedding." She fiddled with the gold band on her ring finger.

"Do you still love him?" I asked, thinking about how my mother always asked me.

Claire nodded before I could get the words out, a sparkle returning to her eyes.

The scoreboard lit up the screen, and Claire giggled.

W.A. still topped the chart, with R.J. in second place. I'd had the best score for months until I bragged about it to

William. After that, he came here and topped me. I'd been trying to beat him ever since. I wasn't even getting close.

The mere thought of William made my stomach twist, or flutter, or clench.

"Uhm . . ." I faced my friend. "Would you rather I tell you a secret and you can't tell anyone, or would you rather I keep it to myself?"

She quirked a brow. "Not even Neema?"

"Neema will tell Shaun, and Shaun will freak out even though he shouldn't . . . I mean, he'll hit on anything that moves. We know that so it's not even a big deal," I rambled.

"'He' as in William?" Her eyes went so wide that the whites were visible all around the irises. "*William* hit on you?"

My heart stilled at hearing it out loud.

"No. He just . . . ugh." I groaned, my cheeks heating like a flame. "There was a moment . . . I guess? I don't know."

"I want details. I've always wanted to know what it is about him that has women following him around. Immerse me in this moment. Okay? Start at the beginning."

I slammed restart on the screen. I would need another game for this.

Round 9

Since receiving my warning at work for being too *distracting*, I'd made an effort to blend in as much as possible. Yet whenever I turned around, Jeffrey Markham was there, his eyes searching for something to linger on. He paused behind me and peeked at my emails, made himself a cup of coffee when I went to the kitchen, and timed his lunch break to coincide with mine—all while staring at me with his beady eyes.

And he made a point of never doing it in front of anyone else. I started wondering if I was imagining it.

"Rose," he said, pausing at my desk, "perhaps you could stay late and help me with the I&I report. I'd love to have your input."

I cleared my throat, thankful my black blouse was buttoned to the top. I knew one thing for certain: I would not be staying late to work with him alone.

But I wasn't sure how to say no either.

It was game night, and I had been looking forward to it for ages, but that wouldn't quite cut it as a good enough reason to reject my boss. I&I was one of our biggest clients.

"I could take it home and finish it this evening," I suggested.

"Many hands make light work."

"Mr. Markham." Shaun rounded the corner and turned into our shared cubicle.

Our boss straightened, taking a step back. "Mr. Ashdern."

"Sorry to eavesdrop, but I, uh, heard you mentioning staying late." Shaun widened his eyes in my direction for a split second before narrowing them. "I . . . uhm . . . I need to know because Rose promised Neema she'd help with the wedding arrangements tonight." He turned to Markham and offered him a charming smile. "Maybe I could join you. Three heads are better than two?"

"Oh," Mr. Markham said and tutted.

When I didn't respond, Shaun continued, "Or I could help her finish it up at our place before we jump into the dresses and flower arrangements. We'll have it done long before midnight. Right, Rose?"

I nodded and met Markham's cold gaze. "Sounds great."

When Shaun remained unmoving beside my desk, Mr. Markham lifted his chin and stalked off.

I slumped into my chair. *Just get through the last of the day for game night.*

Only once I walked into Shaun's apartment did it hit me that it was the first time I'd seen William since we . . . I don't know . . . whatever it was that happened when he was . . . nice. When he'd looked at me with eyes filled with light and playfulness and . . .

Did I imagine it all?

Perhaps in my spiral of rejection and shame, I saw something that wasn't there.

I must have because he didn't even turn around to greet me. Although that wasn't unusual for him. He tutted at his screen, and I did what I'd usually do. I approached him, but with caution, as though he were a feral and unpredictable creature. After the last time we saw each other, it felt that way.

"Hey . . ." I said.

The eyebrow closest to me cocked upward as he glanced away from his screen and at my feet. "How's the ankle?"

"Mostly better." The overwhelming urge to address the unspoken lingered between us. "Thanks again for the other night. I owe you."

His focus returned to his game, and the hand resting on his mouse flexed. "I look forward to you paying up."

I leaned my hip against his desk, something I'd done plenty of times before but only to annoy him. That wasn't the case anymore. Perhaps we were done playing dirty. Perhaps Shaun's little game of Playing Nice could continue. "What are you playing? Is it for work?"

One arm zapped behind his head, and he dragged his fingers through his messy dark hair. "Kinda. I'm doing research for an idea I'm toying around with." A sheepish grin spread across his face, and his cheeks pinkened. "Our talk the other night got me thinking about what I want and what I'd like to develop next."

My mouth must have dropped open in excitement because a chuckle escaped him. If it was anywhere near as good as *Walk of Death*, it would have me glued to my screen for at least forty-eight hours.

"Tell me!" I demanded.

"Nope. Not yet. It needs to be perfect." He rolled backward and swung his chair around to face me.

I grumbled. "If you let me play yours, I'll let you play mine."

A wicked expression covered his face.

I cleared my throat. "I have a board game." My chest heated in the most pleasant way. It was weird acknowledging it out loud when I had spent so much of my mental capacity denying it.

William's mouth dropped open, and his eyebrows popped up. "Your game? You'll let me play it?"

His soft enthusiasm only increased the warmth spreading through me at the thought of someone playing my game. But I couldn't ruminate about that. It was stupid and childish. Before he could say anything more, I interrupted him.

"Anyway, when your game is ready, say you'll let me play it immediately? Please. I beg. I concede. You'd win all the rounds of Playing Nice for the foreseeable future and . . ."

William bit down on his lip, his dimple greeting me. "You'll be the first to know."

He held my gaze, his eyes searching mine. I had no idea what he was looking for or what he'd find. He opened his mouth again but whatever he was going to say was interrupted by Patrick's voice at the front door. Like thunder. William spun around and resumed his game without another word.

"Hey, babe." Patrick slipped an arm around my waist, which was out of character.

I leaned into it and wiggled, trying to get comfortable, but I couldn't seem to find the right fit. Instead, I pulled him to the couch and turned to Shaun and Neema. "So, wedding arrangements. Did you really need my help?"

Shaun pressed his lips together. "No, but I sensed you needed mine."

I huffed out a sharp breath.

Shaun clenched his jaw until his expression resembled his brother's. "Rose and I need to knock out a report before we get

started. It shouldn't take too long. I started it at work already."
He opened his laptop and patted the seat beside him.
"Markham wanted her to stay late . . . with him."

I resisted a shudder at the mention of Markham's name.
"To meet a deadline. Which is normal, I think." I scooched
next to Shaun and read through his draft.

Shaun grumbled. "You should report him."

"For wanting to work with his employee?"

"It's the way he looks at you when he requests it."

"He's . . . It's nothing . . . " I left the sentence hanging,
unable to think about Markham for too long. I'd become so
good at avoiding him at work that I managed to avoid him
in my thoughts too. I tried shrugging it off, but my heart
raced with discomfort. "He's my boss. What am I supposed
to do?"

"It doesn't sound like nothing," Neema said.

Patrick inhaled a breath through gritted teeth. "Has he
touched you?"

I shook my head.

"Any weird texts or emails?"

I shook my head again and bit at my cuticle as my anxiety
grew.

"So, he just . . . looks at you?" Patrick's jaw relaxed. Before I
could nod, he continued, "Well, babe, if I were you, I'd let it go.
He hasn't done anything wrong, has he? Not anything you can
prove. You'll look bad."

I nodded. Perhaps Patrick was right . . . but my sinking
stomach said otherwise.

William spun around, his right hand still clenched around
his mouse and his face filled with harsh lines. "She'll look bad?
You're worried she'll look bad instead of worrying about her
well-being or whether she's comfortable or happy?"

Even in our heated rivalry, I'd never been on the receiving end of that heavy tone. I lifted my gaze to meet William's. His eyes were as dark as the night.

"The industry is small. Building her career is part of her well-being." Patrick side-eyed William for the briefest of seconds and then turned to me. "Use them to gain experience and then leave. It would be a different story if he'd actually done something. My dad knows him from golf. He's married with two kids."

A low sound came from the back of William's throat, which, against my will, caused something inside me to flutter. And then his gaze met mine, hard and determined.

Whatever had fluttered inside me full-on started flying.

"If I were you, I'd—" He paused and blew out an angry breath before mumbling, "Pathetic."

Beside me, Patrick stiffened, and his face turned a mottled purple. Placing a hand on his arm to mollify him, I sucked in a deep breath and ignored the way my entire body seemed to hum. I wasn't sure whether William was talking about Mr. Markham or Patrick, and I was even more unsure about what was going on here as a strange tension settled between the two men. If I let it linger any longer, I'd suffocate under its weight.

"Like I said, it's nothing. How about we get started?" I turned to Shaun and widened my eyes. "I'm sure we can finish this report later."

Understanding my expression, he nodded. "Yeah. It's almost done anyway."

Neema must have picked up on the tension too because she jumped into action and started setting up Dungeons & Dragons, her favorite game. It was, by far, the thing about her that shocked people most.

Oh, you were a lingerie model? Makes sense.

You were the guitarist in a band? Totally believable.

You fell asleep in Turkey and woke up in Greece, and you have no idea how it happened? Still completely believable.

You play D&D? Wait, what?

But I knew her before she blossomed into this confident version of herself. Neema and I met at the board games club at college, which is also where we met Claire and Lincoln. Of all the things I learned at San Diego State University, D&D was the thing I least expected.

Since then, every time it was her turn to pick a game, she picked D&D—and she was always the Dungeon Master.

"William," Neema said, tightening her cape, which my mother had helped her make, "you're joining."

"I'm not. I'm working." He gestured to the thing he was shooting on his screen.

"Lincoln and Claire aren't here, and Patrick won't play." Neema gestured to Patrick, who had taken a call on the balcony.

"Can't we play something else? I got a new poker set." William blew out a breath as he shut down his laptop.

"No, because you cheat," I said, hating how he always managed to read my hand.

William met my gaze, albeit for a microsecond, before saying, "I never cheat. I like winning fair and square."

Don't read into that, Rose. You didn't cheat on Patrick. Nothing happened. Nothing would ever happen. Besides, he didn't mean anything by it.

This wasn't a game I knew how to play. I swallowed, unable to find a proper comeback, and resorted to, "Then how?"

"A wizard never reveals his secrets." William swiped the wizard figurine and offered us a wicked grin. There were still elements of his anger in the angles of his face, but with each minute that passed, the playful William I was accustomed to returned and urged the rival in me to join him.

Instead, I hopped up and met Patrick on the balcony. He ended the call and slipped a hand into his pocket. His green eyes were dull, and the bags underneath them darkened. It was clear he wanted to be anywhere but here.

"Sexy Stacey really did a number on William," Patrick whispered, glancing to the door. "He used to be difficult to be around but now he's unbearable."

"He's not all bad." The words escaped before I could stop them.

Patrick scoffed as he shot off a text. The distance between us was growing, and I feared I wouldn't be able to cross it, even if I tried. But I had to try. "Do you wanna get out of here? I'll skip game night for you." I stood on my tiptoes and kissed him.

He sighed, and everything within me shrank.

"I'm exhausted, babe."

"I know." I swallowed around the hard, unmovable lump in my throat and kept my eyes fixed on the way the city bled into the ocean in the distance. I couldn't turn around and face him because, if I did, I feared I'd see his lack of interest and the absence of yearning. The mere thought of it shredded the dwindling remains of my self-esteem. "You should get an early night."

"But then you'll be mad." Patrick ran a hand over his face. "I don't want you to be mad."

I took a sharp inhale and blinked a few times before plastering on the smile my mother had taught me to wear. "I won't be mad."

And for the first time in a long time, I wasn't.

Round 10

It wasn't surprising when Patrick didn't show up to the next game night. No one asked. Not even me.

Luckily, I had enough distractions—such as Neema and Shaun pulling William and me aside with matching grins on their faces.

"Rose," Neema said, batting her lash extensions at me.

"William," Shaun added.

William stood and offered me a cheeky and knowing glance. We both knew what was coming, having bet on it a couple times in the past.

"Will you be our maid of honor?" Neema asked me.

"And our best man?" Shaun asked William.

Of course I would. If I was entirely honest, I wished I could be *both* maid of honor and best man. I had already planned Neema's bachelorette party, and I had a number of suggestions for William about Shaun's bachelor party.

"Yes!" I screeched. "It's on my Life Goals, and I've been itching to tick something off."

I bounced into her arms, and William, in a completely unpredictable manner, pulled his brother in for a tight hug. Shaun seemed as surprised as the rest of us.

"Of course." William squeezed Shaun and suddenly pulled back. "Although I don't know if . . . you know." His voice went soft and hesitant, unlike the free-flowing snark I was often on the receiving end of.

Know what?

But Shaun knew. His smile faded.

Neema and I exchanged glances and took our squealing to the balcony, leaving them alone in their moment.

I shut the door and turned to face her. A breeze whipped by and chilled my core. "What was that about?"

She shook her head. "No idea. But I'll bet it's got something to do with their dad."

"Oh," I said, thinking back through all our conversations. "I don't think he's mentioned him much. Did you know William's mom died when he was little?" I asked, feeling a pinch of sorrow as I recalled his pained expression.

"Yeah, Shaun mentioned it. He doesn't like to talk about William's mom or their childhood. Seems the Ashderns have some issues." Neema chewed on her bottom lip. "I've only met his dad once, and William didn't come up in conversation at all, which seemed . . . weird."

"The wedding's going to be interesting."

Neema's deep brown eyes widened beneath closely drawn brows. "I fear it might be."

My first duty as maid of honor was to arrange and attend pole dancing classes. Neema insisted she needed lessons in preparation for her wedding night—lucky Shaun. She also insisted we take the lessons with her. While I easily agreed to most of what Neema suggested, Claire didn't usually.

"I'm surprised you came," I said over my shoulder as Claire climbed into the backseat.

Her mom and her nephew stood on the porch, waving her off.

"So am I," she huffed out. "But it was either this or playing another round of Mad Magazine with my nephew."

"Ugh." I rolled my eyes. "That game is so chaotic. I hate it."

Neema giggled. "Your mom loves it though."

"Unsurprisingly," I said.

"So does William," Neema added. "Or maybe he loves it because you hate it so much."

My breath hitched at the mere mention of his name and the fact that Neema still had no idea what had happened. Although that made two of us since I couldn't make sense of it either.

A nervous laugh escaped me when I opened my mouth because no words came out. I looked away, but Neema caught my eye, her concern obvious.

"You okay? You've been acting weirder than your usual weird. How are things with Patrick?"

"Everything's fine. I'm seeing him this evening. I'm just a bit tired and overworked." I defaulted to my automatic answer whenever anyone asked me what was wrong and I didn't want to burden them with my actual thoughts . . . or face them myself either.

I didn't want to tell them that my dates with Patrick had become later and shorter, and even when we were together, we weren't. He was thinking about work, and I was thinking about how he was thinking about work.

"You need to unwind," Neema said.

"Yeah." I offered her a smile, and for the last few minutes of the drive, I wondered what unwinding would look like.

I'd completely unravel and end up on an island living exactly the way my mother does—and that was not an option. I had to stay focused, forget the game, finish this degree, get the promotion, get married, buy a house, have children, and raise them in a stable home.

That was still the dream, right?

The car stopped in front of a baby-pink building, pulling me from my thoughts.

"We're here." Neema climbed out wearing her shortest shorts, as instructed.

You need the friction between your thighs and the pole, the instructor had told us.

While I was short, I was not as slender as Claire or as athletic as Neema. I'd need a lot more than friction to get my body to defy gravity.

As soon as we walked in, our instructor shimmied with glee. Her silver hot pants accentuated her gloriously long legs. I could use them instead of the pole.

We greeted Neema's other friends before the instructor addressed us.

"Welcome, ladies!" She stretched one leg high in front of her before taking a step. Spinning once, she pressed her back against the pole and slid down.

She dipped in such a seductive way that my cheeks heated.

"I'm going to teach you a beginner routine with enough twirls and spins to make it impressive."

Her eyes screamed *sexy* while I was sure mine screamed *scared*.

But our first task was simple enough: stretching our arms upward, grabbing ahold of the pole, and lifting ourselves off the ground.

Well, I was wrong. As someone who'd never lifted anything heavier than a laptop bag, this was not going to work.

After a few mediocre pulls—and activating muscles I didn't know I had—I managed to find a rhythm and get the hang of it. But as soon as I'd gained my confidence, the instructor showed us our next move.

The Fireman.

The only problem is that none of the firemen in the videos I often watched ever did this trick.

Following the instructor's step-by-step directions, I mimicked her posture and curled a leg around the cold pole. With a deep breath, I lifted my other leg off the ground. I squeezed my eyes shut—hitting the floor would be less painful if I didn't see it coming.

But I didn't fall.

It worked.

Everyone was as shocked as I was.

"See, Rose," Neema yelled, "you've got this!"

Her other friends cheered, and the tips of my ears heated.

With each move and every spin, I surprised myself and enjoyed the way my heart pulsed.

"Good job, girls," our instructor said at the end of the lesson. "You'll be ready for your performance in no time."

"Performance?" Claire and I asked at the same time, our heads snapping toward a very guilty-looking Neema, who grabbed her things and bolted toward the car.

"About that . . ." she started when we caught up to her.

I was already shaking my head, taking a few steps closer to her.

"I meant to talk to you about this before the class, but you've been so busy and stressed, I thought it better I tell you at a later stage."

"Tell me what?" I glared at her.

"Remember how I asked if we could end up at VOX?" She scrunched her nose and smiled at the same time.

"Yes, for the pizza and live music." I dropped my head into my hands in preparation for Neema's secret plans.

"It used to be a strip club and they still have the poles and I was hoping we could put on a performance and it'll be fun and we need to have a bit of fun, please." She spat the words out all in one breath.

"No, thank you," Claire replied. "I'll cheer you on, but I won't perform."

"Fine. I know coming to this class is already far out of your comfort zone," Neema said and touched Claire's shoulder. "I appreciate you being here. Will Dean be joining the boys?"

"He wants to."

Neema turned her full focus to me. "I assume Patrick will be joining . . . if he's not working." She took my hand, her skin several shades darker than mine but glistening. "I need one of you up there."

"The boys will be there?" I couldn't tell if my heart's speedy rhythm was due to the workout or imagining myself pole dancing on stage . . . in front of *the boys*.

"Shaun's going to want to see me that night, I know him. You need to get William to take him to VOX without giving anything away. Can you do that? Or are the two of you only capable of pulling each other's hair like kids on a playground?" She folded her arms across her chest, challenging me.

"Uhm, we . . ." I stumbled on my words and resorted to a *pffftttt*. Claire went completely silent.

We walked to the car while Neema wrinkled her nose and gave me her best puppy-dog eyes. "You'll be fully clothed. It's a respected sport!"

"You know me—you know I can't do that. My body doesn't work that way. It just isn't sexy. I'll look like a fool." I crossed my arms, my voice dropping in anger. "This is the coat idea all over again, and that didn't work out well, did it?"

The deep feeling of rejection, of how *unsexy* I was, consumed me.

Neema sighed, climbing into the car. "Since you're so sure you aren't sexy, how about a deal?"

Claire and I got in and waited.

"If, by the last class, you manage to master the routine and feel semi-confident about it, you'll do it even if you take one of the poles farther back. I want you up there with me, and I want you to feel sexy because you are."

I grumbled, accepting defeat. "*If* I feel confident—and I won't—but if I do, I'll join you up there."

"Deal."

This was the first bet I was hoping to lose.

I stared at the message again.

> **Patrick:** Babe, this meeting is running over. Breakfast tomorrow?

I stood in front of the mirror, scrutinizing my face and body. My mouth that no one longed to kiss, my waist that had long since been desperately held.

You're being dramatic. Stop it. He's just busy.

To avoid screaming in frustration, I called my mom. That usually did the trick to remind me that I was loved by someone.

"Rosie, Rosie, my little lovely baby, baby," Mom sang into the screen as she answered, her dark hair half the length it was during our last call. "I'm being spoiled with calls. You're all dolled up. Where are you off to?"

"Nowhere." I grabbed my makeup remover and the face scrubbies my mother had crocheted and started cleaning my lips. When my mom stayed quiet, I peeked at my screen and said, "So, what did you do to your hair?"

My mom's little frown softened but didn't disappear. "One of our neighbor's daughters wants to be a hairdresser, so I let her practice on me." She ran her hands through the jagged edges. "Do you like it?"

"How old is she?" My lips curved upward, and my airways opened again.

"She's seven, but I think she's got potential." She admired her own hair in the video.

I giggled, and my eyes welled with tears. I was grateful for my mother's bad internet connection. "I miss you so much."

"Miss you too. How's work and all the usual things?"

"All fine." I tossed the scrubbies aside and climbed into bed with the intention of leading the conversation elsewhere.

We discussed Neema's wedding (my parents were coming!), her current work (painting portraits), her love for my father (unnecessarily explicit), and finally, my board game (she insisted I finish it and submit it to the competition or she'd disown me).

"I mean it, we'll cut you off!" she teased, her voice breaking up due to their shaky internet connection. "I watched you create this game. I watched you build it. You were so little, with no idea what the world had in store for you, and your dreams were uncontainable. Finish it, please. Show the world what you made for them."

I rolled my eyes, even though my chest pounded with want. I couldn't play it down and pretend I didn't want that. "It's not such a big deal . . ."

"For someone who loves these games, you sure are afraid to roll the dice."

"I'll see," I said, wanting to be freed from the truth bomb she insisted on dropping. I was afraid it would shatter all the lies that currently held my life together. "I have to go."

"Do you still love him, Rosie?" she asked before I could hang up.

I paused. My heart raced in the seconds that passed.

The one thing I could always rely on was my mother's intuition. Before I stumbled in search of an answer, she gracefully changed the topic. "I think a ghost visited me last night."

"Tell me everything."

Round 11

Even after I'd backtracked on my concerns about Mr. Markham, Shaun took it upon himself to ensure I was never left alone with my boss at work.

I'd always thought of Shaun as my brother, and I imagined it would feel something like this.

He wheeled over with two foil-wrapped squares and handed me what I knew would be the stretchiest, cheesiest sandwich in town.

"Your unread emails drive me nuts." Shaun peeked at my screen, his mouth full of food.

I tore open the foil with my teeth while scrolling. "I get so much promotional mail."

"Do you know that you don't get a prize for subscribing to everything? Is this one of the strange things you've turned into a game?"

"No, I just don't like missing things."

"As if any of that is important. You've left them unread for a reason."

I huffed and read the bolded text. "There's some useful stuff here. A new *Lady of War* is being released next month, and

there's a discount in this email." I kept scrolling. "And this . . ."
I paused, my heart hopping to my throat.

Shaun's eyes landed on the subject line I had selected:

```
There's still time to submit your original
board games!
```

His chewing stopped.

I ignored the email, like I'd ignored the original one, and like I was ignoring the way my stomach fluttered at the possibility of it.

Shaun grabbed my computer mouse before I could press delete. "Too slow, Rose." He read through the email without stopping until he found the link to the submission guidelines.

I sunk deeper and deeper into my seat. Having Shaun read that email made it feel all too real, as if it was actually possible that I could win.

"You have to do this!" He faced me, pinning me with his gaze. "Aside from the cash prize, your board game would be developed and distributed worldwide. Rose, your game would be played everywhere."

I shook my head despite my fluttering stomach twisting into an ache in my chest. "I don't have time. I didn't have time when they made the initial announcement, and now I have even less time."

I reached for the mouse, and he wheeled away.

"You have to," Shaun said. "Isn't your game like almost done?"

"You know nothing about my game." Anger crept up, but it wasn't meant to be directed at Shaun. The only other person that I'd ever tried showing my game to, outside of my parents and Gandalf, was Patrick, and he wasn't interested in playing it. "This isn't real life." I swiped the mouse and gestured at the screen before closing the window and replacing it with my office emails. "This is."

My throat was thick with fear . . . fear of what? Achieving a dream or failing at it?

Shaun's light blue eyes were soft even though he wore the Ashdern scowl.

"Please go for your lunchtime workout." I turned away, hoping Shaun didn't spot the way I pined for the exact thing he was encouraging me to do. "I have work to do."

Shaun blew out a breath and stood. "Fine. But we're not done here."

"We are. I don't have the capacity to even think about this."

It was an absolute lie, as that was all I did for the rest of the day.

Your game would be played everywhere.

Was it bad that I was happy Patrick was away for work? Was it even worse that, when he returned, I used my MBA as an excuse not to see him? Because that's what happened, and it almost made doing the MBA worth it.

It wasn't untrue. My deadlines were approaching, and I was running out of time. So much so that I was prepared to give up game night. But Shaun and Neema lured me in by telling me they needed my help with wedding planning.

I straightened my fitted black pencil skirt as Shaun opened the door to his apartment. Inside, William was sprawled on the couch, taking up more space than any one person should. His legs were spread wide, and his head dipped back with his eyes lowered to the screen in front of him. It was a miracle he could see through those stupidly long eyelashes.

As soon as I stepped inside, William's gaze snapped up and then traveled down to my heeled boots. "Did you walk here in those?" He glanced back up at me. "Looking to twist the other ankle?"

"Hello, William. It's nice to see you too." I used my snarky tone, maintaining just enough eye contact for him to wonder whether it was true.

It was.

A wide, friendly smile flashed across his face, and it was all too easy to reciprocate.

Fingers tapped across my back, and I spun around to face Lincoln. He lifted a sealed glass container. "Dal for you. My mom wants her container back." He lifted another box. "Jalebi, to share."

"Thank you!" I shrieked, already salivating.

He offered me his trademark half smile and slipped by. Claire came up behind him and pulled me in for a hug. It had been a while since she had joined for game night.

And since Claire rarely gave hugs, Neema joined us, and seconds later Shaun came bouncing over. "You're not group hugging without me." Shaun turned toward us, his arms thrown wide.

William shook his head. "You people are ridiculous."

"Wanna join?" I teased.

"I'd rather drink acid."

I couldn't resist giggling, especially once I caught sight of the light bouncing around in his eyes as he said it.

Playing Nice was so much easier than whatever it was we were doing before. I'd have to thank Shaun for it someday.

A sharp rap on the door, followed by Patrick's business voice, signaled his unexpected arrival. My anxiety peaked, which was one of my newer reactions to seeing my boyfriend. I opened the door to greet him, but he was grumbling at whomever he was talking to, his phone squeezed between his ear and shoulder and his laptop open in the palm of his left hand.

"I'll call you back with an update soon," Patrick barked into his phone before hanging up. He gave me a quick peck on the cheek. "Hey, babe."

"You came," Neema said from behind me, a flash of white as she smiled.

I opened my mouth to say something, but he cut me off and gestured to his laptop. "I have a deadline."

"I see." I searched the depths of my soul for even the slightest desire to offer him a hug or to place my lips against his, but there was no urgency.

How do those feelings disappear? Where do they go? The island with all the missing socks and plastic container lids?

Patrick sat down with his laptop and inserted his noise-canceling earbuds before continuing his work with a deep frown of concentration.

Sitting next to him, I unzipped my heels and curled my legs beneath me. Pulling my gaze away from his screen, I found everyone watching me.

Shaun placed a cup of tea in front of me, and Lincoln pushed the box of jalebi toward me. "Thanks," I said, and despite my spidey sense tingling, I wasted no time shoving the sticky, crunchy, chewy treat into my mouth.

With my mouth full, I finally asked, "What's going on?"

Shaun paled.

Neema and Claire smiled, but their eyes were wide open.

Lincoln removed his glasses and rubbed his temples, avoiding my gaze.

My anxiety heightened. "What is it?"

Shaun made a show of pulling out his whistle to start the game, but there was nothing set up.

"Ey, what are we playing?" I asked.

"You tell us." Neema lifted a tote bag from behind the couch and dropped it on the table. Her concerned expression met mine. "Shaun told me about the competition. You should enter."

My head snapped toward Shaun, who flinched.

"It's my turn to pick a game, and this is what I want to play." He unzipped the bag and lifted out a board more familiar to me than my own hands. I had spent hours painting it with my mother and repainting it on my own. "If you'll let us."

My breath hitched.

He pulled out the pieces, one at a time: the hat, the crown, the book, the sword, and the bow and arrow. Each time he reached inside the bag and pulled out another component, a piece of me went numb.

I lost my voice, my ability to move.

I was vaguely aware of Neema's eager smile, of the guilt in Shaun's expression, and Claire's squeal of delight. Lincoln leaned forward and scrutinized the board while William said nothing, his wide-eyed gaze fixed on the game in front of us.

They were waiting for me to say something, but I couldn't think. All I could hear was the *click-click-click-click* of Patrick's keyboard beside me.

My heart raced with each tap of his fingers, the short pants of my breath coming faster and faster. I was having a panic attack.

I was having a panic attack.

I was definitely having a panic attack.

"I pick this one," William announced, louder than the blood pumping in my ears. He grabbed the hat marker and looked at me. His eyes were lighter than I'd ever seen them. He wanted to play.

But this wasn't one of our silly little games. This was *my* game. And they knew nothing about it. What if they hated it?

"Come on," William chirped at the rest of them.

Neema sprung into action. "I want the bow and arrow."

Shaun grabbed the crown.

Lincoln took the sword and brought it close to his eyes.

Claire picked up the book between two fingers.

"Is it a five-player game?" Neema asked. "Can we add something for you? Otherwise, you can have my bow."

I shook my head, kneeling before the board with limbs that had gone useless. "It's a six-player game, but I've lost the heart game piece."

I thought back to that day so many years ago. Gandalf had taken it, claiming he wanted original memorabilia of the greatest board game to ever exist.

Neema removed the heart charm on her necklace and added it to the starting square. "Here. We can use this."

Tears prickled behind my eyelids. I kept them shut, trying to compose myself.

"Can you two please hold it together?" Shaun said. "We haven't even started."

Neema and I giggled.

"What's it called?" Lincoln trailed his deft fingers across the board, lingering on areas with different textures.

I'd referred to it as my Board-Game-in-Progress for so long that I nearly forgot the name.

"It's, uhm, it's called . . . " I hesitated, begging my voice to stay with me. "Overpower."

Everyone nodded, encouraging me to continue.

"It's a fantasy-adventure game." I turned to my best friend. "Neema, your bow and arrow makes you a warrior. So are you, Lincoln, with the sword." I studied the different regions on the board. "Um, Claire, you're a scientist. Shaun, you're obviously the king with . . . you know, the crown. And uh, William . . . the hat, you're an enchanter."

"Ha!" William offered me a wink, and the anxiety I held on to lessened.

"And the heart?" Neema asked.

"Oh, I'm a medic." I blew out a stream of air, trying to calm my nerves before continuing.

I glanced at Patrick, and my stomach sank. His eyes still focused on his screen. He might as well have been anywhere else for as much attention as he was giving us.

Neema nudged him, and his gaze lifted and met mine.

"What's this?" he asked, removing one earbud.

A part of me ached, wishing he hadn't noticed. He'd spent countless hours in my bedroom and had never asked me about it.

"It's Rose's game." Shaun beamed. "Which we have no idea how to play."

"Cool, babe." He glanced at his phone as it buzzed in his hand. "I have to take this, please excuse me." He answered the call and stood, already rambling off numbers and percentages.

A whip of frustration slapped across my spine, but I ignored it and focused on the group of people smiling at me.

"Okay, so . . . the rules. You probably need the rules . . . which I haven't written anywhere."

I recited them from memory, stumbling and contradicting myself before accepting what I always ended up realizing: they weren't good.

I hopped to my feet, ready to pack it up. "It doesn't make sense. It needs work, and the deadline is approaching. Plus the timer broke. Let's play something else—even Dungeons & Dragons. We could even play *FIFA*." I turned to William. "Hand me a controller."

But William's soft smile stayed fixed. "Nah. We're already invested here, and now we know at least half the rules." Reaching above his head, he grabbed a timer from another game on the shelf behind him. "Are you afraid I'll beat you at your own game?"

His eyes met mine, and my heart thundered.

He raised an eyebrow to challenge me, and it struck me then: I wanted William's approval. Since the day I'd discovered he was a game developer, that he fixed games for a living and was the only one who ever matched my enthusiasm for playing, I'd wanted his approval, but up until now, I was too scared to ask.

If I could get him to like my game—the man who mastered every game—then surely it was worth something.

I wanted this. Holding his gaze and exhaling all the little butterflies flying in my stomach, I whispered, "Let's play."

Shaun blew his whistle again, and the game, my game, began.

It went on for hours—far longer than a board game should. But my friends were laughing, arguing, and at one point Claire even threatened Lincoln. I choked back tears of joy, and my heart swelled in my chest.

But William was taking notes. Each time he wrote something down, I leaned over to see what he was writing, but he shoved his notebook under his thigh, hiding it from me.

There was no way I would touch his thigh.

Despite that, he seemed to be enjoying himself. And everyone reassured me afterward that they had as well.

But there was a huge crack in my otherwise joyous moment, splitting me into tiny pieces. At some point in the middle of the game, Patrick had left.

He hadn't shown any interest in game night in years, so why would this change anything?

But it did. It changed everything.

Round 12

The light pouring in through the window made Patrick's hair look like spun gold and brightened his green irises.

I looked into those eyes that had become familiar to me. I couldn't hurt him. I didn't want to, and I especially didn't want to be alone. I didn't want to be single, to date, or to learn how to become comfortable with an entirely new person—comfortable enough to share my body with them.

I sat down beside him, wishing there was a rulebook, a spreadsheet, or something to tell me what to do next. It was why I loved board games. They were structured, and there was only an expected number of outcomes.

My mind raced with these thoughts as he pulled me close and slipped a condom out of his pocket. Even though we didn't need one, he liked having "double protection."

Patrick pressed his lips against mine, and I panicked.

"Uhm, I'm actually exhausted." I spoke against his mouth, breaking the kiss as soon as possible.

He huffed out a sigh, twirling the shiny square between his fingers.

"I shouldn't have agreed to see you today. I have an assignment to finish, and now there's a deadline for my game too."

The mere mention of it nearly tugged a smile out of me. All I wanted to do was tweak it. It had been a long time since I'd felt so excited about working on something. "I have all these ideas. I was thinking I could—"

Patrick laughed. "Don't get me wrong, I know it's fun, but remember the MBA is more important."

"I know." My enthusiasm dipped to the depths of my stomach.

"What about a quickie?" He kissed me again.

My body recoiled against his touch. Everything about it was wrong. Undeniably wrong. The truth sucker-punched me in the gut, leaving me breathless. It had been wrong for a long time.

"We should break up," I blurted as our lips parted.

"What?" He pulled back, his eyes on fire. "You can't be serious."

My words choked me, and I shook my head, trying desperately to cough out what I needed to say.

His lip curled. "I've been trying. I'm here every Saturday, and some game nights. I watch you and your friends play those silly games for hours." Standing, he shoved the condom into his pocket.

"I know." I fixed my gaze on my hands. "But . . . I'm not happy. *We're* not happy. You don't like spending time with me or my friends. We don't go out on dates. We barely talk." I wiped a stray tear. "And we haven't slept together in a really long time."

"It's not like you even enjoy it, and that's not my fault." He inhaled sharply, as if wishing he could suck back the words.

My mouth fell open, but before he could retract it or before he said something that would hurt even more, I rolled the dice and bet on myself. I wanted more than this.

"I'd like you to leave," I said with no hesitation in my voice, despite my risk-averse brain flagging my words.

"Rose." He looked at me, but I stayed planted where I was. He walked to the door and waited a few seconds with his back to me. "This isn't happening. This can't be happening," he mumbled.

When I didn't budge, he let himself out without a backward glance.

Over the next few weeks, I spent all my time on my work and studies, neglecting both my board game and game night.

Not because of heartache, which there was little of. I'd mourned our relationship long before it ended. But I wanted no one else's voice but my own in my head while I processed it.

Neema, ever concerned, brought me treats and more tea than I could drink, and hugged me at every opportunity. I hadn't been calling my mom, but I could clearly hear her on the phone with Neema, both of them increasingly worried about me.

When I wasn't at home, Shaun fussed around me at work. He had a similar strategy.

Treats. Tea. Hugs.

Once, when he was hugging me, one of our colleagues walked by us and whispered, "So glad you two finally got together."

Even that didn't deter him.

When I couldn't handle it anymore, I showed up at game night, intent on proving to everyone I was okay. Plus, it was my turn to pick a game, and I'd been itching to play Cluedo.

I kneeled beside the coffee table and set up the game. Everyone tiptoed around me—including William, which was strange because he always made his presence known.

Tonight he wore black jeans and a gamer T-shirt that fit him far too well.

"Hot date?" I asked, trying to lighten the mood.

"I'd never miss game night," he teased, ruffling his hand over his hair in an attempt to tame it. At some point, I'd have to tell him how pointless that was.

"It's been a while since you brought a girl over," Neema said, bringing me yet another cup of tea. "I rather enjoyed watching those women slobber all over you. They were always ultra-nice to me in an attempt to impress you."

William rolled his eyes and sat at his desk. "Oh, stop."

Shaun sat down on the couch. "William can charm the pants off the pantsless. That's why I don't leave any of you alone with him."

"Dark magic," I mumbled.

William's groan turned to a laugh, and I was grateful that the focus was on his love life instead of mine.

Our phones pinged simultaneously, and Neema glanced up from her screen. "Claire's texted the group to say she's not coming. Hannah's got the flu. She's really sorry."

"Nothing to be sorry about. Her eighteen-month-old with a viral infection probably needs her more than her adult friend who is *perfectly fine*," I enunciated the last two words and made eye contact with all of them.

I also knew that, if Claire wasn't coming, Lincoln wouldn't come either. Even after all these years of friendship, he still battled with social anxiety. I turned to face William. "And you, I hope you weren't kidding about being excited for game night because now you have to play."

William's mouth tilted upward as he hopped up from his desk and joined us around the game table. "Seeing as you're *perfectly fine*, I won't let you win this time."

He really didn't. Jerk. After losing Cluedo because William caught me out, I walked out to the balcony for a moment alone. There was a slight breeze, but the moon was bright and almost yellow amid a starless sky—which was soon interrupted by William's dark shadow sliding over me.

Leaning his elbows on the railing on my left, he stared out at the ocean ahead. "I'm sorry."

"For winning?" I shrugged. "Don't be. You did it by the book, although I don't know how you keep doing it."

"About Patrick."

I wasn't sorry. But it didn't seem appropriate to say that.

"Love is temporary." I turned and offered him a wink, repeating the words he'd said to me not too long ago.

His dark eyes met mine, and while we'd been talking a lot lately, having his full focus left me speechless. Dark magic. Like I said.

I tucked a lawless tendril of my black hair behind one ear and offered him a smile. "I'm fine. Tell everyone to stop worrying."

His mouth pursed upward to the side, pushing in his deep dimple. He turned back toward the vast ocean in the distance. "Well, that's good to know."

Standing side by side, we drank in the comfortable silence. After the longest time, he gripped his hands around the railing and then turned to face me with one of his black eyebrows arched.

"Are you fine enough for some constructive criticism?" From his back pocket, he pulled out the folded notebook he'd written in while we'd played my game.

A wave of nausea swirled inside me. I wrung my hands. "No. I don't know. How mean are the comments? I know we do this thing where we're mean, but I—" I shook my head. "I'm really nervous."

"We're Playing Nice, remember?" The light in his eyes sparkled much like the stars I'd been staring at.

He flipped through the pages, the chunks of black ink clear on the white paper. "But it's too much to discuss right now." He tilted his chin toward the door behind him. "Sounds like Neema's about to leave."

"That looks like a lot of criticism," I blurted, my gaze still fixed on the little book. "Was it bad? Be honest."

"No." A soft laugh escaped him, and his lips tilted up on one end. "It was good, really good. But if you let me, we could make this game even better."

His voice dropped an octave as he spoke, shaking something inside me.

"I could come by on the weekend, if that's okay?" I pushed myself back from the railing, creating space between us, then I did what I knew how to do best with William—I teased him. "I imagine your day starts at noon, after you've evicted some poor woman from your bed."

His eyes gleamed, and a wide grin crossed his face. It held a dare. "Jealous?"

My heart rate skyrocketed.

I wasn't sure I was ready to play this round with him.

Instead, I retreated to the safety of Round 1. I scrunched up my face and told him to go away.

And he did. He turned around and made his way to the door. "Good night, Rose."

"Wait!"

I caught up to him and he froze, glancing down at me with an expression I couldn't place.

"You didn't say what time," I said. "Should I come here or . . . ?"

"Or?" He grinned. "Am I being invited to your place? Oh my, the Shire. How exciting."

"What time, you miscreant?" I nearly growled and poked his hard bicep.

He flinched and rubbed the spot. "Noon. Because according to you, I have to get a strange woman out of my bed." His lips hitched up before he stepped back into the apartment.

Such an idiot.

Round 13

Neema gulped down the last of her herbal tea, her eyes narrow. "I can't believe your nemesis is coming here."

"'Nemesis' is a bit of a strong term." I slouched over the kitchen table and popped another bit of toast layered with avocado, tomato, cheese, and an incredible amount of ground pepper into my mouth.

"And according to Shaun, he specifically requested that he be alone with you."

"You're making it sound weird."

"It is a bit weird."

I swallowed. "I'm guessing the only reason he wants to be alone is because, if you and Shaun are here, he won't critique it properly. This is business. Simple as that."

Neema hopped off her stool and towered over me like a graceful swan, whereas I was more of a . . . headless chicken. Her eyes were still narrowed. "Okay. But be careful. I haven't met a woman who could resist that troubled man, and now you're single and vulnerable, and I'm just saying . . ."

I opened my mouth to stop her, but she raised a perfectly manicured finger, stopping me. "Don't give in to his charms. If you hook up and it doesn't work out, it'll be a mess. Why do you think I've never introduced him to any of my friends, and—"

"Whoa." I raised my hands. "Who said anything about hooking up? I can handle William. And besides, I'm far from his type. Again, this is business. He made notes, plenty of them."

She hummed and grabbed her keys on the way to the door. "I suppose he is the perfect person to do it. He won't go easy on you. Are you ready?"

I wasn't. How could I ever be ready to have someone tear apart the game of my heart that I'd spent years pouring myself into?

But before I could answer, my phone buzzed. It was strange seeing William's name beside a text message.

"He's here," I told Neema as she opened the door. "I'll walk down with you."

We walked downstairs to the parking garage, where William's car turned into the visitor's bay, the loud sound of the engine bouncing against the concrete walls. He pulled into a space, and everything stilled the moment he turned off his car.

Climbing out of the driver's side, William stretched his long legs and rolled out his neck. It was a mystery how he folded himself enough to fit into a hatchback.

Black jeans. Starfleet T-shirt.

Neema waved at him on her way to her car. "Be nice!"

He lifted his hand and saluted. "We're Playing Nice." He glanced at me, and even in this mediocre lighting, the lines of his face spelled mischief.

My stomach somersaulted against my will.

"Stairs or elevator?" I asked, ignoring the nerves brewing within me.

"Stairs. I sit enough during the day."

His body said otherwise.

Bah. Stop.

I swatted away that thought and raced ahead, but he and his long legs caught up within a couple steps.

Unfair.

William walked into my apartment and looked around. The small kitchen to the left was clean, spotless even. I'd wiped it down before he arrived. Across from it, the living room looked ... well ... lived in. The large, worn navy couch faced a decent-sized flat screen, and underneath it, my Xbox sat on display. I'd left it there for him to see. Between the couch and television was the coffee table with my board game already set up and waiting.

Which was the main focus of today's meeting.

"Have a seat." I gestured to the couch. "Coffee?"

He nodded and walked straight to the Xbox like a magpie seeing something shiny.

I picked up a box of chocolate chip cookies and said, "Think quick," before tossing them at him.

One large hand snapped upward, and he caught it just before it hit him. He fell backward onto the couch and spread out in the way only William did, like he belonged there.

"Thanks, these are my favorites," he said. "Did you get them for me?"

"Purely coincidental. I didn't buy them specifically for you."
I think.

I exhaled a shaky breath. Why did it feel like a job interview or a first date? Neither of which I had much experience in.

William let his gaze linger on my face before he looked down at the cookies and opened them. "Take a breath. I'm not going to kill you or seduce you. This is business."

"Can you read minds?" I asked. That could be a problem.

"No. But I can read you." He glanced over his notes. "Which is why it's so easy to beat you."

"Oh, stop it." I carried over the two mugs of coffee. "You take it black, right?"

"Yes, as you once told me, 'like my soul.'" He flashed me one of those smiles, and a strange tingle spread across my chest. Was this his dark magic at work?

Perhaps sitting as far away from him as possible was a good idea.

I sat on the opposite couch and gestured to the game. "Shall we get started?"

He took a sip of his coffee, and his Adam's apple moved as he swallowed.

Damn you, Rose. Stop it. Don't look.

I stared down at my coffee and took a deep breath.

"I'm going to walk you through my gaming experience." He glanced at his notebook, his voice void of the playfulness I'd become accustomed to. "Your first problem, which I'm sure you're aware of but I'm mentioning it anyway, is the missing written and structured rules."

My face flamed hotter than the mug I was clutching. "I know, I know."

"That way, you won't have to be there to ramble in circles about it every time anyone plays your game." His dimple made a showing while he suppressed a smile. "Although, I imagine if you had it your way, you would be."

He was absolutely right.

He took another sip of coffee and then picked up a cookie and put the entire thing in his mouth. "But, Rose." He paused while he finished chewing.

I startled at his use of my name. When he called me Rose, it was somehow familiar and unfamiliar at the same time. I always expected some variation of "hobbit."

He swallowed the remainder of his cookie and brushed the crumbs off his black T-shirt. "We're not going to discuss the formation of rules now. Today is all about the game, exactly as we played it."

My mind spun, and I couldn't decide whether it was because he was dissecting my game or because I couldn't keep my eyes off the way his T-shirt tightened around his biceps every time he moved. Something inside me coiled tight, and I looked away.

This was a totally normal reaction to a man who was extravagantly handsome.

"You okay?" He leaned forward, and even though an entire coffee table still divided us, it was too close.

I nodded, careful not to look directly at him. Neema was right. It was too dangerous.

"Let's see those submission guidelines again," he said.

Perfect. I needed an excuse to breathe. I scrambled off the couch and toward my room, where I'd left my laptop. His scent followed me. I spun around and found him leaning against the doorway, staring into my bedroom, which seemed to have shrunk in his presence.

I'd left it exactly as it was when I'd woken up. My cheeks flushed further at the number of books, games, and notes scattered over my bed, the chair, and part of the floor. As much as I denied my parents' chaos genes, some of it had slipped through the cracks.

He peeked inside at the bulletin board mounted beside the doorway. "This is in line with what I expected." A hearty laugh escaped him as he traced his fingers over my ticket stubs and photos.

A look of approval crossed his face as he spotted the same bands I knew were also his favorites. I'd seen his T-shirts.

He touched all my Comic-Con ticket stubs and smiled— I'd bet he attended Comic-Con too. His face straightened, and he retracted his hand before grazing a photo booth strip of Patrick and me.

I'd forgotten that was there.

I shoved my laptop against his hard chest and tried to ignore the firmness.

One more inappropriate thought and I'd shove myself into the freezer until after he'd left.

"Out, out, out. Bedrooms aren't part of business meetings."

He laughed, his eyes switching back to playful. "Even if I wanted to seduce you, I can't say it would work among the Pokémon plushies."

"Ouuuut." With a final push, I managed to move his heavy body.

We settled back onto the couch. Opening my laptop, I pulled up the contest rules and scanned over them.

"Okay, so . . . " I leaned back as I read with William sitting beside me, though far enough that we weren't touching. "I need to submit it in about one and a half months. It needs more than five players, has to be played on a board, has to be an original idea, and no pop culture–themed games or new versions of existing games allowed." I cleared my throat. "And no . . . erotic games."

My entire body must have been the same color as the red shirt I wore.

"Damn, well there goes my last note for your game," he said with that now-familiar lilt in his voice. "Fantasy-adventure-erotica board games are coming up."

I couldn't resist the chuckle that escaped me as he laughed with me, rubbing his hand from the back of his neck all the way through his hair, messing it up further.

"You're a fool," I said.

"I know I am. But I am brilliant at games, so you need to listen to me." He smiled smugly. "Before we continue, can I ask why you love board games as much as you do?" He leaned a bit closer, giving me his full focus.

This close, I could see myself in his pupils.

I opened my mouth, expecting to know the answer, but I didn't. I'd never thought about it. Games had always been something I just loved.

"I know you love rules and structure." He tilted his head, observing me. "Is it the social aspect? Because that's exactly why I don't prefer them."

"I think so . . . I was a lonely kid. Traveling around the world, board games were played despite language barriers, with children and adults, sometimes on my own." I cleared the lump in my throat and blinked a few times. I hadn't expected this strange onslaught of emotions I'd buried many years ago.

He bit his bottom lip while I composed myself.

"Lonely kids, assemble." He offered me one of his signature winks.

I giggled, but I couldn't help wondering where Shaun had been to make William a "lonely kid."

He took a deep breath and opened his notebook. "Knowing your motivation helps. So, lonely kid, your current version takes six players, and while it's good enough, it could manage eight, which'll make it more accessible."

"I'd need two new characters that are important, but also not *that* important, so you won't need eight people for every game."

His eyebrows drew together, and he bit the tip of his tongue while thinking.

It was weird seeing William sitting in the exact spot where Patrick had sat not too long ago. Like an alternate reality. With his casual black clothes, messy hair, and playful energy, William was the anti-Patrick.

"Double up then." His voice elevated with excitement. "Two warriors, two enchanters, two scientists, one ruler, and one medic."

"You're a genius!"

"It's a fine line between a genius and a fool."

I nudged him with my shoulder. Bad move. His body was hot with . . . I don't know. It was hot, and it made my body heat up in response. I shifted away to calm my rattled nerves. "Okay, next note."

By the third note, more than four hours had passed, and Neema walked through the front door.

"Oh, you're still here." She dropped her bag onto the counter.

"Imagine if I greeted you like that every time I found you on my couch," William joked.

"You do. You're a menace." She laughed and walked into the bathroom.

"I should get going." William stood and ducked his head down to look at me. "But, uh, if you want to continue, you could come over sometime this week, after work, since it's nearby. Maybe we'll get through another one of my notes." That dimple was working overtime.

"Yeah, sounds good." I stood and craned my neck up at him.

Grabbing his notebook, he retrieved his car keys from his pocket and spun the Dragon Ball key ring around his finger.

"And look, you survived being alone with me without spontaneously combusting."

I grinned as we approached the door, keeping my gaze on the ground. "I guess you're not that powerful."

"I'm as disappointed as you are."

Round 14

It had been days since William sat on my couch, and even though nothing had happened and nothing ever would happen, the memory was crystal clear in my mind.

At least that's what I told myself when Shaun and I walked into his apartment and my eyes immediately landed on William. Standing in the kitchen, he held a spatula while something fragrant sizzled in the pan in front of him.

"Hungry?" he asked.

Was that flirty? Have I completely lost the plot?

Shaun nodded. "Yes, yes, yes."

"What is it?" I set down my bag and joined Shaun at the island separating the living area from the kitchen. The closer I got, the more my mouth watered.

For the food. Obviously.

"Spaghetti Bolognese." William reached into a high cupboard and retrieved three plates.

Shaun closed his eyes, his nostrils flaring. "You're gonna wanna say yes to this," he said to me before hopping off the stool and walking into the bathroom.

As soon as I was alone with William, an easy smile spread across my face. "Well, yes, please. I didn't know you could cook."

His gaze darted up to mine and then to the closed bathroom door. Glancing back down at the sauce he stirred, a provocative smile curled onto his face. "I think you might find that I am multitalented when it comes to satisfying cravings."

His voice dipped as he reached the end of his sentence, and my entire body vibrated.

That was definitely flirty. I was not imagining things.

This wasn't Playing Nice, but something else. A new round . . .

A thrill coursed through my veins as one thing became clear: I wanted to play.

But I wouldn't. It would blow up in our faces, much like Neema had warned.

Why was I even thinking about this? Nothing had happened.

William lifted the plate questioningly, his eyes landing on something behind me.

"Ten," Shaun answered. "Fill it all the way up."

"You?" William held a second empty dish in my direction. "One is a taste, ten is as much as can fit."

"Uh, five?"

He tutted. "You can handle a bit more."

"Six?" I squeaked out, ignoring the way his gaze dipped to my mouth.

He shook his head and gestured upward with his free hand. "Seven?"

One end of his mouth quirked up. "You won't regret it."

When he finished scooping up everyone's meals, he handed me my dish and asked, "Do you want to get started? We could work on the balcony or in my bedroom, but I believe bedrooms aren't part of business meetings."

"Why not here?" I gestured to the living area, where it was safer.

"Because Shaun isn't going to leave us alone unless we can lock him out."

I chuckled. Unable to resist the smell of the food any longer, I took one bite, and my taste buds came alive. Damn this man. Damn him and all his talents.

"Why can't I be involved?" Shaun gulped down a forkful of food. "I know things about board games too."

William smiled at his brother. "Okay, name one thing you'd change in her game."

"Nothing. It was awesome." Shaun grinned at me.

"Exactly."

"Well, at least eat here before you abandon me," Shaun said, shoveling another forkful into his mouth.

"Fine." William turned to me. "But eat fast before the third part of your weird trio gets here."

The door opened, and Shaun smiled as Neema walked in. "Too late."

William threw his head back and groaned.

"Please give me five minutes to catch up?" I said, having already finished most of my meal.

William's brows drew together in confusion. "You live with her."

"Yes, but she left this morning before I woke up. It's been, like, eighteen hours since we've seen each other."

"Rose, can we talk about . . ." Neema gestured toward my outfit, or my hair, or face, or probably everything. ". . . this?"

For a moment, I had forgotten I looked like a used washcloth. Mortified, my cheeks heated. "I had a rough day. My assignment was due, I was thinking about my game, and Markham was creepier than usual."

"What did he do?" Concern laced my best friend's voice.

"Nothing." I shook my head, trying to shake away the memory of his voice and the way he stared at me. "He hasn't *done* anything, but he kinda lurks around my desk, and in meetings, he either sits right up against me or directly opposite me."

William turned to Shaun, the muscle in his jaw flexing. "How are you okay with this?"

"He's our boss, and he hasn't done anything," I said before Shaun could respond. "I'm fine. It's all fine, and everything is fine." I offered William what I hoped was a convincing smile.

The line between his dark brows only deepened.

"Soon enough, he'll realize nothing will ever happen between us. He isn't my type."

"Who is your type?" Neema asked. "You were with Patrick for so long, maybe it's time to date again—for fun, at least."

"How?" I swallowed the last of my spaghetti, wishing I'd asked for more. "I have no idea how to date, and the thought of having to get to know someone new is making me nauseous."

"Use Spark," Neema said.

William cringed and shook his head. "Don't use Spark."

"Why not?" I asked.

"It's good for casual hookups, and according to you, you're not that kind of girl." He stood, and with a final huff, disappeared onto the balcony.

"I think it might be what I need." I turned to Neema and immediately hated the idea of it. "Maybe not. I don't know."

Neema shook her head. She wouldn't take *no* for an answer. Holding out her palm, she said, "Give me your phone."

I handed it over, and within three minutes I had a Spark profile set up with her choice of photo and bio.

"You can go talk board games." She made a shooing gesture with one hand. "I can do this on my own."

I grabbed my game and joined William on the balcony, where he was playing on his phone.

I dropped the game onto the table before closing the balcony door behind me, separating us from the rest of the world. "So, you'll have to show me how online dating works."

He looked up, his eyes dark. "Nope. You can do that on your own."

"Why?" I bristled.

"Because that's not part of our game." He tucked his phone into his pocket, a challenge spreading across his handsome face.

The out-loud acknowledgment of *our* game set me alight. Had I heard him correctly?

I blinked twice, and a wicked expression crossed his face as he registered my speechlessness. He patted the space beside him with a smile so smug that it tore at the part of me that needed to win.

If life was a game, I couldn't resist playing.

Sitting next to him, I leaned toward him and whispered, "Maybe when you're done showing me how to make that game better"—I pointed at my game on the table—"you can show me how to make *this* game better too."

His eyes widened, and I was tickled by his shock.

He turned to face me, his mouth far too close to mine and his eyes changing dangerously between light and dark.

Did I misread that? Does he think I'm a joke?

When he said nothing, I sprang to my feet, but he was faster, sandwiching me between his hard body and the railing. A shiver traveled down my spine and settled in the depths of my stomach, and not because of the cold metal pushed against my back.

With his tan arms outstretched on either side of me and the muscles in his arms flexing, he leaned down and whispered, "I have a few comments on this game too." His voice was thick, his breath tickling my ear and slipping down my neck. I wished it were his lips.

What am I doing?

My brain screamed, telling me to stop. *It's William, your best friend's brother!*

But my body—my body wanted something else as I looked into onyx eyes that invited me—dared me—to do something. William's attention on my mouth, on my lips, on my every move, left me feeling alive and . . . sexy. Something I hadn't felt in months, years even.

I knew I shouldn't play this round, but I wanted to.

So I did.

Before I could change my mind, I lifted my hips toward him, grinding upward ever so slightly until I felt him pressed against me. Lava spiraled from my midsection throughout my body. His already-dark eyes turned black, and a groan at the back of his throat had me dropping down to my heels.

"Oof." He pushed himself back and ran a hand through his hair and down his neck. His chest rose and fell. "I forgot my notebook."

My pounding heart made me dizzy. Spinning around, I inhaled a deep breath, forcing oxygen into the depths of my soul as I tried to clear my mind. I gripped the metal rail and lifted a hand to my hot cheeks, hoping I could cool them down before he returned. But it was no use. My body was awake and waiting for him.

William walked back onto the balcony and held up the little notebook before closing the door behind him. I wanted to throw that notebook into the ocean and continue doing what we had been doing, otherwise I'd have to throw myself into the ocean to cool down.

"We don't have much time." He took a seat beside the game. "We should get started on this."

I nodded, confusion sneaking in. I was afraid speaking would give away how little control I had over my voice.

We spent the next hour deciphering the rules from my brain, and though William's tone was even and calm the entire time, I couldn't help noticing his reddened cheeks and the way his eyes traveled from my lips to my chest.

I avoided looking at his mouth and used all my energy to process what had just happened. What *I* had done and how good it felt. How natural.

William read another note out loud and then bit down on his lip—and the truth was, I wanted to bite that lip.

I swallowed hard. This wasn't a good idea.

"Best man and best woman," Neema yelled, flinging the door open, "we want to ask you about wedding stuff. How much longer?"

William's long fingers leafed through his notes, and he blew out a breath. "We won't finish tonight anyway. Her game needs a lot of work."

I narrowed my eyes to slits.

Dragging his teeth over his bottom lip, he dropped his voice so only I could hear. "Feel free to come by whenever you want to continue, Rose."

I stood, and my knees wobbled, but I managed a brief nod before following Neema into the lounge, where her Pinterest board was open and waiting.

Round 15

It took an entire week to summon the courage to see William again, even though he lived in my every waking, and sometimes sleeping, thought.

What would have happened had we been alone?

I couldn't shake the look in his eyes or the feeling of his warm breath on me. My body was filled with want . . . and fear.

But time was running out, and my game wasn't done yet.

So, after work, I went to his apartment with Shaun at my side. There would be people around, and none of the inappropriate things I'd been thinking about would be possible.

Yet, when I got there, my heart beat in my throat—which was medically impossible.

I did google it.

Stepping inside, I raised my chin, determined not to let William know he'd won the last round. "Hey."

Hunched over his desk, his hair standing sideways, William shut down one of my favorite games. It disappeared from the screen as he spun toward us.

"Hi and goodbye," Shaun said, never looking up from reading a text on his phone. He picked up the backpack he'd dropped on the floor only seconds before and then grabbed a set of keys from the rack. "Neema's car broke down at work. I need to rescue her."

"Wait, uhm, I . . ." I stammered.

"Play nice!" Shaun grinned before stepping out the door and closing it behind him.

Whatever little confidence I had in beating William at his own game was gone the second we lost our buffer.

William stared at me with one dark brow raised as I made it to the couch on wobbly legs.

"What?" I snapped, retreating to the safety of a snarky tone.

"The game?" He gestured to the bag I clutched against my chest.

"Oh."

Smooth, Rose. Really smooth.

I removed the scarf from my hot neck and set up the game before taking a seat directly across from where William had sprawled out, keeping a healthy distance between us.

He leaned forward, his elbows resting on his parted knees while he stared at the board. "No one wants to play a board game for four hours."

I sighed. "I know. There's so much I wanted to fit in."

A smile played on his lips, and his tongue shot out and took a swipe against the bottom one.

My traitorous cheeks flushed.

"Sometimes the fun is better in small bursts." He stretched, and his T-shirt slid up, exposing his Adonis belt.

My gaze dipped to where it shouldn't. It was more of his body than I'd planned to see, and far more than I was capable of handling in this state.

Damn those low-riding sweatpants.

"You okay?" In one swift move, he hopped from his couch onto mine. His movements were careful and intentional as he leaned closer. "Did you hear any of what I said?"

No, I didn't. Not while fighting the inexplicable desire to kiss him.

Instead, I told him another truth. "Your pants are so low, I'm surprised they manage to stay up."

His gaze dropped to my cleavage, and I wondered if he could see my erratic heartbeat.

He rubbed his palms across his thighs. "I'm surprised you couldn't find a shirt with an even lower neckline."

"You wish I had." My breath caught at how easy it was playing with William.

"I really do," he conceded in a voice barely more than a growl.

The depth of his voice snapped whatever it was twisting in my stomach. A soft laugh escaped me, and I turned away to hide what I imagined were blood-red cheeks.

"What are you so nervous about?" A wolfish grin made an appearance on his face. Taunting. Teasing. Wanting. His body was turned to face mine.

"How do you know I'm nervous?" The nerves I was pretending not to have climbed with each careful word.

"Because I know you." He inhaled with a struggle. "I know that little laugh when you're nervous, or how you fidget. You look away when you're lying, and you bite your cuticles when you're planning but also when you're anxious and stressed. But it's different when you pick at them . . ."

My heart jerked almost painfully in my chest, shoving every coherent thought from my brain and replacing it with his words, his smooth voice, and his ability to notice things about me that most people didn't.

Unable to take it anymore, I twisted toward him, tentatively reaching out to touch the arm nearest me. "How do you know all that? Why do you know all that?"

William remained silent while my fingers trailed over his defined bicep that he often flexed for my attention, then found its way to his chest. We froze, and for a second, his heart raced against my palm.

"I like looking at you." His right hand slid to my waist. And squeezed. A gasp escaped me, and I lifted my gaze to meet his.

"If you know me so well, tell me what I'll do next," I managed in a soft, shaking voice.

"I think you're going to kill me." He dragged his teeth across his bottom lip, his fingers pressing deeper into my side with a desperation that flowed through him and into me.

"I want to."

His left hand found the other side of my waist and he lifted me onto his lap. "Do it, then."

There was so much intention and power in his grip. A shaky breath pushed out of me as I widened my legs to accommodate his width and straddled him. An ache of desire burrowed into the depths of my stomach. I tried to look away, but he caught my chin and held my gaze with his obsidian eyes, as if breaking eye contact would break the spell. His thumb traced against the mole on my jaw, while his free hand pulled me closer.

A sound of wanting escaped me. I slid my hands along either side of him, bracing myself against the couch, supporting me so I wouldn't fall into his gorgeous face. His fingers found the small patch of skin where my waistband and the hem of my shirt met. Our breathing synced, deep and wordless.

"Rose," he choked out, his eyes almost black, "you're succeeding."

Strong fingers twisted into my hair, and he pulled me so close I felt his every heavy, struggling breath.

It was my turn.

His mouth was so deliciously near to mine that I couldn't resist. Leaning forward, I kissed him. Softly at first, mapping the shape of his lips, which were new and, somehow, everything I'd expected. The same lips that had pouted and smirked at me for years.

I darted the tip of my tongue across his top lip, then the bottom, followed by the corners where they met, enjoying the way he reacted.

"Rose," he said again, even deeper this time. He slid his hand from my hair to my neck and pulled me against him.

Our mouths crashed together in a hard kiss, desperate and hot. William kissed me as though I were the only person he'd ever kissed with such urgency, such desperation. As if it were something he'd waited for his entire life. His tongue parted my lips, and my breath hitched as it greeted mine.

He tasted like sweet, black coffee, and I wanted nothing more than to keep touching him and tasting him.

William leaned back for air, but kissing him was more important than oxygen.

"More." I slipped my hands into his soft black hair, dragging his lips back to mine. I needed his mouth—needed every part of him—against me. I cursed at the layers separating us.

I didn't know kissing someone could feel this way. And it was William. William Ashdern.

Against my lips, he let out a husky laugh, his palm sliding down my back and playing with the waistband of my pants, edging me closer until we were as close as physics would allow.

But it wasn't enough.

William's eyes, dark and simultaneously playful, met mine, and his expression shifted. Lifting me, he turned and set me beside him on the couch. "I think that's about enough of *that* game. But it's not over." His eyes challenged me to play along.

I struggled to catch my breath, and my cheeks flushed hot with confusion. I'd been rejected by Patrick, but this didn't feel like rejection.

Before I could respond, William placed a finger over his delicious lips.

"Listen." He lifted his hand to the shell of his ear.

Shaun's voice carried from the hall into the apartment, followed by Neema's familiar cackle.

I blew out a breath, willing my brain to form a logical thought. I straightened my clothing while he patted his and shifted around.

"Tomorrow?" he asked, still breathless.

I shook my head. "Pole dancing tomorrow."

His flushed cheeks paled, and he mouthed the words back to himself. I relished in the idea of leaving him with that thought.

"I'll see you at game night," I said, surprised I still knew how to use my mouth to talk.

He leaned down and kissed my cheek only seconds before the front door opened.

Game night came around quicker than I was prepared for, but took far longer arriving than I'd have liked. My heart had pounded all day, from the minute I woke up to the second I walked into William's apartment and he jumped off the couch to greet me.

"Rose." He shrugged, obviously attempting to appear casual when calling me by my name was anything but. Part of me missed being called hobbit.

He shifted on his feet as though staying away from me was taking every last inch of self-control. He threw himself back down on the couch and let his eyes rake over my knee-length gray dress, cinched at the waist and paired with black, sheer stockings and the high heels I'd nearly broken my ankle in.

I bit back a smile. "William."

As soon as Shaun had his back turned, I winked at William, only to catch him winking at me first.

A tie.

Not unheard of for us. In our years of competing, many of our games—both on and off the board—ended in a draw.

But this one wouldn't, so I sat beside him. "What are you playing?"

"I'm working." His tone dripped its usual annoyance, but a coy smile played over his handsome features.

I studied his profile, and heat coursed through my veins. I turned my attention to the screen, where he was playing a fantasy-adventure video game I'd never seen before. "This looks cool."

"It's okay. Good concept, poor execution. The idea I'm toying around with is the same genre but way, way better." His shoulders relaxed, and he turned to me with a childlike smile so different from moments before.

"What made you design a game in the first place?"

He nodded at the bag housing my board game. "What made you?"

"I wanted to play a game that combined my love for fantasy and strategy and, admittedly, economics."

From the kitchen, Shaun chuckled. "That may be the nerdiest thing I've ever heard you say, and based on the fact that you're you, that's saying plenty."

"Oh, shush." My cheeks heated, and I looked down, picking at my cuticles.

"I think it's impressive," William leaned in and whispered.

Pine and lavender. Intoxicating.

"By the way," he continued, gesturing to the screen, "the characters in this game have different strengths and different goals and, therefore, have different routes to winning. I think that might be what we're missing. At the moment, it's far easier to win as a ruler or warrior."

The gears turned in my head as I considered my game. "You're onto something!" I said with more excitement than I'd anticipated. Then I spent the next few minutes rambling off ideas with no stop or pause button in sight.

But William received it all with a wide grin.

"So, when do you need to submit?" Shaun asked, sitting on the couch across from us.

"In about a month."

He sighed. "Good, good. So both of you will have the capacity to focus on the wedding after that."

"When is the wedding?" I asked. "Neema said you guys hadn't agreed on a date yet."

"Well, as of two hours ago, it's about three months from today! Neema's dream venue had a cancellation. It's gonna be a weekday wedding, but we don't wanna wait any longer."

"Three months?" I pulled out my phone and scrolled through my calendar. My brain buzzed with scheduling as I made notes of all the appointments that needed shifting.

"Why'd you tell her now?" William turned his focus back to the screen. "Now she's going to be stuck in her planning mode."

"It's the best mode." Shaun offered me a nod of encouragement and sat next to me as we went through all the appointments I had scheduled for him too.

The apartment door opened, and Neema walked in already talking. "Rose, I hope you're up to the challenge of throwing an amazing bachelorette party within three months?"

Hopping to my feet, I squealed. "Of course!"

"What are you planning?" Shaun asked, greeting Neema with a kiss.

"I can't tell you our plans because that will ruin Neema's surprise, but we'll end up at VOX." Neema and I shared a secret look that left my cheeks burning.

"We can meet you there after whatever William has planned?" Shaun asked.

William shrugged. "Sure. Doesn't change my plans much."

I wondered what he'd planned. Knowing William, he'd make sure everyone had as much fun as possible.

Turning to me, he pointed at Shaun, who was opening their wedding Pinterest board. "We may as well take advantage of them being distracted." His hands breezed against my thigh while he packed away his console.

At this point, I wished I were a PlayStation controller.

I headed straight for the balcony, needing air or anything to cool my overheating body. "Going to discuss some bachelor party things," I shouted at Neema and Shaun. "Stay out."

The balcony door closed, and William reached me in three quick steps. He wasted no time, twirling me out of view and pressing my back against the wall before lifting me. My legs instinctively curled around his strong waist in a way I had been wanting since he'd peeled me off his lap a couple of days ago.

William's warm lips landed on my neck, burning my skin with desire as he ran more soft, slow kisses across my collarbone. His teeth nipped gently, sending lightning shocks throughout my body. A whimper escaped me, and he looked up with wide eyes, an even wider grin, and that cheeky dimple.

I needed that mouth on mine.

Using both hands, I cupped his jaw and pulled his face toward mine, kissing him as if it were our last opportunity. His body pressed against mine through the four thin layers of fabric separating us. I pulled him even closer, and he groaned, my name slipping through his lips. A name he so rarely used.

I wrapped my arms around his neck, running my fingers through his soft, messy hair. I didn't know how to get enough of him. I wanted more from him, and he knew it.

Claire's laughter from inside the apartment pulled me from my desperate thoughts, and I unwrapped my legs, cursing. William lowered me to the ground, a frustrated groan vibrating through his chest against mine. Our gazes met while we tried to catch our breath.

I was sure I'd electrocute anyone who touched me.

Leaning in, he whispered into my mouth before stealing a last kiss. "To be continued."

Round 16

My deadlines had me fully booked over the next few weeks even though all I wanted to do was see William. I considered sneaking out for a quick kiss, touch, lick—I'd take anything. I was seconds away from sniffing Shaun to see if he smelled anything like his brother.

Addiction. Surely that's what this was? I wanted to live and breathe William. I wanted to spend my days in his lap, feeling his hands caress my body and my lips drag across his skin. Any part of it. I needed to catch him looking at me, the way his gaze ate me every time our eyes locked, one small bite at a time, regardless of what I was wearing.

But I was here. Working on my MBA. Staring at my laptop screen, my mind drifted to my game—*to our game*—as I inhaled a slab of chocolate. I remembered when my father quit smoking and took up chocolate in its place. If it could work for nicotine, it should work for William.

How did he manage to infiltrate my every thought?

It didn't help that William had started texting me too.

Memes mostly; he was terrible at texting. But every now and then, a message would come through that only I would understand.

> **William:** I have some more ideas for the game.
> **Rose:** Like what?
> **William:** I think to make it a more immersive experience, we should extend gameplay between rounds.
> **Rose:** I thought you said we need to shorten the game.
> **William:** I was wrong. It's too short. Players get frustrated. So frustrated they may not be able to eat, sleep, or work until they get to finish the game.

My heart beat so fast that I felt it in my flushed ears. If I called a taxi, I could be at his apartment in twenty minutes.

But I'd never do that.

By the time game night rolled around and I walked into his apartment, I worried I may need to be restrained. Predictably, William was in his usual place on the couch—lounging in those damned sweatpants I remembered all too well.

"What's up?" he said.

"Nothing, what's up on your side?" My gaze dipped and I cocked an eyebrow.

A flash of white teeth appeared as he smiled and shifted to create space for me. I scooted next to him.

He shook his head. "Wait until it's my turn."

The underlying threat in his tone tickled every part of me, but before I could question what he meant, Claire and Lincoln arrived. Well, I assumed it was Lincoln behind the tower of pizza boxes and the 30 Seconds booster pack resting on top of it. They greeted everyone and set the pizzas on the table.

I grabbed the booster pack to investigate. "You're picking 30 Seconds, but with a booster?"

"Yep, because you and William have memorized the other set." He held up a long finger to stop William from protesting. "And we're doing unlikely pairings."

"We've never been partners," Claire said to Shaun. "Lincoln and Neema and . . ." She turned to William and me.

"I'll trade with any of you." William grabbed two slices of pizza.

As he lifted one slice to his mouth, I swiped it, and our fingers grazed. The casual contact ignited whatever it was inside me that burned for him.

Brain, focus. It's game night.

And it wasn't just any game. It was 30 Seconds, the game that had us at our most competitive. Each team had thirty seconds to explain as many terms on their cards, ranging from places to musicians, as possible.

And the unlikely pairings were causing a stir. Shaun and Claire made a terrible team with neither understanding the other's hints. Whereas Shaun preferred using facts, Claire gave hints in the form of personal anecdotes.

On the opposite end, Neema and Lincoln flourished where Neema's creativity complemented Lincoln's engineering brain.

While they were busy, I walked to the kitchen and opened a cupboard high above my head. Eyeing a box of cookies far outside my reach, I raised my arms and shouted, "Come!"

Unsurprisingly, the cookies didn't heed my command.

From across the room, William's eyes met mine. Grinning, he dragged himself away from the game and joined me in the kitchen, where he grabbed the cookies with ease.

He opened the box and held it out to me. His voice dipped low. "If you want something, you could ask."

"It's polite to offer." I took a cookie and popped it into my mouth.

"I am not polite."

And I nearly choked.

"You two, stop conspiring," Neema called. "It's your turn."

Final round.

It was William's turn to describe, and mine to guess. We returned to the game, and he rolled a two.

He cursed.

We needed five correct answers to win.

William blew out a breath and turned to me. "Ready?"

I nodded.

Bouncing from one foot to the other, he geared up for his first hint.

Shaun touched the timer, and William rounded on him. "Hey, hey, fast fingers! I haven't looked at the card yet."

"Sorry!" Shaun threw both hands up in surrender.

No one smiled. Once upon a time, this game had nearly caused trouble between Shaun and Neema, and Claire and me. There were a few months where we'd banned it from game night.

William glanced at the card as Shaun flipped the timer.

"The capital of Turkey," William stated.

"Next!" I shouted.

He frowned.

"Next! Next!" I shouted again.

"She's the actress in that movie you love about the blond doctor with the pink—"

"Ray Loffel!"

"Correct." He grinned. "You have like three concert ticket stubs from this band."

He'd noticed.

Not now, brain.

"Lime Park!" I shouted.

"Correct! It's a fizzy drink, you seem to hate it."

"Coke."

"The full name," he bit out, his tone urgent.

"Coca-Cola," I replied, and then added, "Ankara. The capital is Ankara!"

"Correct and correct. The winners of the last UEFA."

I shook my head.

"It's soccer," he added.

"Liverpool?" My eyes widened. "Manchester?"

"You had a colleague with the same name. You were really sad when she resigned."

"Chelsea!" I jumped up, as if that would get the answer to him quicker.

"Yes!" he shouted as the last grain of sand fell through the timer.

We were already standing from sheer excitement and broke out into our own individual winning dances. His dance was way worse than mine, but he looked better doing it.

Shaun took the card and shook his head. "Nope, Chelsea F.C."

"What?" I turned to him.

"Chelsea F.C." he repeated. "You only gave half the answer."

While I wanted to win, I was a stickler for the rules, and everyone knew it. With a deep grumble, I watched as Neema and Lincoln ended up taking the gold, and William and I sulked over our almost win.

After everyone made peace with one another, I went to the balcony, hoping William would follow me again.

He did.

"Those jeans are against the rules." His soft words, so close behind me, sent a shiver of anticipation down my spine.

Glancing over my shoulder, our gazes locked as he tilted his head to one side.

I giggled, spinning fully around to face him. "We should have won."

A strange sense of weightlessness filled me, scaring me . . . like I might float away.

"I'm counting it as a win." William closed the space between us and handed me a sheet of paper. "I sketched this last night while we were texting. I think this is what you're imagining?"

I unfolded it and couldn't hold back my grin at the squiggly lines and scribbles with made-up names of regions I'd created for my game.

"I love it," I managed.

"Awesome. I'll get someone at work to make it look good."

I took him in, absorbing the sound of his soft, sure voice when he spoke about my game, the twinkle in his eyes when he'd challenged me only moments ago, and the way he leaned against the wall in that moment, just looking at me.

I stepped toward him. "How did you know about Chelsea?"

He bit his bottom lip. "Like I said, you were really sad when she left."

I stood on my toes and kissed the underside of his jaw. His head dipped, reuniting our mouths as his large hands slid across my back and pulled me closer. Hot lips trailed my neck, and the ache within me grew deeper, tighter. His urgent kisses lingered on my skin, pausing to savor me.

"Rose?" Neema called.

We jumped apart, each of us moving to opposite sides of the balcony. My heart pounded, and my head spun with a need I could barely understand.

The door opened, and Neema poked her head out, her gaze darting between us. "I'm heading home. You coming?"

"Yeah." I swallowed hard and glanced at William, who'd managed to close his gaping mouth, but his cheeks were flushed bright red. "I'll see you tomorrow?"

He nodded. "And the day after, and after that, if you so wish."

My already hot cheeks flamed.

William whipped out his phone and opened the Candy Crush app. Long after I'd given up with that game, he'd continued playing.

He was nothing if not determined.

Round 17

All I could think about was being on the balcony with William. We spent weeks fixing my game, talking about it, and playing it before crashing together with our lips meeting and our hands exploring each other a little more.

And now Overpower was ready, but *our* game wasn't done.

Although I'd be lying if I said I hadn't thought about surrendering. I could grab a chair, throw myself over his shoulder, and direct him to his own bedroom. But I wasn't ready for that.

Instead, I went home and called my mom.

"Hey, Rosie. How's my baby girl?" she said, a bustling airport behind her.

"Mom! Are you coming home?"

"Not yet. We're off to London to surprise Aunt Neha for her sixtieth birthday, but we'll be there before Neema's wedding."

"You kinda have to be. I believe you're in charge of the candles."

Her eyes widened. "Ah, yes."

She ordered a coffee from a barista off-camera and then turned her phone and showed him my face, told him I'm recently single, that I love board games, and that I'm her favorite child. She didn't bother telling him I am her only child.

I gave the barista a polite wave, embarrassed this stranger was seeing me in my Hello Kitty pajamas. I hoped she would tip him well.

"How's your game coming along?" she asked.

"I'm submitting it tonight." I blew out a nervous breath. "I'm terrified. William and I have worked so hard on it."

"Oh, yes. Mean William with the beautiful dark eyes." She smirked. "Is there something I should know?"

I knew that would be her next question, so I hoped my tone sounded casual when I responded.

"Nope, nope. What's going on on your side? Dad up to anything interesting?"

"Dad's made a new friend. He's from New Zealand. Look. There they are chatting about rugby." She turned her camera toward my dad.

Dad waved at us, and I waved back.

"If you go to New Zealand, I'd come and visit," I said. "I still haven't seen Hobbiton, feels almost sinful."

"Oh, my little hobbit in Hobbiton. Let's make a plan to do it. You should dress up again. You looked adorable."

"Remember Gandalf?" I asked.

"He is very memorable, Rosie, reminds me of your father."

"Gandalf from that time at Comic-Con, Mom."

"Oh, yes. Well, I remember helping you search the parking lot after you lost his phone number."

"I searched everywhere," I said, thinking back to the heartache that had followed. Gandalf had written his number on a scrap of paper since my phone's battery had run out. "Sometimes it feels like I imagined him."

"You still haven't found him?"

"No," I replied. "How would I?"

"You kids are innovative. Remember how social media connected those two girls who were best friends as kids?"

"I'm not going to do that, Mom. Don't be weird." A laugh escaped me.

"Weird? You're the one thinking about him all these years later." She threw up her hands and grinned.

I shrugged. "Been thinking about him a lot recently, working on Overpower and all."

"You spoke about him nonstop for at least two or three months after that. I worried you might never stop."

I rolled my eyes. "Whatever, Mom."

She paused and then narrowed her eyes, studying me. "So, has Patrick contacted you yet?"

My chest tightened at the mere idea of it. "No, why are you asking?"

"He's going to contact you. That's all I can say, baby."

"Mom, why is he going to contact me? Why do you know this?" Panic raced through my veins.

"Oh, don't worry, but I have been sworn to secrecy." Her eyebrows bounced, nearly touching her hairline before she glanced sideways. "Anyway, gotta run. It's boarding time, and I'd like to use the loo before the flight. I have a runny tummy. Dad told me not to eat the leftovers, but you know I don't like wasting. Anyhoo, love you forever and wherever."

"There are no secrets between us!" I yelled.

I was too late—the call ended.

Frantically, I checked all my social media accounts and emails, but there was nothing from Patrick. *Could she be mistaken?*

I considered texting him, but the idea of doing that filled me with so much dread I had to take one of my mother's emergency Calm Down pills.

This was an emergency. I couldn't think about Patrick. I had too much going on. Patrick and all my work drama would have to go into a little box to be dealt with later.

Or never.

Never was fine too.

The submission process for the game was simple. Enter your personal details and give them two or three sentences about yourself. Upload the game rules, game overview, approximate game length, and photos of the game.

But simple did not equal quick or easy. At least not for me. Not with how much this meant to me. Plus, my mind was hung up on my mother's comment about Patrick, and the rest of me was hung up on William.

After spending forever typing and retyping three sentences about myself, I texted William.

> **Rose:** Describe me in three sentences.
>
> **William:** Short. Dorky. Sexy.
>
> **Rose:** Not three words, you menace. It's for the game submission.

I chewed on my lip to stop myself from smiling at my phone like an idiot.

It took him all of five seconds before he responded.

> **William:** Tell them the truth, Rose. You're the best person to have created this game.

Well, now I was smiling at my phone. It was impossible not to. I was back to my teen years, secretly texting the boyfriend

I wasn't supposed to have and ready to hide my phone the instant anyone walked in.

Keeping his message in mind, I typed up a new bio.

All that was left to do was to hit the big blue submit button, but my hands were shaking. I'd been on edge for the last few hours leading up to this once-in-a-lifetime opportunity.

I read and reread the instructions. I'd followed the rules. All of them. I had thirty minutes left to submit. Pushing myself away from my desk, I walked through the living area and to Neema's bedroom.

The door flung open, and Neema stood before me in her silk nightie. "I was on my way to you."

"Why?"

"I wanted to make sure you submitted your game." She offered me a loving smile before her hands landed on my shoulders and she spun me around toward my room. "You haven't done it yet, have you?"

"I was about to."

"Let's get it over with so we can go to bed. We need to be up early tomorrow morning."

I groaned as I plopped down onto my chair and stared at my screen. My mouse hovered over the button.

Neema kissed the crown of my head, and I clicked submit.

"You've got this," she said. "Now, go to bed. I'll see you at six."

Groaning again, I laid my head on my desk. "I have a few more things to finish before bed, but good night. See you in about six and a half hours."

Round 18

A few more things ended up taking a few more hours, and now I was sitting in Neema's car, very unhappily sipping coffee.

Neema gulped down the last of hers as she reached a red light. "I can't believe she wants to meet this early. But at least we'll get to tick off a whole bunch of wedding things today."

The thought of seeing all our planning come to life for their wedding was enough to shake me awake. When I looked over, her smile reflected mine.

Taylor's Tailor was a small, neat place Neema had heard of through one of her colleagues. An older woman wearing a dark green skirt and a floral blouse came out and welcomed us. A measuring tape was twirled around her neck in a way that was certainly a choking hazard.

We'd barely set foot into the space when she pulled me away and started measuring. Wrapping her tape along my arms, my legs, my waist, and even my head.

Shaun stumbled inside, red-faced and a little disheveled. "Sorry for being late. William's down with food poisoning or something, and I spent the morning trying to convince him through the bathroom door to call a doctor."

"Is he okay?" I asked before Neema could, and I tried to ignore the way her eyes cut in my direction after she walked into Shaun's arms.

"Uhh." Shaun hesitated. "I think so? I don't know. William holes himself up when he's ill." Shaun shrugged, but his brows were still drawn close.

The tailor dragged Shaun off and started measuring him while he rambled to her about how his brother being sick meant he wasn't coming.

My stomach tightened.

Food poisoning. I've had it. Everyone's had it. It's just food poisoning.

I took out my phone and shot William a text to check in, but it wasn't delivered. His phone must be off. The strange tension in my stomach curled tighter. I turned away and drummed my fingers on the table beside me.

Without intending to, my brain noticed the numbers on the tailor's notebook. Aside from my head, all my measurements were larger than when I'd sewn my last Comic-Con costume. Sticky discomfort crawled down my spine. I'd always been happy in my own skin, but right now my sleep-deprived brain was struggling.

Maybe that was why Patrick had lost interest.

"So, we need to pick our own fabric and come back here. Then we can grab lunch, get to the florist, the baker, and the graphic designer." Neema shimmied, her eyes sparkling before landing on me and then dimming with concern. "What's wrong?"

Still reeling from my thoughts, I shook my head. "Nothing. I'm tired. I was up all night, remember?"

"Yeah, I know. But you look upset." She led me outside toward the car and whispered before Shaun caught up to us. "So, you still have no idea what Patrick wants?"

Discomfort soared through me. "Nope, and something tells me my mom wanted to give me a warning. As chaotic as she is, she rarely slips up when it comes to secrets."

Neema and I released the same long exhale.

Shaun reached us and offered Neema a soft smile.

"Uhm . . . maybe I'll skip the fabric store and check on William then join you later?" he said. "Or could we reschedule? I don't want to miss anything but—"

Shaun's concern seeped into me, and before I could stop myself, I said, "I'll check on him."

Two sets of shocked and confused eyes focused on me.

I shrugged. "We're done here, which is all I really needed to be present for."

"But you planned all of this," Neema said.

"For you." I grinned. "You both need to be here, and rescheduling this is a nightmare."

That wasn't the only reason, but I'd seen the confusion in Shaun's eyes with a hint of unease. I hated lying to them, but telling either of them about whatever William and I were doing before the wedding was a disaster waiting to happen—much like William and myself, I supposed.

But it was too late to stop. And he was sick. This was innocent. Mostly.

This wasn't Round 1 or Round 2 of our game. I didn't know what it was. But I knew I wanted to see him.

Neema squeezed my arm and tossed her keys to me.

I gave them my best smile. "Text me everything. I want photos, updates, selfies, and voice messages." I kept rambling until they both chuckled and I was in the car and on the way to William, following the pull in my stomach leading me there.

After a quick stop at home, I went to their apartment and knocked on the door. Only silence. I went through Neema's keys and found the spare Shaun had given her. Barging in wasn't something I was comfortable with, but what if William was unable to walk?

I unlocked the door and cracked it open. "William? I'm coming in."

A shifting sound came from William's bedroom. I dropped my things and closed the front door behind me.

His bedroom door cracked open. "Rose?" he said. His face was unusually pale and sweat glistened on his straight nose. His dark eyes lost focus as they reached mine. "Rose? What are you doing here?"

He leaned his head against the doorframe, looking like he might pass out.

"You need to lie down," I said, leading him back to where he'd come from.

I sat on the edge of his bed and brushed his damp hair out of his face. His eyes closed as I touched him, and he released a soft breath.

"Have you called a doctor yet?"

"No doctor." His lips pressed together, and his hand shot to his stomach.

"Is it cramping?"

He nodded, looking smaller than I'd ever seen him. "I don't want to throw up again. Been throwing up all night, and I really, really don't want to throw up in front of you. It doesn't go well with my sexy, mysterious persona."

I bit back a smile, happy he still had his priorities straight. "Luckily for you, I am well trained in dealing with food poisoning and rarely having access to a doctor." I took out a bean bag, which was one of the things I'd stopped at home for.

William frowned at me in question.

"Because of how much we traveled and the middle-of-nowhere places we ended up in, there were plenty of times my stomach did not agree with what we were eating, and we treated it wherever we were, sometimes with the help of the locals. Other times, I thought I may die or lose a parent." I shut my eyes. "Sorry, I didn't mean . . ."

He smiled a gentle, weak smile that had my free hand trailing up to touch the dip of his now-shallow dimple.

"You had a strange childhood," he whispered.

His hot hand slid into mine, and I tangled our fingers, my heart softening in a way I hadn't expected. I squeezed lightly before releasing him. "I'll be right back."

He swallowed hard, shut his eyes, and whispered as I left his bedroom, "This is kind of like a dream I've had."

I heated the bean bag in the kitchen and prepared an electrolyte mixture using the strange unlabeled sachet my mom had sent me.

When I got back, William was curled up, and my heart sprung from my chest at his unease. I unfurled him and helped him sit before lifting the hem of his shirt and placing the bean bag on his stomach. I averted my gaze, trying not to stare at how even more defined he was than I'd expected.

He noticed and chuckled.

I handed him the drink, which he eyed through narrow slits.

"Trust me on this." I brushed his hair away from his face again—more for myself than for him, if I was honest. I wanted to touch him, not because of all the general reasons I had been wanting to touch him, but for a different reason. Something new and strange blossomed in my chest. Something that shouldn't be blooming for William. But he looked so soft, vulnerable, and open. So unlike the William I was used to.

I shook off the strange feeling that was consuming me. I was simply taking care of a friend. I'd do it for Shaun, I'd do it for Neema, I'd do it for Claire and even Lincoln, if he'd let me. It was no different with William.

But that was a lie.

Everything was different with William.

"You don't have to be here," he said, after taking the first sip and grimacing.

"Is the drink so bad you'd rather send me away?"

He laughed again, and my heart skipped.

"No." He took another sip. "But what about the wedding stuff? Shaun won't be too pleased you're here . . . for various reasons."

"I didn't ask for his permission." I sat beside William with my back against the headboard and our arms pressing together. "And . . . I want to be here. Do you want me here?"

"I do," he said without any hesitation.

I turned my head and kissed his ear. "Consider this payback for the ankle. We're even."

He melted into it and then gulped the last bit of the drink before leaning his head against mine. Heat radiated from him.

I slid my hand up to his jaw to support his head before placing my lips on his forehead. "You're hot."

"Thanks, so are you."

I giggled. *If life was a game, William never stopped playing.*

I propped him up with as many pillows as I could find before slipping into the kitchen and fetching a cloth and some cool water. When I returned, his eyes were closed. One of my most hated memories was waking up to a cold, wet cloth against my fever-ridden body. I took one long look at him, enjoying the slow rise of his chest and the touch of color returning to his cheeks.

I placed the bowl of cold water on his desk and marveled at his collection of . . . well, everything. William had stacks of games, comics, books, trinkets, and superhero figurines. If I had more expendable cash, my room would look exactly the same.

I lifted the latest copy of Haunted Thrones. Of course he was following this series too.

A soft moan called my attention, and I put the book on his nightstand and wrung the cloth before stroking my dripping fingers along his jaw.

"Hey, I'm going to try and cool you down, okay?" I said, removing the bean bag from his abdomen.

He cracked his eyes open, his frown deep. He offered me the slightest nod, and I put the cloth on his forehead. He flinched, but I continued tracing my fingers down his chin, cupping his face before placing a soft kiss on his cheek.

"This is . . ." he said.

When I pulled away to look at him, his eyes had fallen closed again.

". . . nice." He swallowed.

"I'm doing the bare minimum here to keep you alive for my own selfish reasons."

He chuckled and stilled. He didn't open his eyes when he spoke again. "I've never had anyone do any of this for me . . . not since my gran."

My heart cracked open. That couldn't be true. What of his father? Who, it occurred to me in that moment, was a doctor. I stared at him, wanting to ask questions, to do more. But there wasn't much more to do, and I didn't think my intrusive questions were appropriate.

William tilted his head in my direction and opened his eyes. "What did you think of the latest Haunted Thrones? I assume you've read it by now."

I lifted the book and shook my head. "I haven't had a chance. Have you?"

He nodded and then cringed.

"Oh, don't do that," I said.

"What?"

"Don't do that with your face. Now I know someone is going to die. Who is it? No. Don't tell me. Never mind." I put the book back on his shelf and enjoyed his soft laughter behind me.

"My brain feels noisy," he whispered.

"I get noisy brain too." In fact, having not had an inch of sleep all night and a busy start to the day, I was currently fighting it. "I drown it out by watching something familiar I don't really need to focus on." I grabbed his laptop and brought it to the bed. "Wanna try?"

He nodded, and I scooched near him, resting my head on his shoulder. He dropped his head on top of mine while I navigated through the movies he'd marked as favorites.

"I know." He took the mouse and scrolled to a movie I'd have chosen if given the chance.

Half-awake, he locked our hands, our fingers fitting perfectly.

I closed my eyes and gave in to the feeling of peace, knowing William was okay and he was close enough for me to hear every breath.

A few minutes into *The Lord of the Rings*, sleep came for me. Finally.

Round 19

Neema stayed over at Shaun's place, so the next morning, I was knocking on his door because they needed to fill me in on the wedding arrangements I'd missed.

And I wanted to check on William.

The previous day, I'd snuck out of his room the second I'd heard Shaun and Neema enter, and before either of them could ask me anything, I made excuses to leave.

But here I was.

Shaun opened the door, and I peeked inside. William was on the couch, fast asleep. I lowered my voice when I greeted them but Neema turned on the loud kettle.

"He's asleep!" I said.

"Yeah, like a log. You can kick him, and he won't wake up. But he's okay. Your mom's concoction worked," Shaun replied, his voice at regular volume.

I hovered over William, but he barely fluttered an eyelid at Shaun's loudness. He looked so peaceful in sleep—no smirks, no disdain, no frowning. I resisted the urge to place soft kisses all over him and his long eyelashes.

Instead, I pinched his chin.

He groaned and blinked a few times as he came awake.

"Welcome to Neverland." I grinned.

He offered me half a smile, the other half still waking up. "Hey."

"Not healthy enough for a bit of sarcasm?"

He stretched, every muscle in his body flexing until I practically vibrated.

"Give me a minute to wake up."

His sleepy eyes, light and fuzzy, combined with his soft smile, left me wanting to crawl into the small gap between his warm body and the couch and live there.

"How are you feeling?" I asked.

William kicked his feet off the couch and pushed himself upright. He grabbed his glasses and slipped them on.

They made him even cuter.

"Tired, but okay." He took my hand in his, stroking my palm and sending bursts of light up my arm. "Thank you."

We let go the second Neema and Shaun joined us in the living room.

Neema filled me in on everything I'd missed with an emphasis on her wedding website. "It's live! We can track RSVPs and meal preferences. It's awesome."

William stiffened beside me, his gaze lifting to Shaun's, who had been looking at him too.

"Any news?" William asked.

Shaun shook his head, his lips pressed in a thin line. "We'll know soon enough."

While I didn't know what they were talking about, after William's comment yesterday, I wondered if it was about his father. I hadn't been able to shake the sound of his voice and how soft it had been. Only then did I connect the few dots I had. William wasn't in any of the photos of Shaun with his parents. And there were no photos in William's room of his father either.

It was none of my business, but my stomach twisted, and seeing Shaun lose his smile only pulled it tighter.

"I still have you down for a plus-one," Neema said to me.

I groaned.

"I'm going to find you a date before then. I already have one very interested party."

I stammered at the same moment William huffed out a harsh breath.

"Remember Wade, the accountant?" Neema continued. "Well, he's cute and single and has been asking about you since you came to my office party."

"Uhm, thanks. But no thanks," I mumbled, not daring to look at William.

"He's really nice. Plus, he's your type." She nudged me.

"What's her type, then?" William asked, his tone even.

Neema beamed. "He's quite tall. Not as tall as Patrick, but still, tall. Very handsome. And most importantly, he's nice. He's doing his MBA part-time too."

"I'm not interested." It wasn't a lie, and I wasn't ready to explain why either.

"What about sex?" She grinned. "Since you deleted the Spark profile I created, this might be a good way to get back in the game. Rebound sex is excellent."

William's presence grew larger and darker, and he released a grunt.

Neema turned to him. "What's wrong with you? Are you feeling sick again?"

"A little." He stood before making his way to the balcony.

I wanted to join him, but Neema bounced from the couch she was on to mine. "So, coffee? I'll set it up for after work one evening."

"Uh . . ."

"It's just coffee. Unless there's another reason stopping you that I don't know about?" I couldn't tell if I was imagining it, but there was a knowing tone to her voice.

"Coffee's fine." Panicking, I stood, needing to be near William. Immediately.

Out on the balcony, William leaned over the rail. All the color and mischief that had been missing from his face yesterday returned in full force. He glanced at me with eyes alight with that *desire* I lived for.

I slid myself between him and the rail, enjoying the way he reacted to me. He lowered his head and kissed my neck, taking my breath away. I allowed it, giving in to the way he made me feel. How I burned for him. How I'd imagined him doing this.

Goose bumps popped out over my arms. I was definitely not imagining this.

His tongue traced my earlobe.

"I want you," I whimpered.

Clearly disagreeing with me, my brain set off alarms, but my body ignored it.

William's eyebrow arched, and I bit my lip as he cradled my face in one hand. I shuddered with anticipation.

Did he not hear me? I was ready. I wanted it. I couldn't want it more if I tried.

He kissed me again, setting every part of me alight. "Not yet."

"Why?" I trembled as though I may explode. "I need it."

"Not yet. It's not the right time."

I wanted to question him further, to figure out what that meant, but his lips pressed against the curve of my ear. "And,

Rose, when we do reach that round, I'm going to need a lot more than these stolen seconds with you."

My breath hitched.

He took a few steps back and gazed at the sky overhead as he released a long, slow breath. "Besides, what about Wade?"

"Neema was suspicious, so I had to agree to meet him for a coffee. But she's coming along, and she'll see I'm not interested."

William shrugged and pinched his lips up on one side. "You didn't *have* to do anything." He glanced at me sideways. "What makes you so sure you won't be interested?"

"I'm very one-track-minded." I smiled.

His face relaxed at my words. "Okay, but before your date—"

"It's just coffee."

"Before your coffee, I want to see you." His lips curled into something devious, and his eyes held a hint of playful danger, daring me to agree.

And so I did.

Between work and my studies I was swamped, so my coffee with Wade was arranged about two weeks later on my first free evening. I left the office that evening with Shaun, which meant I could easily follow William's request. I hadn't stopped thinking about how he wanted to see me before my meeting with Wade, and my skin tingled at the thought of spending a few extra moments with him. He was up to something, which made it even more exciting.

"Hello!" I called out my arrival, my gaze scanning the living area for William but only finding Neema on the couch.

Neema, who looked stunning at all times of the day because her job required it, looked me up and down, her eyes narrowing at my choice of outfit. "I will never understand how you get away with dressing the way you do."

Grinning, I shrugged and handed her the bag I'd brought along. "What do I need to worry about when I have you to dress me?"

Rolling her eyes, she rummaged through everything I'd brought along, holding each piece up in front of her and studying it long enough to let me know how seriously she was taking her task.

Shaun went off to the kitchen to prepare a pot of coffee.

Standing, Neema abandoned the bag and approached me before pushing my hair away from my face.

William's bedroom door clicked open, and my head snapped in his direction, taking him in. His messy hair stood out on one side, his rumpled shirt looked like he'd awoken from a nap, and his checkered pajama pants hung low on his hips. He'd never looked better.

"I'm surprised you're awake," Shaun said to him. "You haven't slept properly in days."

"I have some more work to do." William's eyes met mine before he slipped into the bathroom.

My body buzzed. Was I the work? Did he have actual work? Did he remember he'd asked me to come over?

The sound of rushing water filled my ears, and I couldn't help but picture William in the shower. People were naked when they showered. Very naked. Fully naked.

Rose, snap out of it.

Neema held up a pair of jeans and a T-shirt. "Try this."

"I'm not getting undressed here."

A light laugh from the kitchen made me look up at Shaun.

"I don't think she meant in front of us, Rose." Shaun gestured toward his bedroom. "You can use my room."

I grabbed the clothing and walked into his room. It was the complete opposite of William's—neat and orderly with a few photos of Neema and his parents and a few business management books. Much like his office cubicle.

After slipping into the chosen outfit, I walked back to the living room and spun around, knowing Neema would demand it.

She nodded and then held up the white dress I'd brought. "Okay, now this one."

This time when I walked out of the bedroom, William was also exiting the bathroom wearing nothing but a towel. I stopped suddenly, afraid if I took another step I'd slip on my own drool.

William's shoulders appeared wider with nothing hiding them, and his tan chest and arms seemed bigger with every muscle revealed. His hair was still wet, sending droplets of water racing down his chest and through the center of his abdominal muscles before disappearing into the towel around his waist.

The towel. That damned towel. The thing protecting his dignity and saving me from going feral.

He cleared his throat, and my head shot up in time to catch his smirk. Of course, this was part of his game.

Without changing out of the towel, William sat on the couch and stretched his long legs in front of him. I swallowed hard—he definitely hadn't skipped leg day.

"Ew, William." Neema scrunched her nose. "Get dressed."

"I want to help pick an outfit." He flashed his dimple, and his muscles danced as he crossed his arms over his chest.

My cheeks heated, watching him watch me.

"Whatever." Neema blew out a breath and began fussing with my hair, trying to tame the riotous mess of waves that defied her efforts. After a long while and what must've been a full bottle of detangling spray, she released my long black hair into a gentle cascade of curls down the center of my back.

William shifted, and the towel moved, but not enough to reveal anything. "I like the dress." William bit down on his bottom lip, his gaze raking across me.

I'd thought the dress was a modest and safe choice. It landed only slightly above my knee and cinched at the waist, and the neckline barely showed anything, but William's obvious desire had me feeling completely exposed. An electric current shot straight from his dark eyes, leaped across the coffee table and beyond the dress, meeting me—touching me— right in the center of my chest. I could feel his need, and I wanted nothing more than to climb onto his lap and live there.

My mind wandered to what we'd do if we were alone. I'd rip off that towel no sooner than he'd tear off this dress. I wanted to touch every inch of his skin and then drag my lips across his damp flesh as my fingers slid through his dripping hair. My body pulsed at the thought, and I was moments away from begging him to put me out of my misery.

"I agree," Neema commented, clearly surprised. "Now, let me fix this face. You're looking a bit flushed. Are you okay?"

"I'm fine."

I looked at William again, wondering how his body was so chiseled. I'd never seen him working out. He was always sitting on this damned couch.

He stretched his arms behind his head and flexed. It was so intentional I burst out laughing. A half beat later, his laughter joined mine.

Neema snapped her head toward William. "Don't make her laugh." She turned back to me and shot me a stern look. "And don't move your face."

Much to my disappointment, William raised his hands in surrender and left the room.

Oh, but he wasn't done yet. Of course not. He returned a few moments later wearing a pair of fitted black jeans and carrying his shirt. Walking to the closet, he removed the ironing board with slow, deliberate movements. My eyes memorized the way his back muscles moved.

What a back, what a good-looking back.

"There!" Neema surveyed her work with a grin. "That should do it."

Satisfied with my makeover, she slipped into the bathroom to wash all her brushes. The second she turned on the water, William's gaze met mine over the back of Shaun's head, urging me to join him in the kitchen. In only a few weeks, we'd mastered the art of speaking without saying a word.

"I'm gonna wash these," I told Shaun, gathering the mugs.

"Don't worry about it. Neema will kill me if you mess up your dress," Shaun said. "Are you excited for the date?"

"Coffee. It's just coffee," I corrected. "I'm gonna wash up. You do it at our place all the time."

Never in my life have I insisted on doing the dishes.

Who am I?

Shaun shrugged and turned his attention to the TV as I joined William in the kitchen.

Setting the mugs in the sink of soapy water, I ran a sponge over one of them. William crowded behind me, the heat from his skin so close I could feel it on mine. His body pushed closer, pressing against me until my nerves fluttered in response. He ran wet kisses below my ear, moving his lips along my jaw before cupping my chin in one strong hand and tilting my face toward him for better access to my mouth.

After a second of pleasure, I pulled my hands out of the soapy water and pushed him away, frantic to be sure Shaun couldn't see us. Thankfully, he was absorbed in a meme compilation on TV. And the bathroom door was still closed with Neema behind it.

This was risky. Which somehow made it better.

I admired William's bare chest up close, running my fingers along every contour, of which there were many.

"Why did you want me here?" I asked in barely a whisper.

"I don't want you to forget about me when you're with him." With one hand, he lifted the edge of my dress and ran the backs of his fingers along my thigh in light, caressing circles, teasing my flesh until tiny bumps rose along my skin. A whimper escaped me, and I slammed my mouth shut as his hand traveled higher.

Curling his lip on one side in a devious grin, William gazed down at me and winked. Then, dropping his hand, he took two steps back and returned to the ironing board.

I closed my eyes and cursed. Because English had abandoned me and curse words were the only words that came to mind. Damn him—my entire body vibrated with desire at a frequency that may very well shatter these mugs.

Furious, I turned to the sink and washed the dishes. They'd shine so brightly when I was done that the next person who used them would be blinded.

Round 20

"How was the date?" Shaun asked, leaning against my desk the next morning. "Neema said you weren't interested, and she can't understand why."

The date started and ended with me thinking about William. *That was why*. And I had no doubt every date with anyone else would end in the same way.

But I couldn't tell Shaun that.

"I'm not attracted to him." I shrugged, taking my seat and setting up my laptop.

Shaun nodded. "Pity. He's great—smart and kind. Perfect for you." He tutted and changed the subject. "What about the year-end party? Are you coming solo or do you have someone in mind?"

I hadn't even thought about that—or about how Patrick accompanied me every year. "Maybe I'll skip it."

"You arranged it, and the theme is right up your alley."

Superheroes and Villains. And while it may seem like I had a hand in that, it was purely coincidental. "Maybe I'll come alone, then."

"I mean, we'll be there. Neema's planning on wearing her Supergirl costume."

I grinned. "That's lingerie."

Shaun returned my grin. "I know."

An email notification pinged on my laptop, and my heart stopped.

```
Board Game Competition Submission: Winners -
Round 1.
```

Shaun leaned over my shoulder and read it before I could swipe the window closed. "You're not going to open it?"

"William needs to be here."

"Oh." Shaun froze, his eyebrows dropping low while he seemed to process my answer. "Makes sense. He worked pretty hard on it. So . . . you're coming over after work?"

I nodded. "But I have to finish all of this." I pointed at my screen.

His jaw dropped. "That's impossible."

"Markham assigned it. I think he's testing me."

"Using you." Shaun shook his head, grumbling under his breath. "Well, I'm here as long as you are."

I turned my focus to the first item on my to-do list, but that contest email burned away bits of my fingers with each key I tapped on the keyboard.

Late that afternoon, when I desperately needed a break, I stepped away from my computer and went to the kitchen. Most of the office lights were off, but a few of the automatic sensors detected my presence as I walked by and turned on. The others remained off, seemingly not knowing I existed . . . or maybe I just didn't meet the height requirement. I swung my arms high, and a few more lights came on.

Popping a coffee pod into the machine, I waited with my cup in place while the machine hummed, the scent of the coffee making my taste buds come alive.

Footsteps echoed behind me, and I called over my shoulder, thinking it was Shaun. "Coffee?"

"Sure," a familiar voice answered, but it wasn't the one I expected.

I spun around and faced Mr. Markham, who stood close enough for my head to snap up to meet his gaze.

"Mr. Markham," I stammered.

"You look beautiful in black," he whispered, his voice thick and low.

A chill raced down my spine. I retreated a step, and the edge of the counter stabbed into my back. "This is inappropriate."

"Oh, Rose. Don't be such a prude." He stepped away and then added with a jovial lilt, "It was only a compliment. I am a man, and I have eyes."

Leaving my cup where it was, I sped back to my desk, where Shaun waited. No part of me wanted to tell him—no part of me even wanted to think about it.

"Are you okay?" he asked.

"I'm ready to leave."

Shaun walked over. "Everything okay? Is it Patrick? Did he finally contact you?"

I shook my head, caving at my mother's vague warning. Shaun and Neema were as worried about it as I was.

"It's not that," I said, but I didn't want to tell him what had happened, so I added, "I just want to read the email. Let's go."

Luckily, that won him over.

If Shaun noticed my silence during the walk to his building, he chose not to say anything. Each step that took me farther from our office lifted the nausea swirling in my stomach.

The second we entered the safety of their apartment, Shaun told Neema and William about the unopened email in my inbox.

While he spoke my heart was raging in my chest, but I wanted to forget Mr. Markham's compliment. That was all it was . . . right?

William's eyes grew wide, and he sucked in a deep breath while I retrieved my phone from my bag.

"Okay, last chance for bets," I deadpanned, but no one laughed. I handed my phone to Shaun and whispered a soft prayer.

Surprised, a smile lit up his face. "Can I read it out loud?"

I nodded and sat beside William. It was only when he slipped his hand between us and grazed my thigh with the backs of his knuckles that my shattered nerves settled back into place.

Shaun cleared his throat and read from my phone. "Hello, everyone! Thank you for your submissions. We loved seeing the passion and creativity poured into each and every game you created. Unfortunately, there can be only one winner." He pulled in a deep breath and took a moment to gaze at each of us dramatically before continuing. "The following five board games will continue on to Round 2. Congratulations to the following people, in alphabetical order."

I inhaled, and the sound of oxygen entering my lungs was the only sound in the room. Shaun stilled, and Neema was quiet for the first time in her life. Even William was, quite literally, sitting on the edge of his seat.

"A Princess's Tale, submitted by Alia Ghoor."

Okay.

"Cats versus Dogs, submitted by Lester Hanning."

Okay.

"Overpower, submitted by Rose Marie Jones."

I jumped to my feet and pointed a finger at him. "Don't lie to me, Shaun!"

"I wouldn't lie to you about this." He beamed at me and pulled me in for a tight hug.

"Don't lie to me," I repeated, unsure of why I was crying. It didn't take much, but even for me, it was excessive.

Neema sprang up and joined the hug.

Shaun glanced at my phone over my quaking shoulders. "Kaleidoscope, submitted by Anita Peterson." He grinned. "And you know what? No one cares what the last game is because you're winning this!"

A harsh sob erupted from somewhere deep inside me. I was entirely overwhelmed. The past few months had been too much, and this . . . this was something that held my heart for a lifetime.

Shaun spun us around, and my gaze met William's.

Told you. He mouthed the words through a huge smile, following it with a wink. His hands were fisted and crossed over his chest as though he were stopping himself from grabbing me and pulling me into him.

I wanted to be there. I wanted to thank him for all the hours he'd spent helping me perfect my game. I even wanted to tell him about Mr. Markham.

I stopped my thoughts right there.

I'd been in a relationship with Patrick for so long that I didn't know what to do in this situation with William. Had he signed up to hear about my every trouble?

My stomach curdled at the thoughts racing through me.

We never went out.

We never discussed what we are.
All we'd done was kiss.

I needed to get ahold of my heart, but . . . I dared a glance in William's direction, and the mere idea of defenses fell.

Shaun cleared his throat, pulling me from my stupor. "Okay, where was I? A follow-up email detailing Round 2 will be sent to the five people mentioned above." He scrolled through my emails. "Let's see . . . Ah-ha!"

I settled onto the couch as Shaun took the seat beside me and opened the next email.

"Congratulations!" He beamed, his voice bright. "We decided your game was worth playing, so that is exactly what we'll do."

The four of us looked at one another as he continued.

"We believe we need to play the game to know if it's the one for us. That is why we'd like for someone, not you, to come to our offices and play your game."

My mouth opened in protest, but Shaun held up a finger.

"Why not you?" he continued reading, and by the tone of the language used, it felt like a casual conversation. "Well, the creator of the game tends to become a bit overbearing, trying to explain things mid-game, and that's not how board games are played."

I blew out a breath. Fair point.

"So, send us the details of someone you trust with your precious prototype, and we'll get them here and get us playing," Shaun said.

William.

That was the first and only name that came to mind.

My head snapped up, only to find his eyes already on me.

"In short, you will be judged on the following criteria: How long it takes to set the game up, deciphering the rules, game enjoyment, game difficulty, and game length. The rest will be explained on the day of. Good luck." Shaun turned to me, his blue eyes wide. "It's signed by Dudley."

Much as I tried to wipe the smile off my face, I couldn't.

"I'll go!" Shaun and Neema volunteered together.

I cut them off. "No. I want William to go. If he . . ." I looked at him. "I mean . . . if you want to."

William's eyes lit up in a way I'd never seen. He nodded, and that smirk found its way onto his face. "I, too, think I'm the best option."

Shaun made a comeback, but I didn't hear it. All I knew was my game had made it. My game was good enough for them to want to play.

My fingers navigated to my mother's contact details, and I hit dial.

And like always, she answered immediately. "Hey, Rosie, your cheeks are looking particularly rosy this evening."

Before I could get the words out, Neema hopped beside me and shouted, "Aunty A! Rose's board game made it to the next round!"

My mother screamed, and a few seconds later, my father ran into the room swinging a spiky branch around.

"What's going on?" he yelled.

"Rosie's game won!" my mother shouted.

My dad cheered in the same way he did when his favorite sports teams scored.

"This *round*!" I shouted, trying to lower their enthusiasm. "I won *this round*! There's another round!"

"It doesn't matter, baby. You won this round. You won. You've proved to yourself you created something of value." She beamed with pride.

I blinked the tears away. "Don't make me cry, Mom. I'm not alone."

"Where is my darling Shaun and that beautiful brother of his?" she asked.

I passed the phone to them, and they greeted my mom like young boys talking to a school principal.

"Goodness, you two are gorgeous," she shouted at them.

Shaun and William blushed in response.

"Rosie," my dad called.

I took the phone from Shaun's outstretched hand and held it in front of me to see his face. "I'm here, Dad."

"I want you to know, when you were eight years old and you asked me if I thought your game was good, I wasn't lying when I said it was. You're brilliant, baby. I wish you took a moment to admire your own brilliance the way you do for others. Not only for this game, but in the way you live your life. You're the strongest person I know, my Rosie, and you make me proud every single day."

My dad was a man of few words, but when he chose to use them, he used them at full impact.

And even though he had no idea what had happened at work, it was as though he knew that, tonight, I needed to hear that.

Round 21

The excitement of the board game win wore off as soon as I saw Mr. Markham. I sat in meetings and avoided his gaze. I did my work. I kept my head down. M&G was one of the top firms in California, and in a few years, my options would open up. But I needed to stick this out.

Finding a new job would be awful. Aside from the fact that having M&G on my résumé was a huge perk, I wouldn't have Shaun, and all the other firms of the same caliber weren't in town.

But this wasn't okay. I wasn't okay.

Without fully realizing what I was doing, I walked to the corner office of Louisa, the HR manager, and knocked.

"Come in," she called.

I pushed the door open and found her sitting behind a large desk, her expression welcoming like a kindergarten teacher on the first day of school.

"Hi." I offered her a polite smile.

"Rose. Please sit down. Would you like a cookie?" She opened the lid of the jar she kept topped up with her famous homemade cookies.

There was no reason I couldn't file a complaint and eat a cookie at the same time. I was nothing if not a successful multi-tasker, and her cookies were delicious.

"Awesome job on the Socials Team, by the way. Everything's coming together nicely. I even have my superhero costume ready." She clapped her hands together.

"What are you going as?"

"Supergirl," she replied. "You?"

I stifled a laugh. Neema had some competition.

"I haven't decided yet, but I'll figure something out. I have a box of wigs and hats and a drawer of face paints. Worst case, I'll go green and wear purple shorts."

She offered me an unsure laugh.

Pulling in a deep breath, I closed my eyes and searched for the fearlessness my parents believed I owned, somewhere deep within me, something I never quite recognized in myself.

"Louisa," I said, "I'm here to make a complaint. Or, more specifically, to report someone for . . . " I paused as my heart rate kicked up. ". . . for . . . harassment?" I said the last word as though it were a question.

Louisa's eyes widened, and her red-lipped smile dropped away. My throat dried at her bleak expression.

"Okay." She enunciated both syllables. "Are you the person being harassed?"

I nodded, but I couldn't help but think: *Was I being harassed?*

"By whom?" Her eyes were so wide that she looked more afraid than I was.

"Jeffrey Markham." I said his name as clearly as possible, but it came out sounding more like a squeak.

Louisa stared at me for what felt like a lifetime—so long I wasn't even sure she'd heard me. Then an expression of dread poured over her face, and I knew she had.

"Can you tell me what happened?" she asked.

I told her everything, and the more I spoke, the sillier I felt. He hadn't done anything. Patrick had warned me not to go to HR, yet here I sat with a mouthful of *he called me pretty.*

"Thank you, Rose. I know that was hard." She pursed her lips together, her eyes joyless. "We'll investigate the matter."

"What happens now?" I brought my thumb to my lips and bit at the cuticle.

"I'll talk to Mr. Markham, and I'll probably need to talk to you again. It's best if the two of you avoid each other as much as possible."

The reality of her words washed over me. My mind and heart raced, and my entire body clenched.

"So . . ." My voice heightened in panic. "I still have to deal with him? Here? Every day until you, or whoever, believes me?"

Fresh tears pricked behind my eyelids, this time fueled with fury.

"May I suggest you take a few days off?"

I shook my head. "I have so much work. I can't afford to."

The sympathy in her eyes incited new waves of anger, and I needed to get out of there. I stood and left before she could say anything else.

When I reached our cubicle, Shaun glanced at me.

"I don't feel well," I mumbled. "I think I'll take a sick day."

He scratched his head, concern covering his features. "You never take sick days."

"I never get sick. But I am now," I said, and with the swirling emotions in my body, it didn't feel like a lie. I was sick with frustration. I started packing up my things. "Can you cover for me? I need you to attend one meeting. I'll take my laptop with me for all the others."

As luck would have it, Mr. Markham zoomed down the corridor, avoiding my gaze. My stomach roiled like I might see my breakfast again.

"Let me take you." Shaun stood, his hand going to his pocket for his keys.

"You have to attend my meeting in five minutes." I leaned forward and squeezed his arm. "I'm okay. You don't have to be nice to me all the time."

"Oh, you think I'm doing this for you? No, my fiancée will kill me if she knows you took the bus," he teased, pulling out his phone.

I turned around and shoved my laptop into my backpack while he mumbled into his phone.

"Hey, could you come and get Rose and take her home? Straight home. Yeah, at work. Now. Right now." He hung up and turned to me. "William will be here in a minute."

"William? I thought you called Neema."

"Neema didn't answer, and Lincoln's stuck on site in the middle of nowhere. That leaves William." He studied me. "That okay?"

"Yeah." I nodded.

Shaun scrutinized my expression, and I left, wanting to escape this building with no destination in mind.

The hum of a familiar car pulled up next to me, and an even more familiar voice carried through the open window.

"Did you decide to make a run for it instead of letting me give you a ride?" William leaned across and opened the passenger door from inside.

A smile broke onto my face, stifling the lingering anger. "Your long arms allow chivalry shortcuts," I teased as I climbed in.

The car stood still as he surveyed me for a few seconds. "Are you okay?"

I shook my head. "Not really."

I didn't mean to tell him the truth. I meant to tell him I was fine. That I was okay. But the crack in my voice had him leaning closer, and his soft, intoxicating scent pulled the truth out of me until I told him everything—from the very first incident to the last. Because, for some reason, when William's dark eyes were on me, my walls crumbled.

He didn't say anything, somehow knowing not to push. Instead, he slid his hand off the steering wheel and onto my leg where my hand rested, covering it with his own. Warm against my icy fingers.

With my heart rate stabilizing, I took him in. His crumpled Doctor Who T-shirt, his checkered pajama pants and sock-clad feet resting on the clutch and accelerator.

"Why didn't you change your clothing?" I asked.

He chuckled, a slight redness creeping onto his golden cheeks. "Shaun said it was an emergency, and I was barely awake enough to hear what he was saying."

"I'm sorry." I bit my lip and stared ahead. "I told him I could take the bus."

He squeezed my hand under his. "Don't be silly. Why would I miss the opportunity to finally have a moment alone with you?"

My cheeks heated at the suggestion.

The car launched forward, turning back into the lane, and with his full focus on the road and a seductive grin on his face, he said, "I had a dream about you."

"Oh yeah? Tell me about it." It surprised me how natural it felt flirting with William. How safe.

A hearty laugh escaped him, nearly vibrating the entire car. "Not that kind of dream." He shook his head. "I shouldn't play *Until Dawn* before bed."

Laughter bubbled through me, washing away more of the anger and frustration. With William, I was able to tuck away the memory of Mr. Markham, work, my future, and all my stresses into the deepest depths of my mind, where I felt no fear. With William, I was present. It was all about the here and now, the same way it felt when I was playing a game—which, I suppose, we were doing.

"Hey," he said, drawing my attention back to him, "are you sure you want to go home? I have a tank full of gas, and I've cleared my day. Name a place, and I'll take you there."

"I still have work to do." I gestured to the backpack I was still wearing.

He pursed his lips. "Screw work. Didn't you take a sick day? Shaun mentioned something like that."

"William," I chided, "not all of us have developed a bestselling game with profits we can comfortably live off."

"Okay, fair point." He pulled to a stop and lifted one finger. "But first, you're on your way to developing one."

His words sent a gentle flutter throughout my body.

He raised another finger. "And second, I think you need to blow off some steam. And while I have many ideas of how I could help you with that"—his naughty gaze met mine—"I have a feeling that's not what you need right now. These cuticles need a break."

He reached for my hand and lifted it to his mouth, his warm lips pressing against my thumb below the nail. The one I'd been biting. A foreign comfort spread from my thumb, up my shoulder, and to my chest, where it finally settled.

"How about a coffee at the Arcade Café?" I asked.

He looked down at his pajama pants, and I opened my mouth to retract that idea, but he chuckled.

"You know what? They've seen me in worse."

My head rolled back with a giggle. "How do you do that? How do you not care about what people think of you?"

With a destination in mind, William shifted up a gear, and the car bolted forward, sending a flutter into my belly.

"I care." He looked my way. "At least about what *some* people think."

My breath hitched.

"But for the rest of them … they don't care either. I keep my distance, and there's little to no consequences." He finished with a shrug.

"Games have no real consequences," I said, almost to myself. "It's why I love them. I get to take risks and quite literally roll the dice. Whichever way it turns out, I still have fun."

William stopped the car outside the neon-lit café and smiled at me with gorgeous eyes. "That's the same reason I play. Except instead of dice, I know that if I mess up or die, or kill someone, they'll respawn or restart or whatever. I can't really hurt anyone there."

The pain etched in his words had me undoing my seat belt and leaning over to place a soft kiss on his unsmiling cheek.

He twisted his head and whispered, "I'll have you know, I brushed my teeth before leaving." Then he captured my mouth in a kiss and brought his hand to my chin, keeping me there a minute longer.

William made it feel as though he appreciated every part of me I gave him. As though a kiss were something more than lips touching.

Round 22

With William in his pajamas, and me in formal beige pants and white blouse, we must have looked like quite the pair walking into the café.

I set my laptop on my regular table, and William's brows drew close.

"I want to check my emails," I said.

"You can work. I'll play." He smiled his teasing smile that always gave my stomach tingles.

I expected a kiss or a wandering hand, but William always surprised me. Instead of acting on the mischief I'd noted in his words, he walked up to the arcade machines and started playing Puzzle Bobble.

Technically, I should have asked Mr. Markham for permission to take sick leave, or at the very least made him aware I was leaving. So I opened a new email and typed in his address, but my fingers froze over each key.

I didn't want to.

Ahead of me, William stood looking too large beside the kid playing on the machine next to him. I left my laptop on the table and ordered both our coffees before joining him.

He lowered his glance beneath his long dark lashes. "Are you coming to see my strategy?"

"How? How is your score so incredibly high? I was number one for years, William. Years."

He only chuckled, making me want to growl. He exited the game and stepped aside, gesturing for me to play. "Let's see how you do it."

I took my place and rested the fingers of one hand over bright red and yellow buttons, while I held the joystick with my other.

Admittedly, there wasn't much strategy to the game—only patience and a fairly good aim. But with each falling bubble, each flash of additional points, my body found peace and the adrenaline of the day's events seeped out of me.

"Mr. Markham called me beautiful," I said as a new round pixelated onto the screen. My throat was tight as I spoke, feeling stupid saying it out loud. "But it's just a compliment, and I can't figure out why it makes me feel the way it does. You've complimented me, and it's different. Even before this, before . . . us . . ."

The words fell from my mouth as they often did when I was playing a game. I think it stemmed from my early years when my mother gave me a toy before asking a series of questions she worried would make me uncomfortable.

"Maybe I'm the problem," I continued. "I overthink. I overdo. I'm a lot. I'm too much. I know that, and maybe this is one of those moments."

A deep and almost animalistic huff pushed out of William. "Rose," he started, and when he used my name, it jolted something strong in me. "You are a lot. And you do overthink, and overdo, and the rest of it, but you are never too much. And you are *never* a problem. I will happily tell anyone who thinks, or dares insinuate it, that they're wrong."

I kept my focus on the game, even though I could feel my heartbeat in the palm of my hand as it shifted the joystick to the left.

"Compliments are meant to make someone feel good, and when I compliment you, Rose, I mean it. You *are* beautiful. That is a fact, rather than someone's opinion. But if it's leaving you feeling the way you do now, then it wasn't just a compliment. It was said with an underlying motive—a hope of something coming from it—and that is not okay."

I dropped the game and wrapped my arms around his waist, pushing my face into the soft T-shirt he wore. His strong and sure hand slid to the back of my neck as he leaned down and kissed the top of my head.

I stayed there for a few deep breaths, and his grip never wavered. I released him after taking one last inhale of his scent, making a mental note to buy lavender and pine essential oils, shampoos, conditioners, soaps, laundry detergents, et cetera.

"Have you considered resigning?"

"I can't afford to leave my job. Not only because of finances, but it would make me so far behind on my Life Goals."

I grumbled as I lost my last life, and the machine flashed GAME OVER.

"What are your life goals?" William asked.

"Oh, you know what, I'm not going to explain. You don't need to know that part of me."

Tilting my chin upward, he let his gaze focus for several seconds on each part of my face. He stared into my brown eyes as if they were something to marvel at. His soft gaze dipped to my cheeks, slid down the sharp slope of my nose, and ended on my full lips, where it usually lingered. Eventually, he said, "I plan on knowing all parts of you, and for what it's worth . . ." He took a deep breath and glanced back at the game. "I didn't achieve that score. It's impossible. I tried, and I got damn near your score but couldn't beat it. So . . ." He scrunched his nose.

I pinched his arm, and he chuckled. "You cheated? You said you never cheat!"

"I was going to tell you, but it was so easy to frustrate you."

I pinched him again. "William. You absolute scoundrel!"

He flinched and then his hand slid up my arm, leaving goose bumps in its wake. "I'll delete my score. I . . . I liked that we had our own . . . thing. Without anyone else."

My face heated again. William romanced me in my own language.

I pulled him back to the table at the same time my favorite waiter dropped off the cups of coffee I'd ordered and offered William the same large, lovely smile that I was usually on the receiving end of.

"My favorite customer," Mac said.

"I thought I was your favorite customer," I said, sharing a competitive glance with William.

"You're a delight, honey," Mac said with a gentle touch on my shoulder. "But this one helps me with my IT issues, *and* he fixed the arcade machines."

I narrowed my eyes at William, who only laughed.

"Call me if you need anything else," he said as he left.

William slid his chair next to mine and peered over my shoulder as I opened my laptop. "So, life goals."

Reluctantly, I opened my spreadsheet. "You're going to think I'm ridiculous. Everyone does."

"I like that you're ridiculous."

Tilting the screen so he could see, I handed him my mouse and shut my eyes. I didn't want to see his reaction. I was already regretting this.

"Okay," he said, his tone holding a repressed laugh. "This is more ridiculous than I'd thought."

I snapped the screen closed. "Now you know."

"Why do you do this?" he asked in the gentlest tone.

His face was so close, and his expression so soft, that it sucked the truth out of me.

"It makes me feel like I have some control over my life. I like having a plan. I thought everyone did this. Don't you think about your next step?"

He shook his head. "Not really."

"So, you don't think of promotions, or what you'd like to achieve?" I took a sip of my coffee.

"Nope, I like my job." He shrugged, taking a sip from his own mug. "It's fun, and it's pretty hard to ruin anything big."

"Those are really strange requirements for a job. You're not worried in a few years they'll replace you with someone younger and cheaper?"

"I'll cross that bridge when I get there. But I am hoping to have developed another game or two by then anyway."

The nonchalant way he said it confused me.

"I am terrible with the whole 'go with the flow' thing," I admitted. "Shaun always tells me that. He goes with the flow quite easily. Must be genetic."

William glanced away. "I don't like to think of the genes that bond us."

"Oh."

When he turned back to me, the smirky, cocky William I was accustomed to was gone. In his place was a troubled boy. Instinctively, my hand searched for his.

"My, uh . . ." He cleared his throat. "My relationship with our shared parent isn't very good."

"How so?" I entwined our fingers.

"It's nonexistent." He blew out a long breath and then scratched the back of his neck with his free hand. "I'm the bastard son who showed up and inconvenienced his otherwise perfect life with his perfect wife and his perfect son."

A shudder traveled down my spine. I couldn't find any words. None. I simply stared at the side of his face while his gaze stayed firmly fixed on his steaming coffee.

He continued. "I don't think of the future because, as a kid, I didn't think I'd have a very good one."

"Shaun never mentioned—"

"He wouldn't." William gave my hand a gentle squeeze before releasing it. "It makes him pretty uncomfortable."

Opening my screen again, he took another moment to read my spreadsheet. Releasing another heavy breath, he mumbled something I didn't hear.

"What?" I asked, trying to analyze his frown.

The disdain I'd once seen on his face returned.

William shook his head and offered me a halfhearted smile. "Nothing."

He looked away from the spreadsheet, the lines of his frown still visible.

I closed my laptop and shoved it into my bag. "I find it impossible to be spontaneous or let life take me wherever it may because I spent a lifetime literally doing that." I inhaled deeply. "I like checking things off. I feel good about it."

His charming smile returned. "Yeah, because it's like rounds in a game with little side quests in between for the smaller goals."

No one had ever explained it to me that way.

"Except now I don't know where to go next. I'm questioning the entire life I've built. So yes," I said, my heart hammering against my chest, "I'm stressed out, and I would really like it if you'd kiss me hard enough that I could forget about it, even just for a moment."

William gulped down the last of his coffee. "Well then, let's get you home. If I need to kiss you like that, I'm going to have to do it with no kids around."

Round 23

With William's playful energy returning, my mind eased in to the safe state the same way it did when I played games. And the one I played with William was, by far, the best. Every move was calculated for the outcome resulting in the most fun.

I leaned over the center console and kissed the corner of his mouth, which immediately flinched upward. His hand flew from the steering wheel to the inside of my thigh, and my breath caught.

With William's excellent driving skills, we were in Neema's parking bay in no time. Rushing out of his car, I dragged him to the stairwell, barely making it up one step before he pushed me against the wall and pressed his mouth on mine, hot and urgent as if he'd been holding back the entire morning.

I had.

Between heavy breaths and roaming hands, we finally made it to the apartment, but still he didn't slow. His lips roved over every part of exposed skin—my neck, my ears, my arms, the inside of my elbow. Each new kiss sent an electric current to my fingertips, which he also kissed when they weren't pressed into his skin.

I stumbled backward onto the couch, pulling him along with me, wanting to feel him on top of me. His hands shot out, bracing himself to keep from crushing me.

Leaning over me, he nibbled my earlobe, and my body shuddered. I curled a leg around him and pulled him closer. His hips rocked toward mine, and I reveled in the power I held. I pushed myself against his hard body, relieving some of the tension he caused, but it only created more. My pants threatened to tear. A worthy sacrifice.

Light danced across his dark eyes as he leaned in and caught my mouth with his, parting my lips with his tongue as he hungrily searched for mine.

He released a delicious sigh. For the briefest moment, I wondered how many times he'd done this before with other women, but the thought vanished as his warm mouth pressed against my throat, ceasing any chance of coherent thought.

William released a deep, guttural groan.

Through a thick fog of lust, I barely registered a strange vibration against my thigh.

Bodies didn't vibrate. Did they?

Oh wait, it was my phone. Probably.

It couldn't be more important than kissing William.

The vibration continued, and with an exasperated breath, I dug my phone out of my pocket and glanced at the screen.

Neema.

Apparently Shaun had told her I'd gone home sick so she'd sent multiple texts letting me know she was on her way home.

Dropping my head onto William's shoulder, I held up my phone and showed him the texts.

Releasing a frustrated sigh, William pulled away and pushed himself upright. "It's probably for the best."

"What?" The old familiar feeling of rejection sneered at me.

William paced the living room, lines of thought spread across his face. "It's just . . . there's . . . it's . . . "

From a man who always had a comeback, his stumbling words sent a shiver of unease through me.

"Ah!" I grumbled. "Well, I can't stand the teasing anymore." Pushing myself upright, I swallowed hard. "You're all talk and no action, and I'm starting to freak out that, by the time we go any further, it's going to kill me. Is that your plan to get rid of me? Death by pleasure?"

His dimple made a deep divot in his cheek, and he released a low laugh. I bit my lip—even his laugh was turning me on. I needed a release.

Pausing his pacing, he tilted his head at me in a curious expression. "Wait—so I turn you on, and you come home frustrated. What do you do?" He wore his naughtiest grin now.

"I call my mom."

William burst out laughing. "Really?"

"It usually does the trick to switch it back off."

He laughed harder, finding way too much humor in my situation.

I pinched him. "Stop making fun of me, and finish what you start."

"Believe me, I will." William's voice dropped low, the playfulness in his eyes replaced by darkness, unlocking an unexplored side of me. Bringing my hand to his lips, William kissed my fingers. "Because you're the sexiest woman I have ever seen." Wetting his bottom lip, he leaned forward and placed his lips on mine, nibbling first on my bottom lip before sucking it gently. His mouth moved to my ear. "But it's not just about that."

A key jiggled in the lock, startling us so badly that William and I nearly tumbled off the couch. He scrambled to his feet and pulled me upright. I barely had my blouse straightened properly before Neema breezed in.

"William, you're in my parking spot." She turned to me, her eyes softening. "Are you okay? I'm sorry I missed Shaun's call. He said you were feeling ill."

"I'm fine," I said, greeting her with a light hug. I glanced around her shoulder at William.

Face flushed and his hair sticking out with an adorable cowlick, he smiled like he was keeping a huge secret.

Pulling away from our hug, Neema turned to William. "Thanks for picking her up." Her eyes narrowed. "Are you wearing pajamas?"

He shrugged. "This is what I wear to work."

"What are you doing here?" I asked Neema.

She undid the top two buttons on the blood-red shirtdress she wore and loosened the belt. "Well, I wanted to check on you. I thought you'd be here alone." She glanced at William. "Didn't realize you were going to stay."

"We had game things to discuss," I fired out.

Her eyebrows popped up, but her eyes narrowed again. "Okay, if you say so. Anyway, my day is pretty empty, and I wanted to take a moment to start going through the RSVPs. But I can do that in my bedroom. So . . ." She waved her hands between us. ". . . continue."

William shrugged. "It's okay. I should get going." Turning to me again, his lip quirked up on one side in a suggestive half smile. "I think if I stick around, Rose'll explode. I've given her plenty to think about."

Biting my tongue, I managed a polite and sincere, "Thanks for bringing me home."

His smile was as sweet as sugar, but the wink that followed was full of mischief.

"When are you going to present her game?" Neema asked him, while setting up her laptop.

"In a week!" I walked William to the front door. "I'd like to run through the game once more."

"Maybe we should play it at game night," she suggested.

William and I nodded, and I realized I didn't want him to leave.

"Give me your keys," I said to Neema. "I'll pull your car into your spot once William leaves."

"Oh, awesome." She tossed her keys at me. "It's in Tilly's spot."

Dangling her keys between my fingers, I followed William down to the parking garage in silence as my thoughts raced through good things, bad things, and scary things. It was fast becoming hard to control anything around me.

William's fingers weaved through mine as we entered the parking area. He didn't say anything, but it was enough to slow my thoughts.

I tried to think of what I'd say when we reached his car, but before I could come up with anything, he pushed me against the driver's side door, his mouth claiming mine.

Too soon, he broke the kiss and swiped his thumb over his bottom lip. "I'll see you soon."

William's "soon" would never be soon enough.

I was so flustered by the time he left that I'd made it up an entire flight of stairs before I realized I hadn't moved Neema's car.

This man was all-consuming.

Later that evening, I lay in bed and stared at my ceiling while thinking about William. Everything about William.

Frustrated, and almost angry, I turned onto my stomach and shoved my face against the pillow, willing myself into a dreamless sleep.

But my mind had other plans.

And maybe it was because of the emotional day I'd had, maybe it was because of the thoughts I'd had before bed, but he snuck into my dreams.

A thrill ran through me, and my body tingled while he kissed me, touched me, held me, gripped me. I dreamed of his mouth and that tongue—that stupid tongue he used to lick his pouty lips.

Those lips.

My eyes flung open a moment too soon.

Round 24

"Good morning, Rose," Mr. Markham greeted me as I entered the office kitchen. His eyes traveled down my body, but he said nothing else and left immediately after.

Still, I recoiled.

I had awoken wanting to feel sexy, which resulted in me wearing a little black dress I hadn't worn since Neema hosted a Spice Girls–themed party. Now, after Mr. Markham's eyes were on me, I regretted it. Never mind wanting to rip off the dress, I wanted to rip off my skin so he'd have nothing to look at.

It didn't help that Louisa avoided my gaze as we passed each other in the hallway. She didn't need to spell it out for me to understand: Jeffrey Markham was the boss.

As usual, work was a *wonderful* place to be.

But it did have Shaun.

"The RSVPs are dribbling in." His blue eyes brightened. "It's starting to feel real."

We spent the remainder of the workday sprinkling in talk about wedding plans, and it was exactly the distraction I needed.

"Did you bring your game?" Shaun asked later that afternoon.

"No, Neema is bringing it later."

"I'm super-excited to play it again. Especially now that you and William have fine-tuned it. Don't tell him I told you, but he's really excited about this presentation. He won't stop talking about Overpower and the themes. I swear I can hear him talking about it in the middle of the night." Shaun let out a laugh. "And while he can be really annoying, there is no one better at games than he is."

Shaun beamed, clearly proud of both me and his brother.

Was it normal for a stomach to flutter at the mere mention of a name? Did I need a doctor? What if something was medically wrong with me?

"I know," I almost whispered. "He's the best." I couldn't trust myself to say more about William. Not anymore.

When we arrived at Shaun's place, Neema's car was already parked, and Shaun barely stopped his own car before sprinting upstairs in search of her. My heart twinged at his never-ending enthusiasm to see the person he loved.

I was left behind wondering what silly comment William would greet me with. What secret game we'd be playing today that we were yet to figure out.

But instead, when I walked inside, he stared at me. His gaze roamed over my body, beginning at the top of my head and then trailing over my chest and down my hips, over my thighs, until finally reaching my feet. Then he slowly reversed direction until his eyes met mine again.

He brought his knuckles to his mouth and bit on them.

And now I didn't regret the dress anymore.

Neema gave me a once-over. "I love this dress."

"Well, I only have it because of you," I reminded her.

Claire and Lincoln arrived a few seconds later, and William timed them while they set up the game. It only took a few minutes, but they had played it once before. I couldn't imagine total strangers playing Overpower, especially without me there. It could be a train wreck, but the pride in William's eyes said otherwise.

The game lasted thirty minutes longer than William and I had planned. Glancing at the time, I bit my nails.

"Thirty minutes is nothing." William picked up the pieces. "Plus, I've got a few ideas of how to lengthen or shorten it as we go along."

"Care to share?"

"Nope." He smiled.

"It's really good." Claire gave me a tight squeeze. "I mean it. I'm not saying this because I'm your friend. If I didn't absolutely have to go home, I'd stay for another round."

"Really frikken good. It's brilliant," Lincoln said, which was uncharacteristic for him.

Hearing him speak with that much enthusiasm warmed my heart. I launched myself into his arms. He allowed it and patted my head, a soft laugh escaping him.

"Your genius engineering brain likes it? Or is it because you won?" I asked.

"Both." He sighed, shaking his head. "I especially enjoyed learning the characters' backstories as the game progressed."

William's chuckle echoed through to me. "Yeah, those backstories nearly had Rose shoving me over the balcony."

"It was a gentle nudge," I replied and peeled myself off a silently laughing Lincoln. His vibrating chest brought me an incredible amount of joy.

As soon as I stepped away, Lincoln reached for his backpack and made a strange struggling noise. "I probably should have given you this before we started playing but"—he shifted on his feet while pulling out a small cardboard box—"I know you made the gaming tokens, so I wasn't sure if like . . ." He swallowed.

This may be the most Lincoln Carden had ever said to me.

"Is this for me?" I asked, extending my palm and taking the box from his hands.

He nodded. "I drew them up and used the 3D printer at work. You don't have to use them. Just kept thinking about your game . . ." He trailed off again.

I lifted the lid, and my gaze fell on the hat, the bow and arrow, the heart, the book, and the crown. My eyes welled up.

"Please don't cry," Lincoln said, his dark brows pulling together.

"Too late," William said with a guffaw as he made his way next to me and investigated the contents of the box.

"I love them," I croaked out, and because I wasn't sure Lincoln would accept another hug, I walked into Neema's and Claire's arms and wondered how in the world I'd gotten so lucky to have these people as friends.

When I said goodbye to them, Claire shifted her eyes from mine to where William stood and back to me. One brow cocked in question.

There was so much I wanted to tell her about, but telling her more than she already knew felt like a betrayal to Neema and Shaun. I was already keeping secrets from my best friends but . . . this was between William and me, and until we figured it out, I didn't want to involve anyone else.

The wink she offered me let me know she understood that.

And then Lincoln shooed her out of the apartment.

I went out to the balcony, hoping William would follow, and he did, except Shaun and Neema were right behind him, rattling on about whether they needed both a photographer and videographer for the wedding.

"It's unnecessary," Shaun said. "The photos capture everything. We're never going to watch the video."

He would regret saying that as Neema whipped out her phone and navigated to YouTube, and I was sure she was going to show him all of her favorite wedding videos, of which there were about two hundred. I knew this because, for as far back as I could remember, she'd spent every first day of her period crying in front of a breathtaking wedding video.

"I'm going to make some tea," I said, slipping away, entirely uninterested in reliving those moments. Wedding videos were of extraordinarily little interest to me at the moment.

And apparently to William too.

"Tea? Coffee?" I turned to him as he came around the kitchen island.

Walking toward me, he crowded me against the countertop and placed his hands on both sides of my hips, locking me in place.

My breath caught at the unfiltered desire in his eyes and the heat pressing through my dress where he pinned me.

His gaze dropped to my cleavage, and he bit his bottom lip. "This is unfair."

"Whatever do you mean?" I batted my eyelashes.

"This dress. Come on, is this how you're going to win? Because it's working." He slid his hand down my waist, over my hip, and squeezed. "One bend, and I'm throwing you on the couch and having my way with you. I wouldn't even care if they walked back in."

"I kinda had a dream like that last night," I said, losing myself in his dark, lust-filled eyes.

"Don't tease me," he breathed. The tip of his tongue swiped over his bottom lip, his gaze boring into me like he had other places he'd rather use it.

I liked seeing him flustered for a change.

"Well . . ." I looked over my shoulder and checked that Shaun and Neema hadn't come inside. Satisfied they were too caught up in their debate on the balcony, I stood on my toes, gripped his T-shirt, and pulled him close, touching my lips to the shell of his ear. "Best dream I've ever had. I wonder if the real thing will live up to it."

He swallowed a struggling sound.

I put the kettle on before turning back to him. His eyes were lit up so brightly that I had to look away or I thought I might spontaneously combust. His hands stroked over and around my waist like he couldn't get enough of me.

He groaned. "Okay, game over. I can't take this any longer. I submit this round."

My laughter was cut short when William dropped to his knees. My heart leaped to my throat, and I looked down at him, alarmed to see him kneeling in front of me. My head whipped back to the living room, but it was still empty.

A wicked smile spread across William's handsome face. "I don't think I can resist you any longer."

I tried to respond, but my words left me hanging as, inch by inch, he slid my dress high.

He looked up at me, asking permission—silently begging me to let him continue. Even in my shocked state, I wanted him. My heart pounded against my chest, and my blood rushed through me. My entire body was a heartbeat. I nodded.

Turning his head, he ran his nose along my inner thigh, leaving tiny kisses in his wake. So soft. Softer than I'd have expected. I flooded with warmth. If he stopped now, I'd have to kill him.

"William," I whispered, my mind fuzzy with unbearable want. My heart fluttering with the gentle way he held me.

"Shhh." His lips climbed once more, his fingers following until, once again, he'd found the lace edge of my panties.

And then, painstakingly slowly, he pulled my underwear down, and the rest was a blur as my brain short-circuited. I trembled, my hands falling to the counter and searching for support. A thrill coursed through me, and with every passing moment, the tension grew, twisting inside me in a way I couldn't make sense of.

"Rose, could I please get a cup of tea?" Shaun's voice traveled through from the balcony.

A shock jolted through me, and my body straightened as Shaun walked across the room to his bedroom.

Shielded by the island between the kitchen and living area, William's hand found one of mine and entwined our fingers. My heart skipped.

"Yes, sure. Earl Grey?" My voice sounded unsteady to my own ears, and I nearly choked on air.

"You know it," Shaun said without looking at me while entering his room.

"Anything for Neema, while I'm here?" I squeaked out, suppressing a wild giggle that teased.

"Nah," Shaun called out.

I was hyper-aware of William. My body was a giant, shaking nerve.

"Where's William?" Shaun asked, walking out of his bedroom with a portable charger in his hand.

William looked upward, a wide grin spreading across his face before yelling, "Down here, looking for the syrup. I've almost got it."

Another giggle strangled me, fighting to escape.

"Maple? I'll take some in my tea, actually," Shaun said, and slipped through the balcony door.

I wanted to shriek with delight, with laughter, as a lightness overcame me.

He gripped me in place and gently bit the inside of my calf before opening the cupboard. When he stood, he held in his hand a jar of maple syrup.

"Found it." His words were breathy, and a dangerous smile spread across his handsome face.

I leaned against the counter, unable to move. My legs wobbled at the mere thought of walking.

William's gaze met mine, but I turned away. I didn't know what to say or do.

"Don't look away," he whispered. "I love seeing you like this."

It would take me a while to recover.

"Did you enjoy that?"

I nodded. "Uhm, thank you."

"Don't thank me." He leaned his head against mine and gazed directly into my eyes. "That was for me."

With those words, he washed his hands and then prepared Shaun's cup of tea.

With syrup.

Round 25

Without thinking, I followed William out to the balcony and silently watched him deliver Shaun's tea while willing the blood in my body to return to my brain. William had left me dumbfounded and useless in a way I'd never experienced before, and I wasn't sure I'd ever recover.

"Dad RSVPed no, by the way," Shaun told William. "My mom said he's got some medical conference."

William nodded; the joy I had seen in his eyes a moment ago was replaced by pain and then almost immediately with relief. "Well, great."

Shaun attempted a smile. "Yeah, guess so." Changing the subject, he turned his attention to me. "Have you decided what you're wearing to the office party?"

I searched into the depths of my being for a coherent thought. The year-end party meant nothing to me right now when all I wanted was to join a cult dedicated to William's mouth.

"I don't know," I eventually managed as I sat down next to Neema, afraid if I sat next to William I would implode.

"You're the only reason we have office parties. Plus it's where I first met Neema, thanks to you." He looked at Neema with all the love in his eyes I'd come to expect.

"I haven't had time to get a costume. And I RSVP'd with a plus-one, and I don't want to go alone because . . . " I didn't have to finish my sentence. Shaun knew exactly how I felt around Mr. Markham. He also knew that Patrick had always been my plus-one.

And despite my mother's warning, Patrick had not reached out. I checked all my social media accounts and my three email addresses. He hadn't called or texted. Nothing.

"Take William," Neema said, pulling me out of my thoughts. Her eyes met mine in a way that had me questioning her motives.

Maybe I was imagining it or being paranoid.

"I know for a fact he has a Batman costume." She laughed. "One day he wore it around the house for no reason."

"It was expensive, and I was having a bad day." William laughed and turned to me. "Would be nice to put it to use. I haven't cosplayed in a while, and you won't be alone."

He said "alone" knowingly—protectively—and I let out a breath, still recovering from what he'd done to me, for me, moments ago.

"Plus we could easily throw together a Catwoman costume for you," Neema said. "I'm sure you have a black turtleneck and boots, and I know you have leather pants. We can make a mask—she wears, like, an eye mask, right?"

"And the cat ears!" Shaun added.

"I have cat ears, of course," I said.

"I'm more interested in the leather pants." William grinned, flashing his dimple.

"They were for a *Grease*-themed party." My cheeks reddened at the way he looked at me. Like he hadn't had enough. Like he may never have enough. I stood and walked over to the railing, creating more distance between us.

William laughed again. "Of course they were."

"Oh, you're one to talk," Shaun teased, leaning back and wrapping an arm around Neema. "You have, what? Four or five costumes at the back of your closet?"

"I bet Rose has more," William said, his eyes playing with me.

"Oh my goodness. She's got one closet entirely dedicated to costumes, and a good percentage of her day-to-day clothing is costume-inspired." Neema pointed at my outfit. "Like this dress."

I leaned against the railing. "Why am I being roasted?"

"We both dressed up as Captain Hook for the Fun at Sea–themed party," Shaun said. "Although hers was far more authentic than mine."

I rolled my eyes.

"What else?" Shaun bit on his lips while thinking. "I remember a few superheroes . . ."

"Hobbit," William added, clearly enjoying this.

"Two different hobbit costumes, William." Neema cackled. "Who has *two* hobbit costumes?"

"You're all mean. There are plenty of hobbits. I could have at least seven hobbit costumes, and it would still make sense."

"What's been your most elaborate costume?" Shaun asked.

Before I could answer, Neema said, "Probably that *Spirited Away* one." She then turned to face Shaun and William and added, "And no, she didn't dress up as the human characters you'd expect. She chose those little soot ball things."

"Of course," William said, laughing, and I just knew he was picturing it. When he looked back at me, he asked, "And your worst?"

"I may or may not have shown up to a *Twilight*-themed party dressed as Edward, glitter and all, and . . ." I cringed. "I may or may not have been the only one in costume."

Shaun's eyes widened. "No."

I nodded. "Oh yes."

"You were Princess Elsa too, remember? For that *Frozen* promotion while we were studying," Neema mentioned.

"No. I was Olaf because they needed someone taller for the princesses."

To this, William held his hand to his chest and looked like he may have a heart attack if he didn't release the laughter he was suppressing.

In the end, he failed and shook with his chuckles. "Surely there were better jobs out there?" William asked after calming down. He was doing that thing where he was entirely focused on me, and Shaun and Neema didn't exist.

"It paid well! My parents accidentally got locked up in Kenya and needed money."

This, as usual, launched us into a conversation about my parents and their interesting lifestyle.

"Rose had basically seen the world before she got her first period," Neema said. "She had the most interesting childhood."

"A bit too chaotic for my liking," I replied, shaking away the anxiety linked to it.

"We moved around a few times, maybe four times, but nothing like you." Neema gestured toward me. "Our biggest move was from Tanzania to the States. But I was a kid, so I don't remember much about it."

"I lived in the same house from the time I was born until I moved out to go to university," Shaun said.

I looked at him and then William. "Gosh, it must be nice having a proper home."

"It wasn't my home." William's jaw stiffened, and his head tilted downward.

Shaun shifted, tugging on his collar. William's expression was hard and his scowl deep. I wanted to trace those lines and soften them. I wondered what he was like as a child. Probably a bit of a menace.

"I spent all of my time at boarding school," William said.

I knew Shaun never went to boarding school. He gnawed at his bottom lip, and his shoulders slumped. My eyes searched William's, and he stared down at his hands, clenching and unclenching his fists. I couldn't help thinking about what he'd said under the influence of food poisoning. My heart ached at the distance that seemed to grow between the brothers.

I cleared my throat and changed the subject, hoping to wipe the pain from William's face. "Anyway, has Fun&Games emailed you at all? I know you forwarded one to me. Was that it?"

William looked up, some peace reentering his eyes. "We've been emailing a lot, but there's nothing for you to worry about. It's going to be okay. We're going to be playing a game. I can do that."

"Promise me you'll be nice to them," I said, trying to lift his mood. "Even if they use the word 'irregardless.'"

He smiled. *Success!*

"I can't promise that." He laughed, but it didn't reach his eyes.

"William, you do come across as a jerk sometimes," Neema said. "Took me a few months of coming over almost daily before I understood you don't hate me."

William rolled his eyes.

I wanted to hold him, tell him I would fix whatever was wrong, and if I couldn't fix it, I'd find someone who could.

His eyes met mine, and he gave me a half smile. "You're going to win this. It's my job to know when a game is good, and this game is perfect."

"I couldn't have done it without you," I said.

A warm and delicious blush crept into his cheeks, but his frown was still deep. His shoulders still tense.

Neema yawned. "I'm going home tonight, love. I have a meeting in the morning." She kissed Shaun goodnight and turned to me. "You coming?"

I nodded before looking at William. I tried my best to comfort him with my eyes, to kiss him with a stare. His gaze kissed me back, and some part of me relaxed.

"So, to confirm, you'll be my plus-one?" I asked him. "It's tomorrow."

He nodded. "Yeah. Wanna know why?"

"Why?" I asked, already knowing how he'd reply.

"Because I'm Batman."

I would never tire of this man.

While I was sitting at my desk that evening, Neema knocked on my bedroom door with two mugs in her hands.

"Some hocho?"

She knew I would never say no to hot chocolate and handed me the mug before I could answer. "So . . ." she started.

I took a sip, burned my tongue, and instantly regretted not having enough patience to wait a single minute longer.

"So?" I turned in my chair as she settled on the edge of my bed.

"How are you?"

"I'm fine. How are you?"

"Fine . . ." Her warm brown eyes pinned me over the rim of her mug. "I've lined up a few dates for you."

"I'm really not interested in dating right now. I have so much on my plate." I took another sip of the scalding hot chocolate, hoping I appeared nonchalant.

"Is there something I should know?"

The urge to tell her swelled in my throat, but we were so close to the wedding and my nerves were growing with each stolen kiss. I shook my head. "Nope. Nothing."

"We don't keep secrets from each other."

"I know ... but I don't know what to tell you ... " I took a deep breath, thinking through what I could tell her. William and I were ... we were ...

Not dating. Nor had we ever been on a date.

We weren't even having casual sex.

We were ...

William and I were playing a game. And that wasn't something Neema would understand. No one in the world understood games the way William and I did.

"There's a lot going on. Give me a chance to figure it out?" There was an ache in my soul as I said it. A pressure growing in my chest.

She nodded and pushed my hair over my shoulder. "Okay. But know I'll kill him if he hurts you."

And with that, she left me and my burning tongue stewing in the mess I'd created.

Round 26

Helping everyone all the time was not conducive to getting anything done, and now it seemed I wouldn't be able to get home and back to work before the party.

Shaun walked past me on his way out. "I'm going to get ready and pick up Neema. What's your plan? You look knee-deep in so much mess, I don't care to mention it all."

I laughed and stepped away from two people I'd been helping with last-minute costume ideas. "Can you ask Neema to bring my costume along with her? I'll get ready here."

Walking back to my desk, I opened my task list and dove back into work, knowing I had about another hour before Neema showed up.

I was off by five minutes. Shaun and Neema arrived sixty-five minutes later. Already dressed in her Supergirl lingerie, Neema was guaranteed a prize of some kind. Shaun was in his Superman costume, which looked a lot like the Superman Underoos.

Absolutely adorable.

Neema pulled out the black turtleneck, and I eyed the three fresh slits across the chest. I lifted a brow at her.

She shrugged. "I improvised."

"Of course you did."

"Wait until you see the boots."

I dug inside the bag and found the boots in question. Instead of the lower-heeled, sensible boots we'd agreed on, Neema had packed a pair of sky-high boots. I wasn't mad about it.

Slipping into a bathroom cubicle, I changed out of my office clothes and into my costume. Sucking in my stomach as much as possible, I kicked each leg into the tight-fitting leather pants.

It only took four jumps and three squats to get the pants over my hips, but now that I had them on, they weren't going anywhere. I tucked the turtleneck into the waistband of the pants and shifted the slits, hiding as much of my cleavage as possible. I stepped into the badass boots and zipped them all the way to the tops of my knees. Taking one last look in the mirror, and assuring myself I was properly put together, I exited the cubicle.

Neema let out a whistle followed by a howl. She was a wolf, and I was the full moon.

"Stop it." I blushed.

"What's going on in there?" Shaun called from outside.

"I'm creating a masterpiece," Neema replied.

That silenced him.

Finally ready, I opened the bathroom door, and the music from the roof flooded through to the office. William, or someone I assumed was William, stood next to Shaun in the best Batman (*The Dark Knight*, of course) replica costume I had ever seen.

"Rose, whew!" Shaun teased.

Neema laughed and stepped into his arms.

Shaun lifted his keys and wallet toward me. "Can you keep these? Neither of our costumes have pockets."

I sighed. No wonder people thought we were a throuple. We certainly functioned better that way. I opened my small leather backpack, and he dropped them inside.

I looked at William, relieved his costume gave me access to his eyes and mouth. My cheeks heated as memories of our kitchen encounter made my knees weak.

"William," I said, grateful my mask hid some of my blushing face.

"I'm Batman."

I giggled.

Shaun and Neema got swept up by one of our colleagues, and William slipped an arm around me as if that was where it belonged. I looked up at him, taken aback by his touch but yearning for it, nonetheless.

His eyes raked along my body, and he leaned down until his lips grazed the shell of my ear. "I like this costume, so do be sure to keep it."

My cheeks flushed again, and my leather pants felt impossibly tighter.

I led William upstairs, pleased to see everyone having a good time, and even more pleased at the superhero-themed banners and giant cutouts hanging prominently around the area. They were probably intended for carnivals and children's parties, but it worked.

William's grip loosened until my hand fell into the crease of his elbow. I kept staring at him, confused about how any of this was happening. Every now and again, I questioned my reality and was stuck wondering.

What was William doing with me as my plus-one at a work party?

What did we do in his kitchen yesterday?

Should I tell Neema?

Should I tell Shaun?

If I killed Jeffrey Markham, who would help me hide the body?

I could, at least, answer the last question.

As if reading my mind, William glanced down, catching me in my William-obsessed thoughts. His eyes were playful. I didn't know what outrageous thing he'd think of saying or doing this time, but I knew it was coming. Leaning down, he whispered in my ear, his breath making me lose my senses for a moment.

"Sorry, what?" I blinked. Between the music and the way he made my brain turn off, I hadn't heard a word he had said.

He smiled, letting me know he was onto me. "Would you like something to eat or drink?"

I accidentally tutted with disappointment at the sheer normalcy of the question.

William's mouth turned up in a smirk. "You see, the problem is I am starving. Starving and dehydrated because I haven't been able to use my kitchen. It doesn't feel right without you in it."

There it was. He never disappointed.

I was like a cat with the clink of a tuna can. My head shot up, and I'm sure my fake feline ears twitched.

"That's not going to work for me." I bit down on my lip, trying to stop myself from saying these things. William had a way of drawing it out of me, but he wasn't the only one who could play this game. I ran my gaze over his body, starting at his head and moving down his suit before rising back to his eyes. "You have a body I need you to maintain. I guess I'll have to come over."

"Please." He whispered only the one word, begging, and once again won our game.

"Rose, is that you?" Mervyn from reception lifted his Zorro (not really a superhero or a villain) mask. "It's me, Mervyn."

I nodded and shouted over the music, "Yeah! Hey, Mervyn!"

He turned to William. "Oh, Patrick! It's nice to see you again."

My body collapsed in on itself.

Mortified. There wasn't another word for it. If the ground were kind enough, it would open and swallow me whole—or even in bits, I wasn't picky. Either way, it would save me from having to explain this situation.

A sigh escaped me as I thought of Patrick being Patrick. He'd always come to my work parties ready to leave a good impression on everyone and everything. Every year, without fail, he found a new client too. He took networking very seriously.

I was too afraid to look at William. I needed to say something.

"Hi, Mervyn," William responded in a jovial tone I didn't recognize. "It's so great to see you. Please excuse me. I won't be shaking your hand. I've picked my nose."

Mervyn, like any regular person, laughed politely and made an excuse to leave while my hand shot up to my mouth, covering my squeal of laughter.

"William!" I shrieked.

He rubbed his palms together, his smile wide and his dimple deep enough for me to live in. "Oh, this is going to be fun."

William had found his game.

Thankfully for me—and for Patrick, I suppose—there were enough people who didn't recognize me and didn't bother asking me to reveal myself. The conversations were all general nonsense, enough to keep the smiles on their faces and keep them distracted from asking me, or William, anything else.

At the other end were people who did recognize me, and each one assumed it was Patrick at my side. Granted, I couldn't blame them. Patrick had been around for as long as I had.

"Patrick! How are you?" a man dressed as the Flash asked.

"I'm Batman," William replied.

The man laughed. "Ah, good one. We haven't seen you in a while. How are you?"

"I'm Batman," William repeated, expressionless.

Unable to hold it back any longer, I slipped away where I could laugh out loud without an audience.

Lydia approached me dressed as Catwoman. Besides myself, there were at least three other Catwomen and six Batmen.

"Rose?" she asked.

I nodded. "Hi, Lydia."

"Where is Patrick this evening?"

William waltzed over, and I started giggling before he even reached my side.

Lydia looked up at him. "Patrick! I took your advice and moved my little Patrick to a different school."

"Oh, how old is he now?" I asked, stealing the conversation before William could say anything outrageous.

"He's almost seven years old," she squealed.

"What? Time flies! He must be so big. The last time I saw him, he was permanently attached to your boob."

Lydia laughed. "Oh goodness, remember that?"

"I was breastfed until I was ten years old," William inserted.

I choked back a laugh.

"And then my mom had my little sister, and she was breast-fed," he continued. "Ah, I hated that she got the milkies and I couldn't have any."

I couldn't do it any longer. Pulling him aside, I wiped away my tears of laughter and straightened my expression into one I hoped resembled serious. "Stop your nonsense."

William laughed, nearly doubling over. He thought he was hilarious. "Oh, come on. Do you really mind if they think all these things about Perfect Patrick?"

"No." I smiled. It was impossible not to smile around him. "But I mind that they think I would still be dating someone like that."

"Fair point. Guess you shouldn't have dated Patrick, then. He's a weird guy, I hear. Did you know he spends his free time tracking bigfoot?"

I shook my head and leaned against him as his arms slipped around me.

"William, don't say that to anyone." I bit back another laugh. "Oh my goodness, you're out of control."

He kissed my cheek and whispered, "No, I'm Batman."

I laughed. It was funny every single time.

The music picked up, and Neema zigzagged through the crowd toward me and pulled me onto the dance floor. We danced together until Shaun joined us, openly grinding against Neema. I could not resist searching for William. He stood a few feet away, smiling and watching me in a way I'd come to crave. I motioned for him to join us, but he shook his head.

Letting the music course through me, I skipped toward him. He put his arms out defensively, but I grabbed ahold of them and pulled.

"No, no, no," he murmured.

"Oh, come on. I've seen your victory dance more times than I'd have liked."

He laughed, unconvinced.

"If it's that bad, people will think Patrick can't dance," I teased.

"The problem is . . ." He allowed me to pull him onto the dance floor. "I don't want Patrick taking credit for my smooth moves."

He wiggled his body, and I joined him, swaying to the music as the weight lifted off my shoulders. William's big, stiff body slowly loosened up. Then it loosened more, and I was confused at how he could move so much in a suit that appeared so restrictive.

He danced up behind me, close enough for our bodies to graze each other, but not close enough to attract any attention.

I'd been drinking so much water that I needed to pee. It was an event peeling these pants down and dragging them up again, but I'd waited as long as I could. I left William to third-wheel Shaun and Neema's best enactment of sex on the dance floor and went to the bathroom.

After what felt like an hour of struggling with my costume, I hurried out and found Mr. Markham waiting outside the door wearing a Superman T-shirt. His eyes were glossed over and his cheeks red. It wasn't surprising, considering how much alcohol he consumed at every office party he attended—alone, despite everyone being encouraged to bring their partner or a friend.

His eyes roamed down my body, and an unpleasant smile spread across his face. "You tease."

My heart rate picked up, and I took a step back against the bathroom door. "You're drunk. Go away."

He took a step closer. "You reported me, you little tart. As if you aren't part of this, with your cleavage out and your constant smiling . . . your sugary-sweet voice that I can already hear moaning my name."

My legs wobbled, and nausea built in my stomach. I couldn't think over the panic pulsing through me.

I turned on my heel and walked away, but he was fast and grabbed my wrist in a tight squeeze. The smell of strong liquor washed over my senses.

"Stop it," I choked out and wrenched my arm futilely against his tight grip.

"Let go," William's voice boomed from behind us.

Mr. Markham spun around to face him. I struggled to breathe or swallow in the seconds that passed.

William walked around Mr. Markham and stood between us. His eyes, even from where I stood, were focused and harsh. "And apologize to her."

"Stay out of this," Mr. Markham spat, a crude laugh—if that's what it could be called—escaping him.

"Apologize," William said again. There was no room in his tone for negotiating. "Now."

"Make me." Mr. Markham took a step toward an unflinching William and shoved him.

A muscle in William's jaw flexed, and he widened his shoulders. Mr. Markham tried again, but William was an unmovable mountain.

A sneer crept onto Mr. Markham's face. His fist curled at his side, and then he threw a punch, making contact with the underside of William's jaw.

William's head snapped to the left as a gasp was pulled out of me. Finally gaining control of my limbs, I ran to William. In a flash, he was holding Mr. Markham in the air by his T-shirt, his legs dangling like a rag doll's. As though he'd done it a thousand times, William craned his head back and then snapped it forward, headbutting Mr. Markham before throwing him to the ground.

I grabbed William by the wrist, his fists still curled, and dragged him away. In a situation of fight or flight, I chose flight. My parents never hit me, they rarely even raised their voices, and I'd never in my life witnessed something like this.

"Let's go," I said as two people approached Mr. Markham, who was struggling to sit up.

William tore his gaze away from them and met mine. He inhaled sharply, and his expression froze. "Shoot, Rose. I didn't mean to . . . That was instinct. I—"

His voice shook with adrenaline almost as much as my legs shook beneath me.

I swallowed, but it did nothing to soothe the stark dryness.

We kept moving until we were in his car and on the way out.

We drove in silence as I ran through thoughts of what I'd seen. A quick glance at William had his full focus on the road, his chest rising and falling as quickly as mine.

He pulled into Neema's parking spot, and I turned to face him. Anger lingered in his flared nostrils and deep frown.

"Are you okay?" I asked.

He nodded, swallowing hard. "Are you?"

I nodded.

"I didn't mean to react. I . . ." He blew out a long breath.

His phone vibrated, and he let his head fall back on the headrest as he dug it out. Shaun's face covered his screen.

"Shaun's going to kill me."

When William didn't answer, my phone rang. "We should take this."

William nodded through closed eyes, and I slid my finger across the screen.

"Rose, are you with William?" Shaun asked without preamble.

"Yes," I answered, controlling my breath.

"Could he turn around? You have my car keys in your bag."

I forgot about that.

William was close enough to hear Shaun's request and released a loud huff.

"Oh, and we won Best-Dressed Couple!" Shaun happily announced before hanging up.

"I don't think he knows," I said to William.

He opened his eyes and shook his head, his white knuckles gripped tightly around the steering wheel. "Guess we'll see. I think you should stay here."

I dropped the keys in the console and then leaned over and kissed the spot I knew would be bruised in the morning.

Round 27

Anxious thoughts ran free as I walked into the office the next morning. William and I hadn't chatted last night, and neither had Neema and I. I'd been too afraid to ask them anything.

My desk was as I'd left it. Thank goodness the party hadn't moved inside the office as it had a few years ago when, the following morning, everyone arrived at work not only tired and hungover, but then had to clean up dirty cups and leftover pizza from their cubicles.

One guy even found a used condom. No one ever owned up to it.

After dropping off my bag and setting up my laptop, my next stop was the kitchen. I turned on the coffee machine and inhaled the delightful aroma of freshly ground beans. The tapping of footsteps carried over the purr of the machine and paused. I glanced over my shoulder in time to see the back of Mr. Markham as he sped away.

When I got to my desk, Shaun's lips were drawn down in a deep frown. I swallowed hard, waiting for it.

"Rose, was it William? They're saying one of the Batmen assaulted Mr. Markham. Was it William? Is that why you left?"

It must have been written across my face. Before I could answer, Shaun dropped his head into his hands. "Oh no, oh no, oh no."

"Did he not speak to you last night?" I managed, taking my seat.

Shaun shook his head. "Neema and I had no idea what happened. I only heard about it this morning through gossip. A Batman. Rose . . . what happened? They're saying Batman beat him to a pulp, and he had to be rushed to the hospital. Someone else said Batman pulled out a gun and threatened someone, and Mr. Markham managed to disarm him before being punched or something."

"That's ridiculous!"

"No," Shaun said, his face red and his chin trembling. "What's ridiculous is that my brother punched our *boss*." He rubbed his palms across his pants. "This is typical."

"Typical? William is not violent." My need to defend him jumped out.

Shaun's gaze finally met mine, full of apprehension and fear. "I wouldn't call him violent, but he sure as hell isn't afraid to throw fists—or receive them."

Frustration banged against my chest. "William is not the villain in this story."

Inhaling a sharp breath, Shaun dropped his eyelids and let go of the breath he'd held. "What happened?"

"I don't condone violence." I opened my laptop and stabbed the power button. "But Jeffrey Markham, our *boss*, sexually harassed me, and when William asked him to apologize, he punched William. So you decide."

He slapped his hand against his forehead. "I should have led with that question. Are you okay?" He wheeled over.

"I'm still processing, but without William there, it could have been a lot worse."

The entire day went by without having to face Mr. Markham. I heard some of the rumors that twisted and turned with each new person, and none of them were the truth.

By the time Shaun and I walked back to his place, we still hadn't figured out how to deal with it and hoped it would blow over. In all the rumors, no one had figured out which Batman it was, and it seemed no one knew I'd been involved either.

Beside me, Shaun's walk was stiff, and his jaw muscles were working harder than usual. He hadn't let William off the hook just yet.

"How come you two are so different?" I asked.

He glanced over at me, his face scrunching in pain. "It's a long story, and it's not really mine to share."

"I know his mom died when he was young." I sped up, trying to keep up with Shaun.

"Did he tell you that?"

I nodded.

"Oh." Shaun's eyebrows, which had been permanently down all day, popped up. "He doesn't like speaking about her—or anything from back then, I guess."

"I've gathered he has a weird relationship with your dad," I said as we reached the building, choosing my words carefully. "But you seem close to your dad."

"We have the same dad, but really different versions of him." Shaun's voice dropped lower with each word as we approached their apartment. "It's not something I fully

understand." His shoulders tensed, and he gave me an appre-
hensive look before unlocking his front door.

Entering the apartment, I inhaled the scent of soy sauce
before I spotted William standing in the kitchen.

The kitchen. *That* kitchen.

Get it together, woman.

"Hungry?" William slid his hand across the counter where
I'd gripped for my very survival only a few days earlier.

Was it hot in here? The cooking must've heated up the
area.

Apparently, it took extraordinarily little for me to forget the
current shitshow that was my life.

Shaun threw his backpack on the couch and approached
the counter wearing the same frown he'd worn that morning.
"Always."

"What's with you?" William asked, taking in Shaun's
expression as he stirred vegetables into a skillet.

"You beat him up?" Shaun rested his elbows on the counter
and rubbed his hands over his face. "We work for him, man."

Shaun blew out an irritated breath before walking away
toward his bedroom.

William froze and inhaled a shaky breath. Even though
Shaun had left, William still spoke softly, as though wishing
Shaun could hear his thoughts rather than his words. "I
wouldn't have done it if he didn't hit me first. I swear."

"I believe you," I said, walking into the kitchen and placing
my hand on William's tense back.

"I didn't mean to cause any trouble."

"You haven't."

William turned to face me, and the area beneath his chin
was colored in a rainbow of blues and purples. "He shouldn't
get to talk to you like that because he's your boss. That doesn't

make him above the law or more important than your rights. And I'll bet you're not the only woman he's doing this to."

"You're probably right," I said.

William paused as though he wasn't expecting me to say that.

"He's lucky all he got was a broken nose," I continued, examining his bruises. "And maybe a concussion. I've never seen anyone headbutt another person in real life." I released a long sigh. "I wasn't raised with violence."

William's eyes turned glossy as he looked beyond me instead of at me. "I'm sorry." A darkness clouded over his gaze as though his mind was somewhere else.

"Does it hurt?" I touched the spreading deep blue across his skin.

"I've been through much worse. This . . ." He gestured to his jaw, and pain flashed over his black eyes. ". . . is nothing."

Every time William spoke of his past, I pieced together another part of his upbringing, and it all equaled something I could barely imagine.

I opened my mouth to say something, but he stopped me.

"Stop distracting me before I burn this."

The heavy concern in my stomach relaxed. "Anything I can help with?"

"No, thanks. I've seen the contents of your fridge, and I'm guessing you survive mostly on grilled cheese."

"And mac and cheese, or sometimes just cheese." I leaned on the counter, watching him focus on the meal. "When did you learn how to cook?"

"At my school, once you were around sixteen, you had access to the home ec rooms, provided you bought your own ingredients." Grabbing a spoon, he lifted a piece of onion out of the pan and brought it to his mouth. "Hmm . . . it's missing something." That wicked grin covered his face as he lifted an index finger. "Maybe some maple. I think you know where it is."

"Ungovernable man." I smiled, my cheeks flushing.

I leaned down in the same place William had kneeled not long ago and searched for the bottle. Finding it, I straightened and handed it to William.

Shaun came out of his room, now wearing loungewear after changing out of his work clothes.

"You could put your pajamas on. No one else is here," I told him. "Look at William. He doesn't care that I'm here. He's in pajamas." I pointed at his bare feet. "He's not even wearing any shoes."

"Pajamas are for sleeping," Shaun said, his tone still clipped. Patrick used to say the same thing.

"Could you help me with the seating chart?" Shaun asked me, making a point of avoiding William's gaze.

"Of course." Approaching Shaun, I pulled him close. "He wouldn't have fought if Markham hadn't started it."

Shaun's glare softened, and a huge sigh escaped him. "Still, he shouldn't have . . . Never mind." He shook his head, but instead of leading me to the couch away from William, he pulled me up to the kitchen counter and climbed onto a bar stool.

Sitting across from the kitchen was a bad idea. I could barely focus on the seating chart. Instead, I kept stealing glances at William as he cooked. I couldn't help smiling at the way he frowned into the wok as if offended by it or when he inhaled through his nose and then scratched around for some spice. I could never tell what he'd chosen, but he'd pour the powder and herbs directly out of the jar, mix it in with the vegetables, and inhale again before his frown lines softened. He repeated this process multiple times until his frown lines disappeared entirely. That was when I knew it was time to eat.

"How much out of ten?" He turned to me with a bowl in one hand and a serving spoon in the other.

"Ten!" I shouted.

He gave me a nod of approval, scooped a healthy serving of vegetable stir fry and noodles into the bowl, and then reached across the bar and handed it to me.

The maple syrup and soy sauce combination titillated my senses. I'd have to add this to the long list of things I desired from this man. Another craving only he could satisfy.

"Shaun, how come you've never cooked for me?" I asked, twirling noodles around my fork.

"I'm not really good at it."

"That's putting it lightly." William smiled, staring at Shaun, who was looking down at the chart. His voice softened. "Sometimes I think it's the only reason you moved in with me."

Shaun finally looked up to meet his gaze. A silent conversation seemed to happen across the island, and the tension in Shaun's shoulders dropped.

"Dude, the spaghetti and meatballs you made on the first night?" Shaun kissed his fingers. "You won me over instantly."

William beamed in that special way he reserved for his brother. My heart reached out, wishing he could always smile like that.

"When did you move in together?" I asked.

"Funny story actually." Shaun side-eyed his brother and grimaced. "In my first year at college, I found an apartment, paid the deposit, and when I showed up with the moving truck, there was already someone else living there. I tried contacting the landlord, or who I thought was the landlord, and surprise surprise, the number had been deactivated."

"What?" I nearly choked on a long noodle. "You got scammed? Didn't you view it beforehand?"

"I did." He sighed. "It's a pretty elaborate scam. They give you the official viewing date, so I rocked up to an open flat with a few other people. They assume you'll contact them directly if you're interested. Maybe I was a little gullible."

"A *little* gullible?" William gave Shaun a smug grin.

"Wait, what happened? What did you do?" I had reached the last sliced pepper in my bowl and wished there was a bit more.

Without asking, William took my bowl.

"Well, I couldn't get my deposit back, so I was completely broke and too embarrassed to tell my parents," Shaun explained. "I knew William was studying, too, and I assumed he'd be staying nearby, so I took a chance and called him."

"It was a mistake giving you my number." William handed me another bowl of food. "I let him in for one night, and then he never left."

I smiled at William, enjoying the story and thankful for the second helping.

"Thanks, man, for helping me out," Shaun said. "Even though . . . you know . . . you didn't have to."

William shrugged, his discomfort apparent again.

While I wanted to know everything about him, I didn't want to force it out of him. He also had no reason to tell me. It was easier keeping it on the surface level, where perhaps he wanted it to be . . . where it should be if we were still playing.

Sometimes it didn't feel like a game.

To me.

"With these delicious meals, I'd never leave either," I said, hoping to ease the strange ache in my stomach.

Even though no one had knocked, Shaun hopped up from his meal and opened the front door. Neema walked in, ignoring us, and followed the delicious aroma of William's cooking into the kitchen.

She breathed in through her nose, her eyes lighting up. "Thanks, William. You sure you don't want to live with us after the wedding?"

A stone dropped into the deepest part of my belly. Logically, I knew there would come a day when Neema wasn't my roommate anymore and I'd need to get my own place. I always figured Patrick would ask me to move in with him before she moved out.

"Thanks for the offer, but I'll be fine. Besides, I expect you'll need to accommodate your adopted adult child over here." William gestured toward me.

Neema and Shaun laughed.

I rolled my eyes. "I can take care of myself. I am a grown woman."

"Growing stopped early, though," William teased.

I shot him a dirty look. "Oh, someone is feeling very funny today."

He smiled at me, and all was forgiven. Damn, I was easy.

"Have you decided what you want to do?" Shaun asked, cozying up against Neema on the couch. "I know we're joking about it, but you're more than welcome to stay with us."

"No way. I did the math a while back. If I get the promotion I'm going for, then I could afford our place by myself. Worst case, if I don't get the job, I could afford a studio." Though I tried to sound confident, the thought of moving had my nerves frayed. "Have you found a place?"

Neema clapped her hands together in excitement. "Oh, I forgot to tell you! We were thinking I'd move in here since the wedding's so soon. It's close to both our offices, and to yours, which means you can come here after work every day."

"Even if you stayed in a different country, I'd find a way to be there every day. But thank you for making it easy." I turned to William. "You're moving out? Where?"

His unconcerned gaze met mine. "Haven't figured it out yet."

"You don't seem stressed enough for someone who'll be homeless in a few weeks." My anxiety built. I had been so busy lately that I'd barely thought about how things would change after the wedding. "I have a place to stay, and it still feels chaotic."

"I love chaos."

Well, he didn't have to tell me that.

After dinner, William walked out to the balcony—a signal he'd like to see me alone.

"Hey," I said, using my most seductive voice as I closed the door behind me.

"Hey," he replied.

Our eyes met, and all I saw was discomfort. Which seemed to be the theme of the day.

"I, uh . . . wanted to talk to you about something." He swallowed hard and looked away.

He was going to break up with me. Well, we weren't dating, so maybe not break up, but he was quitting the game we'd been playing. I knew it.

"You want to end this?" I tried to hide the fear in my voice.

He frowned at me. "What? No. Do you?"

I shook my head. "Then what?"

He hesitated before blowing out a deep breath. "I don't think I should be the one representing your game."

My eyes widened. "Why?"

"I don't know if I'm the right person to do it. Earlier you spoke about your spreadsheets and your future plans." He exhaled, turning away from me. "Rose, there are things you don't know about me. I'm . . ."

"You're what?"

He gazed across the rail toward the city lights. "The stakes are too high, and I'm worried that I'm not good enough."

The statement was so ridiculous that if his voice wasn't filled with so much pain, I'd have laughed.

"Send someone else," he said, in an almost childlike tone. "I don't want to mess this up for you."

I stood beside him, our arms touching. "I don't understand what's going on here. Don't you want to do it? I asked you if you wanted to do it, and you said yes."

"I know. I do want to do it. I love this game, and I love . . ." He paused and looked at me for a long moment.

My heart stood still, and time stretched out before me.

He blew out another breath. "I love making games better. But it's never mattered before, not like this. This is your dream."

"Do you have some kind of stage fright? It's not a presentation." I gnawed on my lip, wishing away the rising panic. "If you're worried about the bruise, just tell them you do martial arts or you hurt yourself saving a baby from an angry lion, or something."

He did not laugh. Instead, fear overtook his usually confident expression. "No. It's . . . I know how it sounds, but what if I'm not the right person? What if you're supposed to send Shaun?" He glanced at me. "I have a record of ruining lives. Ask anyone."

"Shaun? Really?" I studied him, not certain he was serious. When he didn't react, I added, "How would you ruin it? You know it as well as I do."

I searched his eyes for answers. There were none. He barely looked like the William I'd come to know. Instead, he looked young and afraid.

"You'll have to trust me on this," he continued. "I will ruin it. Somehow. And if I do, I'll never forgive myself."

"And you have to trust I would never risk my board game. I chose you because I believe, without any doubts, that you are the best person to do it. Overpower is as much yours as it is mine."

My heart hiccuped as I said it.

I stood on my toes and gave him a quick kiss, hoping my kisses made him feel as invincible as he made me feel. He kept his eyes closed after our lips parted.

"You're perfect. You're not just good enough. You're the best," I said, my tone brooking no argument.

Perhaps he needed to hear me say it.

He leaned his forehead against mine, his eyes still closed as though trying to block out his own pain.

"Please say you'll go." I hoped he couldn't hear the desperation in my voice. "You're the only one I trust. Plus it's this Monday, so you're cutting it a bit tight."

He opened his eyes and stared into mine. Finally, he blew out a long, slow, and defeated breath. "I'll do my best."

When I pulled him back into the living room, Neema looked up at us. "What time is the game thing?"

"Eleven," we answered in unison.

"What time are you leaving here?" I asked William.

"Maps say it takes about forty-five minutes of driving, so I'll leave just after nine. An hour's cushion should be enough to get there and find everything."

Had it been me, I would have left the night before and set up a tent in front of their offices, protecting my game with my body. But to each his own, I guess.

"This is so exciting," Neema squealed. "I can't believe your dream is coming true!"

"I can't even think about it," I said. "It freaks me out too much. What if it fails?"

Beside me, William went ramrod straight.

"William, play nice. No heckling." Shaun gritted his teeth. "Or punching."

"May the force be ever in your favor," Neema added.

We all stared at her until she realized what she'd said. "I mean . . . ugh, you know what I meant."

William smiled, but there was no dimple. He still didn't seem confident about this, and his fear escalated my own anxieties. And to make matters worse, he didn't kiss me goodbye that night. Not with his mouth, his hands, or his eyes. He seemed to want me to leave, and I couldn't understand what had changed.

Round 28

Sleep was still giving me the cold shoulder. My mind was buzzing like an itch I couldn't scratch. William was that itch, and he was giving me complete radio silence.

As was my mother, who still had nothing to say on the ominous Patrick-related warning. I'd even considered texting Patrick myself but thought it better to let sleeping dogs lie.

Instead of obsessing over that, I texted William. Regardless of what was happening with *our* game, this was my game, and it was important to me.

Rose: Hey, good luck for today. Please keep me updated.
William: Thanks. Will do.

He responded immediately, so I guess he could have been texting me all morning but was choosing not to. Annoying. He knew what this meant to me. I stared at my phone, willing it to vibrate with another message, but there was nothing. That was all I was going to get.

I may as well have stayed home today because I couldn't focus on my work. My mind kept wandering to William playing Overpower with a group of strangers who may or may not turn it into an actual board game.

Another excellent reason to stay at home would have been to avoid Mr. Markham. There was mild swelling on his nose and bruising around his right knuckles—which was the hand he had used to hit William.

My buzzing phone called my attention.

William: I'm here. Stop stressing.

I would most certainly continue stressing, but he didn't need to know. He'd been so freaked out last night that I didn't want to make it worse.

Rose: Thanks for the update and thank you for doing this.

Three tiny dots appeared on my screen, indicating he was typing a response, but nothing came through. My chest grew heavy. Something was very wrong, but I couldn't figure out what it was.

Every fifteen minutes, I checked the time only to find the clock had advanced by five minutes. The laws of logic and time worked differently when your dreams were on the verge of coming true.

"It's eleven o'clock." Shaun spun in my direction, his hands rubbing up and down his beige chinos. "Any news?"

"He's William. What do you think?"

Shaun laughed. "Told you to send me."

I smiled, but I knew William was the right choice.

"I'm kidding." He grinned. "I'd have picked him too."

I returned his grin, and my mood lightened.

But the second the sun started shining on my worried soul, the rain threatened.

"Rose, could I talk to you privately?" Mr. Markham poked his head into our cubicle space, acknowledging Shaun with a curt nod.

"Of course." I stood, my legs quivering as I followed him into his office and took a seat in one of his chairs.

"I'm going to get right to it." He offered no smile. None of the awkward pleasantries I was accustomed to. "On the night of the office party, I was assaulted by a Batman." He cleared his throat. "Now, I know there were a few Batmen, but one of them arrived with you, and you happened to be there when it took place." He paused. "Is that correct?"

I stayed silent, and he grimaced. The bruising along his nose spread on either side underneath his eyes.

"I also understand that you have made some very serious allegations about me, and if you're wise, we could figure it out here and put this all behind us."

"What do you mean?" The air squeezed out of me.

"I am confident enough to assume it was Mr. Patrick Bailey who assaulted me on the night of the party. Multiple people conversed with both of you over the course of the evening." Mr. Markham tented his fingers. "I won't stop at pressing charges. I will ruin his career and take his father's company down with him."

My chest emptied as a huff of breath was pulled out of me. I couldn't breathe. I couldn't move. I could barely think. I could only hear what he was saying, and I couldn't make any sense of it.

"I'm here to offer a trade: Drop your allegations against me, and we'll forget about this." He gestured to his face. "We'll cover it up with a happy story, and everyone will go off living their pathetic lives as they were."

Knowing I'd manage no words, I pushed myself up. I couldn't be there a second longer.

"Wait." He bared his teeth and continued, "I meant what I said about you being a good employee. I know you've been working hard. I've seen your timesheets. I also know you're very close to completing your studies, and I want you to know I was considering you for Matt's position when he leaves."

I stared at him, trying to register what he was saying. A department head position was one position higher than the promotion I was aiming for.

"Don't answer me now, but have a think about everything we've discussed." The smile on his face was forced and twisted. "And make the right choice or I'll make you and your boyfriend pay."

The bile rose in my throat, and my eyes stung in panic. But I wouldn't let him see it. So I turned around and left.

At 2:30 p.m., William texted.

> **William:** On my way back. It went well.

It went well?
It went well!
I needed more information, but judging from his brief message, not to mention he was probably driving, I wouldn't get it out of him now.

> **Rose:** Thank you, x

Oops. I didn't mean to send the x. For all I know, after our last encounter, we'd never "x" again. But it was too late to delete it now.

Shaun eventually returned from a meeting and dropped into his chair. Spinning to face me, he raised his brows. "What was that about with . . . ?" He lifted his chin in the direction of Mr. Markham's office.

I shook my head and changed the topic. "William should be home by now." I gestured to his bag, which I'd already packed for him in my anxiousness to leave. "Can we go? I know it's early."

"Why do you look as though you're about to vomit? Did William not say anything?" he asked as we walked.

"He said it went well," I replied, a strange smile making its way onto my face.

"That's amazing!" Shaun cheered and high-fived me before gushing on about Overpower and how he was sure it would win. There was something special about having a hype team.

When we reached his apartment, he asked, "What's bothering you? Something happened with Markham, didn't it?"

"Well . . ." I paused outside his apartment door. "They have a witness linking Markham's face to *my* Batman's fist."

Shaun's eyes popped wide.

"There's more." I looked upward, blinking away the panicked tears that prickled. "They think it was Patrick with me, and Markham's threatened Patrick and his dad's entire business."

"Whoa, slow down. You're saying way too much, too quickly." Shaun lifted his hands. "Okay, so what do they want? To press charges against William or . . . Patrick?"

"And then he said he'd drop the charges if I dropped my allegations." I leaned my head against the wall and shut my eyes.

Shaun's blue eyes widened. "No."

"Yep," I replied. "But that's not all."

Shaun's face turned a light shade of green. He scratched one side of his head, his lips drawn down in an angry frown. "I'm literally sweating. Tell me."

"Well, after laying all that on me, Mr. Markham offered me Matt's job. He said I should—and once again, I quote—'make the right choice or I'll make you and your boyfriend pay.'"

Shaun's eyes widened further. He was eyes mostly, with a side of face. His mouth dropped open, stuttering and stumbling before finding his words. "I knew this would blow up. Oh no. No chance you recorded any of that, right?"

I shook my head.

"What are you going to do?"

At that exact moment, it was as though the coin that had been spinning inside me for the last few months finally dropped, picking a side. "I'm going to resign," I said with more clarity than I'd expected.

I glanced at Shaun, and his concern made my throat constrict and my eyes sting. He pulled me into his arms.

"I'll quit too," he said. "They don't deserve us."

I blinked against the stinging sensation. "You're getting married and starting a life. Don't quit your job in an economic crisis on my account."

"How am I meant to work for him?" His panic was clear as his heart beat rapidly against the side of my face.

I didn't have an answer for him, but I was sure of mine.

Round 29

The door flung open, and William's eyes darted between Shaun and me until we stepped apart.

"I heard voices. What's going on?" William asked, taking me in as he always did.

I passed Shaun the quickest of looks, and he understood it. After years of working together, Shaun and I could basically communicate telepathically. I didn't want William to know about my conversation with Mr. Markham. Knowing what I knew now, he would feel responsible. Or worse, like he'd *ruined* everything.

"Nothing," I said. "Work sucks, and I really want to hear about the game review. Please put me out of my misery."

William's eyes narrowed, his expression hard and unplayful. But William was William, and we had been playing our game long enough that I knew which moves would suck him in.

I shot him a coy smile and pushed past him with a whisper. "William, I struggled to sleep last night, plagued by too many dreams, and now I need you to come and talk to me."

I sat on the couch and waited, watching as he fought back a smile and dragged himself to the couch, falling into a heap beside me. He was warm and sleepy, the smell of pine and lavender still lingering around him. It must be his shampoo.

"Well, they loved it. They literally told me so." He turned to me, offering me his sweet dimple. "I could see it in the way they played."

"No, no, no." I kicked off my shoes and curled my feet underneath me. "Start from the beginning—from the instant you stepped into their offices. What was it like? Had they already played the other finalists' games? How old were they?"

William's eyes lit up, and he threw his head back before giving me a dramatic sigh. "Fine. It was a beautiful morning. The sun was shining, and the flowers were in bloom. I approached their office and rang the buzzer. The buzzer had thirteen buttons and—"

"William!" I poked at his ribs.

He flinched away but immediately came back as though there were something pulling him toward me. I wanted to move closer to him too, to sit in the bend his chest made when he slouched forward.

He wiped his face with his hands. "They called me in at exactly eleven. There were five of them, ranging from about early twenties to late sixties. I'm not sure. They all dressed very casually. It reminded me of my office."

He paused as Shaun passed him a cup of coffee. I waited, resisting the urge to grind my teeth as he took his time inhaling the scent of the rich brew and blowing over the rim of his cup. He was doing it on purpose.

"I'll remember this." I raised an eyebrow at him.

Now I had his attention.

"Okay!" He laughed.

Such a delightful sound.

"So," he continued, "I handed them the game, and they used the same rule and instruction sheet you submitted to set it up. It took them a few minutes, maybe two minutes longer than Lincoln did the other day. One of the men timed it and made note of it, but he nodded while doing it. It seemed positive." He took a sip of his coffee. "I let them pick their markers. I ended up being the scientist. The game lasted for about two and a half hours or so, pretty much on schedule with what we predicted. But there was some conversation in between, which also seemed like something they were marking on."

"What do you mean?" I gulped down the rest of his coffee. It was hot, but my entire body was already burning with excitement.

"Some of it seemed rehearsed. I think they were testing to see if chatting throws the game off or if it enhances it. I don't know. They wouldn't explain it."

I huffed out a frustrated breath.

"I did ask," he offered.

"You didn't fight them about it, did you?" Shaun asked, obviously still unimpressed at William's physical altercation.

William side-eyed his brother and then turned his focus back on me. "When it ended, they asked me a few basic questions about you—why I think you created this game, and why I think you should win, et cetera." He bit down on his lip, his playful eyes wide-awake now.

"Curveball. I should have sent Neema."

"What did you say?" Shaun asked him.

"Oh, I told them she's the most ridiculous woman in the world and they'd be better off letting her win instead of trying to explain why she didn't." He smiled, nudging me with his shoulder.

It felt so good having him here. I considered nudging him again, just to touch him. "That's it?"

"That's it." He studied me again, glancing at Shaun briefly as if wishing him away. "Are you okay?"

"Did they say when they'd let us know?" Shaun asked.

"They said they needed to play another two games. They wouldn't tell me which ones, either." William huffed, clearly annoyed with the secrecy in how the games were being judged. "But it shouldn't take long."

Before I could question him further, Neema texted, letting me know she was downstairs to pick me up for our last pole dancing class. With everything going on, that had completely slipped my mind. I made vague excuses to leave since the boys still had no idea what Neema had in store for them this weekend.

"I'll come down," Shaun said, happily running ahead.

I turned to follow, but William pulled me back into the apartment and kissed me until my entire body hummed. When our lips parted, I gazed into his eyes, searching for answers. But I saw as much confusion as I felt.

I turned to leave, but he tugged me back for another kiss, his hands touching all the places my body had missed him.

"One second you're giving me one-word texts, and the next you're doing this. I'm getting emotional whiplash."

He frowned. "I'm sorry. I thought you'd want me to tell you about it in person."

"Obviously. But you could have, like, added an x or an emoji or something to your texts," I said angrily.

"This one?" He made the silliest kissy face, which was also somehow incredibly attractive.

Silly, silly man.

"Yes, that one," I replied.

"Wanted to do that in person as well." His lips kicked up on one end.

I rolled my eyes. "And last night? What was going on with you?"

"That's a long story, and I'm trying to figure it out. I have a plan, kind of. I'll be good enough. I just need some time to finish it . . ." He glanced away and, before I could question his statement, he turned his gaze back on me. "What was going on with you and Shaun when I opened the door earlier?"

"That's a long story, and I'm trying to figure it out. I have a plan, kind of," I mimicked.

We tutted at each other, and I wrenched him toward me for one last, frustrated kiss. If I was not getting answers, I would still get kisses. As I pulled away, ready to storm off, he wrapped his hand around my wrist.

"I was scared last night." His features contorted as though admitting it caused him physical pain. "I don't get scared often."

I touched his chest, feeling the vulnerability radiating from him. It left a surprising taste in my mouth, and all I wanted was to protect him. "What do you mean? What were you scared of?"

"Of ruining this opportunity for you."

His tone was softer than ever before. I wasn't sure I'd heard him correctly.

"William." I gazed up at him, searching for the words that would make his pain go away. Searching for a way to shield him from his own thoughts.

Swallowing hard, he said, "There's something I need to tell you, but I just . . ."

Before he could say whatever was on his mind, Shaun's footsteps echoed down the hall and William loosened his grip.

Approaching us, Shaun casually slapped me on the shoulder as he walked inside. "Neema said you'll be late for your Pilates class."

"Yeah. Okay." I looked up at William, hoping he'd tell me whatever he'd planned to say.

With half a smile, he leaned against the doorframe. "Another time. Good night, Rose."

Rose. Would I ever get used to him calling me that?

What was it William wanted to tell me?

The question plagued me all the way to pole dancing class, which, even I had to admit, was fun.

This week we were working on the final move, what the instructor called the Ballet and Inside Hook. While I still felt like a child applying their mother's makeup and putting on a fashion show, I had to admit the progress we had made was phenomenal.

When we began learning this move, the instructor had us plank. Invariably, I'd collapse at the twelve-second mark and lie there waiting for the buzzer. Now I could do it a full sixty seconds while still having control over my limbs the next morning. I was shocked and amazed I didn't have six defined abs already.

While we rehearsed, I told Neema everything William had reported about the meeting, only leaving out the thing he'd left unsaid.

"In all the years I've dated Shaun, I can count on one hand how many times William has been awake before noon. I imagine he drove there half-asleep." She laughed. "I guess he really likes your game."

A warmth crept into my chest, and I found myself unable to keep the smile off my face. It was becoming a habit at the mention of him. "I guess so."

Neema shot me a suspicious look, but then I landed a wicked spin, and she paused to cheer me on.

"Last chance to let me add a few sexy moves into this routine," the instructor said in almost a plea.

"Nope. I don't want my girls to be uncomfortable," Neema said, making my heart soar. "Rose has tried backing out several times already."

"Thank you, and I'm sorry," I said. "I know this routine is kinda boring."

The instructor brought her thumb and forefinger together. "Just a lil' bit. Let's add some spice."

But Neema reached out and pinched my arm. "I love this routine. It's fun and silly and kinda impressive, and that reminds me of us." She turned toward the instructor. "But I will be using those other moves for the private show."

I burst out laughing.

"Besides, we could go up there and do nothing and the boys would love it," Neema said, her eyes shooting over to mine.

My throat went dry, and I looked away first before spilling all my secrets.

But she wasn't wrong. The boys would love this.

When the endorphins eventually wore off, I curled up in bed wearing my favorite dinosaur pajamas and stared at my phone. William and I weren't done talking. There was so much left in the air that we wouldn't be able to walk through it without hitting our heads on something. I typed out several texts, deleting each one over and over.

My finger hovered above the dial button, but I didn't want to do this over the phone or text. And I knew, whatever it was, he'd have told me by now if he wanted to.

I wanted to see his face. I wanted to feel his warmth. Hear his laugh. I wanted that pine and lavender smell to rub off on me.

Since I couldn't have any of that, I called my mom.

"My Rosie!" she shouted into the phone.

"No, *my* Rosie!" my dad shouted, challenging her immediately.

"Hello, Mom. Hello, Dad," I said to their faces in the camera.

"I was starting to get worried! You haven't called us in ages," my mom said.

Because of my mother's warning about Patrick and the relationship of sorts with William, I struggled to face her. I either wanted to force her to tell me the truth about Patrick or force myself to tell her the truth about William. I wasn't good with secrets.

And if there was anything I knew about my mother, it's that she wouldn't break a promise. Assuming she'd promised Patrick she would keep his secret, it was certainly safe with her.

"I have been texting," I said.

"How's the game, sugar?" my dad asked.

"Sugar?" I swallowed my laughter.

"Oh, just go with it." My mom waved her hand as if my dad wasn't seated beside her.

I launched into the full story, giving them every bit of information William had given me. My mom and dad gasped and cheered at all the right moments. Talking to them was like talking to the small part of me that loved myself.

My dad wandered off mid-call for a smoke after saying, "Good night, sugar."

"He lasted three months this time," my mom said proudly. "Next time, I think we'll hit six."

Every year, my dad swore he would give up smoking, and every year he did—for a few months before taking it back up again with the most elaborate excuses.

"What was his excuse this time?"

She looked around, making sure he wasn't within earshot. "He said he remembers I thought he was sexy when he smoked. But it was the eighties." She shrugged. "Anyway, how's work?"

I suddenly regretted this call.

"Next!" I shouted.

"How's Patrick?" She glanced sideways while asking, ensuring I could read nothing from her eyes.

"He hasn't contacted me yet. Mom, please tell me what this is about. It's been weeks, and I'm on edge."

She frowned, and I thought perhaps I'd get something out of her. Instead, she yelled, "Next!"

Well played, Mom. Well played.

Round 30

I woke up knowing one thing for certain after years of doubting every decision: Today was the day I would resign.

Staring at my laptop, I navigated to my incomplete resignation letter. The thought of being unemployed left a bitter taste in my mouth, but the idea of staying strangled me.

Nothing at work mattered to me anymore. I didn't care about my projects or my deadlines. I was worth more than this. More than the way they treated me. It was a strange realization, and it was refreshing knowing one thing for certain in these uncertain times.

I looked down at my clothes. Somewhere along the line, I had subconsciously begun *un-beiging* myself. Today I was sporting a pair of purple stockings with a black dress and a pair of black sneakers. Everyone who walked by stopped and stared a second longer than usual. Everyone except Mr. Markham, who, to my absolute pleasure, still avoided me.

Because of my allegations. Because of William.

My heart fluttered. At this point, I was sure all this heart fluttering was a medical condition that needed to be cured with a pill or, I don't know, surgically removing my heart—whatever worked.

"Check this out," I whispered to Shaun.

Wheeling himself to my desk, he read over my shoulder and then blew out a long breath. "When are you going to do it?"

"Right now. I considered waiting a week until after the wedding, but I don't want to."

"Whoa." He scratched his head. "I'm going to start my job hunt after the wedding. Have you found something?"

"Nope."

"So, *the Rose* is going to be unemployed for a while?" His eyebrows were perched up high. "You're braver than I am, Rose Marie Jones."

Brave? *Pfft.* I was terrified.

"*The Rose* is slowly starting to figure out what she wants and doesn't want," I replied, despite the way my anxiety soared.

"Who's going to listen to me whine?"

"Still me, probably, but it'll be via text or after hours." I flashed him a smile and hit the print key for my resignation letter.

Taking my letter from the printer, I folded it into thirds, making sure the edges met before slipping it into one of the envelopes I kept in my desk drawer. I inhaled all the confidence I could find and tapped the letter on Shaun's shoulders as I walked out of our office. He nodded at me, somehow both sadly and reassuringly.

I clutched the letter while walking all the way down to human resources, but as I turned the corner, I nearly smacked into Louisa. "I was on my way to see you."

"Oh," she said, her eyes wide. "I was on my way to see you too." Her lips parted as though she could barely hold back whatever she needed to tell me.

She gestured for us to walk back to the safety of her office and closed the door behind me. She sat, and her voice dropped to a whisper. "Would you like to report another case of harassment against Mr. Markham?"

I swallowed hard. I'd been planning to, but I was hoping to resign first. I slid the envelope across the desk.

Her mouth curved downward as she read it. "You don't have to leave. I have a feeling the M in M&G will fall away soon."

I leaned forward, and so did she.

"I couldn't tell you this before because I had to keep it confidential, but you aren't the only person being harassed by him, and after the news spread about the altercation at the party, someone else stepped forward and wanted me to tell you that she believes your story, and stands with you. She's been on the receiving end of his unwanted attention for years."

My breath caught.

"I'm about to send multiple reports to Mr. Ganz, who, I'm sure, will not take kindly to continuing a partnership with him. Between you and me, Markham was already walking a fine line." She leaned back and blew out a long breath. "So, if you'd like to stay, I trust that it will become more pleasant in the near future."

I shut my eyes, and all those early mornings and late nights I'd spent here flashed behind my lids. Shaking my head, I said, "I'm happy with my decision." Each word lifted a weight from my shoulders. "And . . . I'd like to exercise my right to leave as soon as possible. Friday will be my official last day at M&G."

"I'm sure Mr. Ganz will be more than understanding." Louisa nodded, smiling now. She took my resignation letter and signed it.

"I've summarized my projects to make handover as easy as possible."

She waved me off. "I'll reach out to your clients privately and have them write letters of recommendation, if you'd like?"

"Thank you." I nodded and stood, but there was a fire growing in my chest. I placed one hand on her desk and said, "Oh, and yes, I would like to add to my account of what occurred at the office party and thereafter."

The second we walked into Shaun's apartment for game night, I let my eyes roam across the furniture in search of my favorite tall, dark-haired, and handsome man, but he was nowhere to be seen. His bedroom door was closed, but the bathroom door was open.

I waited a beat to see if he'd come out after hearing me arrive, like he usually did.

Nothing.

"Is William here?" I asked, with a weak attempt at keeping the longing out of my voice.

"Nah," Shaun said. "I didn't see his car downstairs. He's been out since morning. He's been really busy lately."

I swallowed my bitter disappointment.

He could come back. The night was still young.

Every time I heard movement at the door, I hoped it was William. The first time, it was Neema unlocking the door for herself.

The second time, someone knocked, and even though William wouldn't knock, my unreasonable heart still wished it was him. It was Claire and Lincoln.

By the time the game started, I was quickly losing hope that I'd be seeing him this evening.

The conversation shifted from wedding arrangements to my resignation, which ultimately had the conversation circling back to William in a Batman suit headbutting my boss.

And then I missed him again.

Even though we texted occasionally, we hadn't reached the level where I felt comfortable texting him out of the blue. I knew he wasn't much of a texter, but I needed to touch base— as if a part of me needed to make sure he was real, that we were real, and not some figment of my imagination.

I took out my phone and typed a message with speedy fingers and a speedier heart.

> **Rose:** Missing my favorite rival. The games are too easy with this lot.

I held my breath, watching the message say *delivered*. Three dots appeared immediately.

> **William:** I prefer the term "archnemesis."

Another reply came through a second later.

> **William:** And I miss you too.

It was real. Really, really real.

Round 31

I was buzzing with excitement for three reasons: One, it was Friday; two, it was my last day of work, and I was leaving early; and three, it was Neema's bachelorette party.

Despite the multiple stressors banging on the inside of my cranium, it felt good to focus on celebrating my best friends' upcoming marriage.

Shaun eyed me the entire day in a poor attempt to milk information out of me.

"We're ending up at the same place. That's all you need to know," I said.

He scrunched his nose. "Fine. Then at least tell me what William has in store for me."

"I don't know," I replied honestly, my heart turning at the memory of William's pained expression.

"Then what the heck do you keep discussing on the balcony?"

Oops.

"Okay, you got me," I said. "But I promised not to tell you."

He blew out a long breath that almost looked like relief. I felt a tiny bit guilty for taking advantage of how trusting he was.

I turned around and packed up my things.

"This is the last time I'll see you do this," Shaun said.

"Oh, shush. You'll still see more of me than you planned for." I pinched his shoulder, and while I'd thought I might be sentimental about it all, I wasn't.

I was nervous, yes, but more so, I was excited, and today was going to be awesome. Grabbing my bag, I yelled, "See you later, Terminator," and left.

Once I got outside, Neema climbed out of the car and handed me the keys. "And you're done!"

"I'm done!" I said, climbing into the driver's seat and tossing my box of belongings into the back. We took one long glance at the building that I'd spent more time at than my own home.

Neema's smile was wide, and she didn't bother asking me where we were going. She knew I wouldn't tell her anyway. After collecting Claire, our first appointment was a group massage. We needed to loosen up, and I was sold on the five-star review that consisted of no fewer than fourteen exclamation marks.

Once we were thoroughly relaxed—the poor redheaded massage therapist had to summon her inner strength to remove the knots in my body—we showered and changed our clothing before the hair and makeup appointments I'd arranged.

I slipped on my bachelorette outfit: a short red skater dress, cinched at the waist, that looked to be made of glitter and provided enough flexibility for the routine. I pulled on a pair of leggings underneath since I wasn't prepared to flash the entire club while doing my twirls.

"You look hot," Neema said, walking out of the changing room in a sparkly gold miniskirt and a black blouse. She let loose a whistle. "The men are not going to know where to look."

My entire body became a live wire imagining William's hot gaze. It was his turn to drool, and my turn to tease.

"Big time," Claire said, straightening her tan knee-length skirt. "I've asked Lincoln to record your performance since I can't be there."

I opened my mouth but she raised a hand. "Don't worry. Lincoln will delete it the second it's sent to me. I think having to record it is going to have him bursting out in hives."

This sent us into a fit of giggles.

After a light sushi dinner where we met the rest of Neema's friends and bid farewell to Claire, we made our way to the final round, VOX, where our names were on the guest list since I'd called ahead with details about our plan.

"A group of women offering to pole dance for free?" The owner's voice had shook with excitement.

I'd explained the situation, and he'd let out a cheer.

"It's going to be a busy night at the club," he'd said. "There's another bachelorette party, bachelor's party too, and a surprise proposal. But with pole dancing involved, you get first prefer-ence for anything!"

With his level of creepy enthusiasm, I was glad the routine wasn't sexy at all.

The opening band, Chaotic Sweet Dreams, started warm-ing up the crowd, and Neema pulled me onto the colorfully lit dance floor.

VOX had high ceilings and dark wood furniture. The wait-staff wore whatever they wanted, but their hair and makeup were glamorous and added to the overall vibe of the club—somewhere in the middle of tacky and luxurious.

The boys arrived as the main band took the stage. Neema launched herself into Shaun's arms, and he swung her around.

William's gaze took its time greeting my entire body. When his eyes locked with mine, he motioned for me to twirl.

After entertaining his whims, I walked up to him and searched his dark eyes, which matched the rest of his clothing, black jeans and a well-fitted black T-shirt with *NPC* printed on the front.

"Can we talk?" I asked.

He frowned but nodded. "We will. We have to." The frown softened before he added, "But not here, and not while you're wearing this. I won't be able to make sense of any of my thoughts."

His eyes settled on playfulness, and it woke up a part of me that enjoyed playing with him. Despite the chaos, I could always rely on William wanting to play.

"This dress is also against the rules," he said.

"I'm breaking a few rules tonight, just you wait and see." I bit down on my lip to stop myself from telling him all about it. Excitement boomed in my chest.

But my excitement was also fueled with white-hot nerves. What if I face-planted on stage in front of everyone? Granted, it wouldn't be the most embarrassing thing I've ever done, but it would probably place in the top three.

William pulled me closer and grazed my ear with his lips. "Tell me more."

His hungry eyes made everything disappear. I was the center of his attention. As if I were the only woman here.

Liam, one of Shaun's other friends, interrupted us with a drink. "Hey, Rose. Good to see you again. I got you a rosé." He grinned. "Get it?"

William narrowed his eyes and gave him a menacing stare. "She doesn't drink."

"It's true," I told Liam and offered him a polite laugh.

His smile faltering, Liam gave an awkward nod and made a swift escape.

I smiled up at William and bit my lip. Jealous William was sexy. It was a turn-on I hadn't known about since Patrick had never expressed jealousy—of course.

"Where were we?" William smiled down at me, refocused, and pulled me into the space only we shared.

"Wait and see. What did you do before this?"

I leaned in to hear him over the loud music, wishing we weren't surrounded by people so I could lean in a bit more.

"Laser tag and dinner," he said sheepishly. "I organized a private one so I could create the challenges for each round. I based it on his favorite shooter games. It was pretty cool." A shy smile crept onto his beautiful mouth.

I knew how much Shaun loved laser tag.

Thoughtful William was far sexier than Jealous William.

The next band stepped up to the stage and introduced themselves as Raggedy Andy, which was our cue. Neema exchanged looks with those of us who'd attended pole dancing lessons with her, and those who were still willing slipped backstage.

My gaze fell on Lincoln, who had his phone outstretched and wore a grimace if I'd ever seen one. I was so distracted by his obvious discomfort that I forgot all about my nerves. His gaze met mine, and I started laughing. His signature half smile appeared on his face while he shook his head.

Raggedy Andy opened with a silky intro, and my skin shivered with anticipation. I walked onstage and took a pole on the right side. Neema chose the pole at center front.

Finding William in the crowded room was easy. Between his height and energy, I was certain I'd sense him from across the world. He stared at me in disbelief, his mouth openly smiling. At that moment, I decided I would maintain eye contact with him throughout the entire routine. It was my turn to win this dangerous game we insisted on playing.

As music filled the room, we started moving in unison. While I had no idea what I looked like, I felt sexy even though the routine the instructor taught us mostly consisted of twirls and spins. And judging from the sounds coming from the audience, we must've been doing something right.

When our routine ended, we formed a line at the top of the stage, bowing together while the band cheered and the audience applauded.

Climbing off the front of the stage, I walked toward William, who stood with his arms crossed, waiting for me.

"Unfair," he said, his breath quick and heavy.

He threw his head back and groaned, and I couldn't stifle my giggle.

The energy in the room, combined with the heat and desire radiating off William, put me in a daze. I smiled, enjoying the upper hand for once. He leaned in and whispered something else, but I caught a glimpse over his shoulder of someone staring at me from onstage.

"Patrick," I said out loud.

William pulled back, a look of disdain covering his face. "Excuse me?"

I pointed. "No. It's actually Patrick. Onstage."

Round 32

William turned, his gaze locking onto my ex-boyfriend, who stared at us.

"What's he doing here?" William asked.

"I . . . I don't . . ." I stammered, unable to catch up with what my eyes were seeing.

One of Raggedy Andy's members passed Patrick a mic.

No. No. What is this?

"Ahem, hello," Patrick greeted the crowd before turning his attention directly on me.

Beside me, William released a long grumble. Everyone else in the club returned Patrick's greeting.

My beating heart changed gears from excitement to panic at the same speed as my racing thoughts. I couldn't slow it down enough to make sense of it. But I didn't need to because Patrick cleared his throat and spoke again.

"I'll keep it quick. Thanks for the opportunity, everyone. I'm here because I'm an idiot."

He paused and laughed, and a few members of the audience joined him. "I'm an idiot because I had the most amazing woman in my life, and I lost her."

Patrick's gaze met mine, and I looked at my feet, at my hands, at Neema and Shaun—everywhere except at the man onstage or the man standing next to me.

"Babe." He walked toward the edge of the stage and waited for me to look up.

I didn't want to, but the gaze of every person in the room bore into me, waiting for my response. Reluctantly, my eyes met Patrick's.

"I know I never showed you love in the way you wanted. I know you wanted me to love you openly and publicly. So here I am, in front of most of your friends and an uncomfortable number of strangers, and I'm asking you to come back."

A collective "aww" went through the crowd.

Hopping off the stage, Patrick advanced toward me. I took a step back, my eyes scanning the room for an escape.

Patrick stopped in front of me. "We're perfect for each other. My parents love you, and I know yours love me too. We have the same goals—let's achieve them together. I want you to be there for the promotions and the birthdays. I want the house in the 'burbs, and the 1.75 kids with two cats and a dog, all named after fictional characters."

The crowd laughed, but I was frozen under a literal spotlight and withering away as the sole focus of Patrick's attention.

Dropping to one knee, Patrick looked up at me with an intent expression. "Babe, let's tick off one of your Life Goals. Rose Marie Jones, will you marry me?"

My heart froze. Goose bumps flared across my skin.

The music stopped but there was noise in my ears and a brightness in my eyes I couldn't shake.

Patrick pulled out a ring box and exposed a shiny gold ring with a diamond so big I was unsure I would be able to lift my hand if I wore it.

This couldn't be real.

And I couldn't tell if it was a dream or a nightmare.

The words I'd been dying to hear for so long filled me with sinking dread that would have brought me to my knees if Patrick hadn't stood up a second later.

"Patrick." My voice cracked through my tightened throat. "How are you even here?"

He gave the mic to someone and took my hand. "Babe, I may have always been distracted, but I was listening. You've been planning this night for ages, and our calendars are still linked."

"Patrick," I tried again, willing my voice to stay with me.

Before I could finish my sentence, he kissed me, right on the mouth.

The crowd cheered, but my body recoiled. The feel of his once-familiar lips was cold and odd on my own. They were neither the shape I expected nor the ones I desired. I pulled away.

"Don't answer, okay? Not here, not now. Nothing good ever comes from a spontaneous decision, right?" he said, using my own words against me. "Go home, make your pros and cons spreadsheet, then say yes."

His smile was wide and confident, a smile I knew all too well. He handed me the ring and kissed me on the cheek.

"Say yes," he said again, and then turned and left me standing in a stunned stupor.

Neema stepped beside me and gently touched my arm. "Hon?"

I turned to her, my eyes already stinging with tears. "I'm so sorry. I had no idea he was planning that. I didn't mean to steal your thunder. This was supposed to be a night about you, and all of us having fun together." I took a deep, steadying inhale but it did not help.

"Please!" She waved a hand. "Patrick couldn't steal my thunder even if he tried." She offered me a soft smile. "It's not like you knew."

But my mother knew. She could have been far more honest with me. Rage bubbled inside me, and I focused on calming my breathing. Years of therapy had unraveled in literal minutes.

"I'd like to go home," I said. "But I want you to stay and have fun."

I needed to get out of here as soon as possible.

"Party's over, and we have to be up really early tomorrow." She wrapped her arm around me. "Let's go home together."

"Are you sure?"

She nodded and gestured for Shaun to come over.

"We're heading home," she told him.

"Of course, yeah." Shaun leaned in, checking on me. "Did any of you see where William went?"

The mention of William made my legs wobbly. I scanned the room, but he was nowhere in sight. He'd probably seen all of it, including the kiss. I shuddered like a leaf.

Neema dragged me outside toward her car, and I settled inside with a heavy heart.

"Did you say yes?" she asked as she buckled her seat belt.

I knew she'd support whatever decision I made. I turned the ring box around in my hands. "No."

"Did you say no?"

"No."

She bit her lip and gave my knee a squeeze. My brain went into overdrive and autopilot simultaneously. I had no idea how

I got into my pajamas or into bed that night, or even whether I showered or not. The only thing I was aware of was the ring box still clutched in my hand, the edges pressing into my palm. The sound of Patrick's voice proposing to me replayed over and over in my brain. When I closed my eyes, I once again saw the smile on his face and the moment I'd planned a lifetime around.

And it happened. It was real. So why didn't I say yes?

There was no point in trying to sleep. My phone flashed with concerned messages from Claire. Neema and Lincoln had already told her everything, but I didn't want to talk to anyone about it.

Powering on my laptop, I opened my Life Goals spreadsheet.

I was supposed to get married soon. Patrick's name was still on my spreadsheet—I hadn't bothered updating it after our breakup.

My eyes drifted over my career goals, and the already big hole in my stomach grew, eating into my other organs until I was sure the acid churning inside me would burn right through the flesh and muscle.

My career goals meant nothing anymore.

How was this happening when all I ever wanted was a simple, standard life?

The same life Patrick was now offering me.

With shaking hands, I opened a blank spreadsheet.

Pros:
We have history, mostly good history
Handsome
Motivated
I like his family

He wants kids
Well-mannered
Likable
Stable
In line with my Life Goals
Knows how to apologize
Always buys me treats
Buys my friends treats
Knows how to use an Oxford comma

The list went on and on.

My mind raced through a handful of cons, but there was only one important, impossible to overcome reason holding me back. One tall, angry, handsome reason, but I was too afraid to type it out. Because typing it out meant facing something I'd been ignoring, which would complicate the already difficult game we were playing.

But eventually I did.

Cons:

He isn't William

With two clicks, I deleted my pros and cons list and my entire Life Goals spreadsheet.

None of those goals involved William.

If life were truly a game, I finally knew who I wanted to play it with.

Round 33

"Come on, come on." Neema tapped my arm. Then, when it didn't work, my face. "We have to get a move on. The appointment is at seven a.m., and then we can finally go to the venue, and I've made it my mission to take your mind off things."

"It's your pre-wedding getaway. It's not about me." I groaned as I opened my eyes, which burned from the tears shed overnight.

The venue Neema and Shaun booked for the wedding, Villa Erba, was about an hour's drive out of town. They offered two nights' accommodation free as part of the wedding package, but Neema convinced them to give us two rooms for one night, allowing us some pre-wedding relaxation.

For me, it meant the possibility of talking to William and a chance to sort through the inventory of things we needed to discuss, starting with the surprise proposal I'd rather not think about.

But first, we needed to go to Taylor's Tailor for our final fitting.

The tailor stuck a few pins along the bottom of my dress, mumbling under her breath how she was sure I'd been taller when she'd measured me the first time.

"She's shrinking," William said, as he and Shaun walked into the room.

I shook at the sound of his gravelly morning voice. One of the pins poked me, and I yelped.

The woman cackled at my expense and mumbled, "Stop moving."

William offered me a soft smile that I wasn't sure what to do with. After the previous night, I'd expected Angry William or Annoyed William—or, at the very least, Vague-I-Have-Something-to-Tell-You William. Instead, I received the strangest version of him yet.

Soft William.

I glanced at Shaun, willing him away so I could have a moment to check in with his half brother, but Shaun stayed put as the old lady held up the jacket of William's almost finished suit. He slipped into it like it was made for him. Well, I suppose it was, obviously. He flexed, running his hand through his hair, and I worried his arms might burst the seams of his jacket sleeves.

The sleeves survived. I, however, did not.

As if sensing my silly thoughts, he looked at me and chuckled.

My anxiety edged away with each smile or wink he so generously offered me.

Neema emerged from her private fitting, beaming. She wouldn't let anyone except the dressmaker see her, and I was both a bit hurt and more than a little excited to be part of the big reveal on the day of her wedding. She was going to be the most beautiful bride ever.

"How about some breakfast before we hit the road?" I said, my stomach grumbling.

We walked out to the cars, and Shaun paused. "Wait, Rose. When I texted you earlier, you said you were running late because you were having breakfast. So, this would be your second breakfast then?" Shaun smiled at his brother.

William caught the *Lord of the Rings* reference, and his dimple made a delicious dip on the side of his handsome face.

"The jokes write themselves," William said. "I'm not even going to add to that. It's perfection. It is art."

I punched him, but he caught my fist and let it go almost immediately. His eyes jumped to Shaun, who glanced over at us.

Neema tossed the keys to Shaun. "Since you're jumping in with us, you can drive. I'd like a nap."

Shaun nodded, and I turned to William.

"Aren't you coming?" I asked, failing to hide the disappointment in my tone.

This only made his lips curl up. "I am. But I have something really important that I need to finish first. I'll be there a bit later." He held my gaze a second longer than usual before lifting his hand in a wave.

I sucked in the deep desire I had to be close to William and climbed into the backseat, trying not to mope about it.

When we arrived at the venue, I took a moment to admire the beauty of the old, rustic building covered in dark green flowering vines. Images of my own planned wedding, with Patrick as the groom, sprung to mind. I shuddered at the thought.

Carefree Rose. Casual, carefree Rose. This is about Shaun and Neema. Not about me. Or Patrick.

I repeated it to myself, hoping at some point I'd believe it.

"So, what's William busy with?" I asked.

Shameful snooping and yet I couldn't help it.

"Dunno. I asked and he said 'work,'" Shaun replied, his tone hiding a hint of frustration.

At that exact moment, the events coordinator appeared with a list of questions. We volunteered Shaun's services while Neema and I went upstairs to check out our bedroom.

"I can't believe Shaun doesn't want to have sex until our wedding night." Neema tutted, throwing herself onto one of the beds.

I collapsed on the other. "I think it's sweet. It's only a few more days. If I've survived this long, you'll be okay."

Grumbling to myself, I thought of all the times I'd tried to rabidly climb William, and each time we were either interrupted or William had cooled us down just as we'd begun firing up.

Neema shot me a look and then rolled over and shoved her face into the pillow with a loud groan. "Don't confirm any of this, because if you do, I'll have to tell Shaun. But, Rose," she said, her voice muffled by the pillow, "I am not blind, and I see how you glow in William's presence. I'm all for fun, you know that. You deserve it. But right now you're a little sad, and I think it's because he's not here. That tells me it's more than just hooking up." She shoved her face deeper into the pillow. "And now, a wild Patrick has appeared, and I don't know if you can handle this level of chaos."

I was completely unsure how to respond.

"So?" she asked, lifting her head in my direction while holding the pillow against her face.

"You said not to confirm anything." My mouth had gone dry. I kept my gaze fixed on the crystal chandelier above the bed, grateful she couldn't see me.

"Tell me you both know what you're doing, and you know what you want. Tell me you've discussed *something*, and this isn't going to blow up and make us all awkward with one another."

When I didn't say anything, she lowered the pillow until her eyes peeked above the satin edge. Her brows drew together upon seeing my face.

"I don't know what to tell you." My heart banged against my rib cage, a call for help. "We haven't spoken—"

Neema let out a high-pitched squeak and lifted the pillow to shield her face once more. She blew out a frustrated breath. Suddenly, it dawned on me how selfish I'd been. I had ignored how this thing—this unnamed thing between William and me—would affect her and Shaun, or Shaun and me, or her and William.

If William and I ended things, was game night together still an option? If I was engaged to Patrick, would we still hang out together? Would Neema have to coordinate which nights I could visit and which nights William could?

A soft whimper escaped me.

This time, she tossed the pillow aside and faced me. "You're already emotionally attached, aren't you?"

The corners of my lips flicked downward even though I tried to keep a straight face. I imagined I looked a lot like a sad, guilty puppy.

Her expression softened, and she jumped from her bed to mine. "Oh, hon."

"Are you going to tell Shaun?"

"I can't start a marriage with a secret that absolutely affects and involves him."

A number of powerful emotions fought within me for supremacy. Sheer panic seemed to be winning. But fear wasn't far behind.

"Can you give me a few days? I want to speak to William and respond to Patrick. Please? It'll be sorted before the wedding."

"Have you figured out what you want to say to Patrick?" she asked.

"I wish I didn't have to think about any of this."

Neema sighed, and when she spoke, her voice was free of concern. "You deserve to shut down that brain of yours sometimes." She grabbed my hand and gave it a squeeze. "So, is he as good as we all assume he is?" She wiggled her eyebrows.

I burst out laughing and shook my head.

"It's not?"

"We haven't actually done that, yet. But . . ." I hesitated as blood rushed to my cheeks. "He's very good at other things."

"Dammit, I knew he would be. That jerk." Her laughter shook the bed. "I was really hoping he'd suck at something."

I hated secrets, and being able to have someone—especially Neema—know about William sent a whoosh of air back into my collapsed lungs.

"So, what's stopping you anyway?" she asked.

"I don't know . . ." I thought about what William kept saying. "We aren't ready, yet." To lighten the mood, I added, "And for your information, you're constantly getting in our way."

Neema grinned. "What? When?"

"Literally every time we're alone. That day you came home and found William there . . ." I covered my fiery face.

"No, what?" Her eyes grew wide, her smile even wider. "You were supposed to be sick."

My cheeks were so hot that I could fry an egg on them. "Even the balcony."

"Rose! You saucy minx!" A shocked laugh escaped her. "I can't even picture you doing that."

"I don't want you to picture it!"

As if a pipe had burst on the secrets I held, I told her everything: when things started with William, where it started, about the secret kisses, and even the dreams about William.

I did, however, leave out the part about the syrup.

That was our little secret.

Round 34

Our gossip was interrupted when a knock on the door jolted us upright.

Neema stumbled to the door, red-cheeked from all the laughter, and found the events coordinator.

"The area's been prepared for you as per your fiancé's request," the woman said with a beautiful smile. "If you're ready, I can take you down there now."

We followed her outside to a flat, green, and very well-maintained lawn where the ceremony would take place. Stretched behind it was the villa itself, which served as a stunning backdrop.

Rows of white chairs were assembled on either side of a long aisle leading to a white arch decorated in pink flowers. Lining the courtyard were flowering dogwood trees, scattering white across the green. We were assured everything would be lit by fairy lights. The goal was "magical," so that last point was nonnegotiable.

Giddy with excitement, the skip in Neema's step returned, and the thought-nado, as my mother called them, in my head slowed the moment my eyes found William. It was like a part of me slotted into place when he arrived.

And I realized I needed to tell him that. I wanted to tell him that.

"Williaaaam," Neema called, a playful smile on her face. "You made it!"

My stomach pulled tight. *What if Neema accidentally exposed us in front of Shaun?* While her intentions were always good, she occasionally ran her mouth a little.

"Come and pretend to be my dad," she begged. "Please walk me down the aisle?"

William sighed and glanced at me. I tried to avoid his gaze, needing more time to figure out what my next move would be and what his intentions were, but he caught my gaze and his eyes initiated a game. And all I wanted was to play with him.

"Some grooms walk down the aisle too," I whispered to Shaun.

"I haven't decided what I'd like to do." He stood next to me as Neema dragged William down the aisle.

"You know the answer to this question," I joked.

"Ask Neema?"

I laid my first finger over the tip of my nose with a grin. "Bingo!"

Laughing, he called out to her. "Love, should I walk down the aisle on the day?"

"Try it out. See how you feel," she called back.

Shaun offered me his elbow, and I hooked my arm through, looking up at him as we walked together. My best friend was marrying my other best friend. Aside from the crazy life I was currently leading, that was enough to keep me happy.

"You two need to practice." Neema pointed at William and me. "You're both stiff as hell. One time at least."

I should have known Neema would do something like this. William offered me his elbow, and I weaved my arm through his. This time when I looked up at my escort, shivers ran down my body.

William was ridiculously handsome. The bright sun turned his tan skin golden and lit up his angled features. His dark brows were a shade darker, and the jaw I'd spent so many moments kissing was stubbled with fresh growth. I bit down on my lip, remembering how his straight nose brushed against mine when our mouths met.

"I'm glad you're back," I confessed.

Smiling, William gazed down at me, and my heart fluttered in the most absurd way.

"You're hiding something from me," he said, reading me like an open book.

If he only knew.

"I could say the same about you." I gave his arm a gentle squeeze, hoping to relay my thoughts before I found the courage to say them. "When are you going to tell me all these horrible secrets?"

His mouth kicked upward again. Then he bit down on his bottom lip. "They're not all bad. Some are good, hopefully—really good. I'll explain everything. I promise."

"If secret-keeping were a game, you'd win."

He threw his head back and laughed, almost carelessly. The pressure in my chest grew with each laugh of his I was privileged to hear, as though my body were storing them.

We reached the end of the aisle, and Neema hooked her arm into mine before whispering, "You look good together."

"You're not really helping to keep me away from him."

I tried to pull her away, but Shaun ran up to us.

"I have a surprise. Follow me," he said and turned on his heel.

Neema dragged me back to create distance between us and them. "I thought I'd discourage it. It's a really, really bad idea.

A terrible idea, but . . ." She dropped her voice to a whisper. "But then I saw the way you smiled at him."

My cheeks flushed hot.

"I can't believe Shaun hasn't figured it out. It's so obvious. You practically drool while looking at William."

"I do not," I said, knowing full well I absolutely did.

"You do, and he has his tongue wagging every time you walk by. Maybe you two need to release that tension." She pursed her lips upward in thought. "Clear your minds. I think it's the only way to figure out if you want to get back together with Patrick or not."

"I want to, but I don't think I can. Does that make sense?"

Even though I'd tried to initiate it, I knew that I'd regret it immediately after.

"Because of how much it'll mean to you?" she asked.

I swallowed the lump in my throat.

Neema squeezed my hand as we went down another flight of stairs, this time in silence.

With the lights dimmed low and the room filled with bulky furniture that must have been older than my great-grandparents, the basement had a dungeon-y feel. If I squinted my eyes, I could imagine prisoners and dark smears of blood.

William and Shaun were already seated at a large table decked with roast lamb and vegetables, freshly baked bread, cubes of cheese, and an assortment of drinks.

Shaun pulled out Neema's D&D set. "Dinner and Dungeons & Dragons. D&D&D."

She slipped the cape he'd brought along over her shoulders and beamed up at him with a sureness I could feel in my heart. The certainty terrified me. I hazarded a glance at William, who was already focused on me with the very same look in his eyes.

Or was it simply a reflection of mine?

Neema confiscated our phones in preparation for the game. She let loose a loud whistle, and it was officially time to begin.

The game went on for hours, longer than usual since we paused to eat and drink and burst into fits of wedding excitement. Beside me, William stroked my thigh under the table. I lifted my left leg and draped it across his right leg, allowing his hand to wander dangerously higher.

I could barely enjoy my meal. Everything was dulled in comparison to the way he made me feel, and he didn't even know.

I glanced at him throughout the game, aware of how my body lit up each time he looked my way. I wondered what unattached sex would be like and whether I could keep my heart out of it.

Would that finish the game? Was that the final round?

Would we pack it up and never return?

No.

No part of me wanted to accept that. There was no way that, after we finished it, we'd squeeze all these feelings and memories into a little box on the shelf that we'd forget about. I wanted to play this game over and over. I wanted to play it forever. And I wanted to play it with him.

I only hoped he felt the same way.

When the D&D session eventually ended, Neema handed back everyone's phones, and I checked my emails while she checked her wedding website—which she'd checked obsessively since the minute it was up and running.

One of my unread emails was from Fun&Games. I dropped my phone on the table, and everyone's focus snapped up from their own screens.

"Final results," I managed.

Beside me, William stiffened.

"Do you want me to read it?" Shaun reached for my phone.

I shook my head and pulled it out of his reach. Then I leaned back in the chair and brought my knees to my chest. "I want to read it this time."

They all nodded.

> *Dear all,*
>
> *It is our pleasure to announce the winning board game is . . . (drumroll, please) . . .*
> ### ***Kaleidoscope, submitted by Anita Peterson!***
> *We'll be in touch with Anita to arrange getting the game developed and distributed as soon as possible so you all can experience the fun we had.*
> *Thank you for all the submissions. Each game we played had brilliance and heart, but there could only be one winner.*
>
> *Keep playing.*
> *Dudley*

A chill covered my skin, sunk into my heart, and reached my eyes, bringing on a wave of unwanted tears. I inhaled a deep breath and counted to ten before exhaling. Disappointment sat heavy in my chest—aching, gnawing. When I looked up, three pairs of eyes were fixed on me.

William pulled my chair toward him and curled his arm protectively around me.

"I didn't win," I mumbled.

His face twisted in anguish. Neema and Shaun let out a long sigh and a string of curses.

I shook it off—emotionally—and then stood and shook it off physically as well. "No. I'm okay. It was a long shot, anyway. Let's not let it ruin our night." I looked at Shaun. "Come on—where's dessert?"

Who cared about it anyway? I knew I wouldn't win. It was a silly childhood dream. Something I should have outgrown a long time ago.

"I'm so sorry, Rose." William's head hung low.

"It's okay. I said it's okay. People lose things all the time." I was rambling, but I couldn't stop.

"Your game was perfect," he continued, his voice quiet as if talking to himself. "I must have done something wrong at the presentation. It's the best board game I've ever played. I even . . ."

"Don't be silly," I interrupted. "At least wait until Kaleidoscope is produced. Maybe it's phenomenally good. Maybe it's so good it's going to be the game that finally makes you admit you love board games as much as video games."

The lines of pain on William's face, combined with the loss of the game I'd spent my entire life creating, was the last straw. It wasn't good enough, and this competition—which meant more to me than I could ever explain—was over.

Rejection filled the hole in my heart where possibility had resided for years.

Round 35

So." I clapped my hands together. "What's next on the agenda?"

Their sympathy-filled eyes, minus William's, were still locked on me. The despondency weighing on his slumped shoulders was so thick I wanted to grab it and shove it off him. I nudged him. His gaze dropped to mine with a look so far away that I feared I wouldn't be able to find him.

"We are not going to sit around moping about this. I am sad . . ." I said.

William curled deeper into himself.

" . . . but I'll get over it. And right now, I'm with my favorite people in the world, and I would really like some cake and some wedding chatter as a distraction." I turned to Neema. "How many people have confirmed they're coming?"

She smiled and unlocked her screen, the wedding website already open. "One hundred and two people." She looked up at Shaun. "Oh, and that includes your parents."

Shaun and William froze. It was as though the air shifted, bringing with it a heavy stillness.

"What do you mean?" Shaun scratched his head, his jaw clenched. "My mom said my dad was scheduled to present at some medical conference in Rome or something. They declined the invite and made apologies."

"Yeah, I know." She nodded and read from her phone. "But your mom changed their RSVP and left a comment to say your dad made special arrangements to be here."

Shaun and William shared a look, but neither of them said anything. Their shoulders squared and stiffened, and their frowns deepened, both ready for battle. But who were they fighting?

"Rose, do you wanna come with me to the ladies?" Neema asked, reading the same tension I'd picked up.

I hopped to my feet and followed her, but we hadn't even made it halfway up the stairs before Shaun's and William's voices rose in a heated argument.

"What do you want me to do?" Shaun's voice fluctuated between anger and disbelief. "Uninvite my own parents?"

"I don't care what you do," William huffed. "We had a deal."

"You can't make me choose."

"You can't make me face him either." William's tone was furious. "He won't want me there."

"This has nothing to do with what he wants. It's not fair. You're punishing me because I want our father *and* my brother—who, let me remind you, is my best man—to both be at my wedding?" Shaun's voice was so loud that we had no difficulty making out every word from our position at the top of the first staircase.

Neema and I froze, partially from shock and—if I was being honest—out of curiosity.

"I'm not making you choose," William said, both calm and vicious. "I can't be there. Besides, he's *your* father. It's not like he was ever there for me. I don't want to see him."

"You're my best man!"

"I don't care."

"You're such a jerk," Shaun snapped. "Maybe that's why you don't get along with him, because you have the same foul temper."

Quick footsteps thumped on the wood floor. "You know nothing about his temper," William growled, his voice cracking as he reached the end of his sentence.

Shaun's tone twisted and mimicked William's. "I know he was only ever angry around you. The only time there was ever any conflict at home was when you were there."

A dry laugh escaped William. "I know. Nothing he hasn't told me before. I ruined his life. And you were his perfect boy. The son he wanted. The one I was constantly compared to and could never live up to. I'll bet he's paying for this place."

Shaun was silent for the longest time before finally responding. "So? What's wrong with that, huh? Why don't you get all your resentment out and hit me like you hit my boss? Rose's boss! She's gone through such trouble because of it—because of you—and now she doesn't even have a job. Do you care about that? Do you care about anything?"

Shaun paused but William said nothing.

He then continued, his voice lower and more threatening. "You think I haven't figured out that you're hooking up? And I know you met Stacey in the parking garage the other night too. This isn't a game, William. You don't get to play around with Rose. She's my best friend and the only person I ever asked you to stay away from. You couldn't even do that for me."

The air was sucked out of me in the seconds of silence that followed. Neema's hand shot out to cover her mouth.

"Look at what it's resulted in," Shaun said.

"She lost her job?" William asked with much less bite.

"I asked for one thing. One thing. I told you, Rose is good. She's too . . ."

"Too good for me," William interrupted.

"That's not what I said."

"That's what I'm hearing." William's voice shook as he spoke. Nearly as much as I was shaking.

There was a brief silence followed by heavy footsteps stomping toward us. Neema and I flew up the next stairwell and hurried to our room.

Shutting the door behind us, we stared at each other in silence.

Neema rubbed her hands across her face, her breath coming out in quick bursts, much like my own.

My heart pounded against my chest, and Neema found her words before I could. "Shaun told me William and their dad don't get along, but what was that? I mean, that's—that's not simply not getting along. Am I being too sensitive?" she asked. She was rarely anxious, but with the upcoming wedding, her emotions had been on show and emphasized—all of them.

I tried to find the right words to say, but my mind had caught on something Shaun said, and Neema picked it up instantly.

"And Stacey? Rose, did you know?"

This was not part of our game. I didn't know how to play this round. I knew we weren't exclusive. We hadn't discussed it. We didn't go on dates. He was William—a charmer. And my ex-boyfriend proposed in front of him. I was in no position to be jealous over a man who hadn't made me any promises. Yet I was horrifyingly jealous.

My silence answered her question, and she blinked away the same tears I was holding back. In all our years of friendship, Neema had been the strong one. The tough one. Whereas it only took a gentle breeze to twirl me into a spiral.

I reminded myself this wasn't about me. Or William. I swallowed the lump in my throat.

"They're big boys. They can figure it out. This doesn't affect you and Shaun," I whispered, steadying my voice. "You two are perfect. And I'm fine. You don't have to worry about me."

"I thought Patrick's proposal would be the curveball. I didn't expect this." Neema shut her eyes, taking deep, intentional breaths.

"There are still a few days before the wedding. Maybe they'll sort it out. I hear siblings fight all the time."

She nodded, but neither of us believed that.

The door across the hall slammed shut. Neema and I waited, listening for a second pair of footsteps. A moment later, Shaun entered the room without knocking, his face red with anger and tears shining in his eyes.

"I messed up," he said, avoiding eye contact with me.

The door across the hallway slammed again, and we jumped. William's recognizable footsteps walked past the door and down the hall.

There were a lot of things I wanted to say to Shaun, but he was a broken shell of a man in need of comfort—comfort I couldn't give him and wasn't sure I wanted to. I slipped through the door, leaving them alone to talk. My conversation with Shaun would happen eventually.

I ran down the hall and made my way to the parking area, where William stood behind his car, throwing his bag into the trunk.

"Where are you going?" My stomach clenched with a harshness I didn't know was possible.

"I need to get out of here." He banged the trunk closed and stormed to the driver's side of the car.

I was rooted to the ground, afraid if I took a step toward him I'd fall apart. "Can we talk?"

He fumbled his keys as he attempted to unlock it. I'd never seen him so frantic.

I opened my mouth to ask him about Stacey, but my voice got caught in my throat at the redness in his eyes when he looked up at me.

"Rose, please. I can't do this now." His voice shook.

"Do what now?" I managed, each word almost hurting as it escaped me.

"This. Play this game." He shut his eyes, pressing his fingers against his eyelids.

My heart cracked open at his words. This wasn't a game to me. Not anymore. But when I tried to speak, when I wanted to ask him to reassure me, Shaun's words struck me.

Was Shaun right? Was this a game for William?

The broken parts of me shattered.

When I said nothing, he shook his head and muttered under his breath, "Patrick is still in your spreadsheet, and even after all of this . . . You really don't remember. I'm such an idiot."

"What?" was all I got out, and I must have looked pathetic saying it because William's entire expression softened with one look at me.

"Rose . . ."

He paused, and I thought he might walk over to me. I thought he might hold me. Instead, he froze before going ramrod straight. I turned in time to see Shaun marching up to us.

"I can't be around him right now." William's voice cracked in a way I had never heard before. "We had a huge fight."

Inhaling a shaking breath, he opened his car door and dropped into the driver's seat. "Rose, I just need time. I'm trying here. I'm really trying. I didn't mean to screw all of this up, okay? Even though I should've known I would." He groaned and shook his head. "Shaun was right about one thing: You're too good, and as usual, I managed to ruin everything."

"William," Shaun said upon reaching us, but his brother was already in the car, and the engine drowned out our voices.

Shaking his head, William closed the door and shifted into gear. Then he drove off without another word, leaving me behind to face my aching heart.

Round 36

At some point in the night, I woke up to a chain of text messages:

> **William:** I'm sorry for getting you fired. I didn't think it would come to that.
> **William:** I'll take the fall. Tell me what to do.
> **William:** And I'm sorry for bailing. I'm sorry for so many things, Rose. I never meant for all this trouble.
> **William:** I'd like to talk to you in person if you'll let me. But I need a little more time. Please. And then, if you still want to, we'll talk.

I didn't sleep a wink after that.

The entire drive back was spent in aching silence. As we pulled up to Shaun's apartment building, a long groan escaped him.

"Good luck, my love," Neema said. "What are you expecting?"

"Well, I'm hoping for the silent treatment—gives me more time to figure out how to apologize." Jumping out of the car, he paused before closing the door. "I'm expecting he's changed the locks and left all my belongings in the foyer."

"He wouldn't do that," I said, staring at my hands.

Shaun and I hadn't talked about everything—about William and me sneaking around, and how he'd known. And more importantly, how he had it wrong.

"I said some horrible things." Shaun swallowed, his voice hoarse. "Things I promised myself I would never say. Things I knew would hurt him in a bad way."

Closing the door, he walked to the driver's side window. He kissed Neema and waited.

"Rose?" he said, looking at me through her open window. "I was trying to protect you and us." He gestured between the three of us. "I can't lose my brother again, or you, and now I seem to have messed it up on all accounts."

"Something the Ashdern boys are really good at," I mumbled and released a long breath. I didn't like fighting with Shaun. "And I am mad—really, really mad at you. Not only for thinking you could speak on my behalf, but for doing so behind my back. I can make my own decisions, even if you don't agree with them."

He nodded. "Understood."

"We're not done with this conversation, but you haven't lost me, you idiot, and I'm sure with enough groveling, you'll get William back too." My lungs squeezed breathing his name.

"If he doesn't come around, do you want to be my best man?"

"She's taken." Neema gave him a kiss and pushed him out of the window. "And her maid of honor duties will be keeping her busier than usual."

As soon as we left, Neema turned to me. "Have you spoken to William? Are you okay?"

I shut my eyes and exhaled. "I don't know if we're okay. I don't know what 'okay' is since we're not anything." My voice cracked. All I could think about was *Stacey*. "Maybe we were never 'okay.'" I looked out the window. "It was just a stupid game, and I'm not innocent. I was playing it too, but I think maybe we were playing different games. I don't know. I don't want to think about it." A harsh sob broke from me, and while my mother had always called me a crier, this was excessive.

I had no idea what was going on in William's mind or what he needed time for, but I imagined he wanted to let me down as easily as possible and wait until after the wedding. My heart crumbled as I imagined the pain in his eyes. The regret.

And the mere thought that I had anything to do with that regret drowned me.

I couldn't lose him. I would miss the light in his eyes, the secret smile he offered me and only me, the pleasure of that dimple, the hunger, his strong hands. I would miss everything.

Neema opened her mouth to speak but hesitated before finally saying the words she held back. "Let me know if you need a plus-one for Patrick. Whatever you decide, I'm here." She looked at me, studying me before adding, "I think you're wrong, by the way. I think you were playing the same game, only you were both confused about the rules."

Chewing my lip, I turned my attention to the trees whipping by fast enough to bring on nausea, which was easier than trying to untwist my tangled heart.

Later that evening, my maid of honor duties kicked into high gear, and I was tasked with collecting our dresses from the dressmaker along with the boys' suits. William wouldn't need his now that he'd backed out, but I wasn't about to explain that to the woman who'd spent so much time creating them.

Because Shaun and Neema agreed they wouldn't see each other for the last few days before the wedding, I had to drop Shaun's suit at his apartment. And if I was being honest . . . I was hoping to accidentally run into William. It had been less than twenty-four hours since his text message, but my need to see him grew with each passing second.

My need to tell him he had it wrong. Shaun had it wrong.

William was perfect for me. And I was perfect for him—if he'd let me be.

"Hey, thanks for this," Shaun said, opening the door and taking the bags from me.

I not-so-subtly peeked around him.

Shaun sighed. "He's not here."

"Oh." I swallowed my disappointment.

"In a strange turn of events, he's not mad at me." Shaun released a light sigh followed by a soft smile.

"That sounds like a good thing."

He shrugged and pursed his lips. "You know William. He's pretty comfortable with being mad—it's like his default setting. And this time, I deserve it. But he isn't mad. He's quiet. Quiet and busy."

"Busy with what?"

Shaun looked up and all around before scratching the side of his head. "He's been at work most of the time. He's got a deadline."

The lump in my throat returned, and when I didn't answer, Shaun let out a soft sigh. He placed the suits over the back of the couch. "He still won't be needing this."

"I thought he wasn't mad."

He released a pain-filled laugh. "It's not about me. He doesn't want to be around our dad, and I can't really blame him for it. We had a deal." He smiled, and then his mouth curved downward. "But I had to invite my parents. I thought . . . " He unclenched his fists. "I thought my dad wouldn't make it. He's usually too busy to do anything."

"Were things really that tense at home? Between William and your dad?" I leaned against the wall and checked the time. I had to leave in a minute, but I wanted to hear this.

"I guess it was, I don't know. A lot of their arguments happened behind closed doors. Our dad didn't like for my mom and me to get involved." He inhaled a deep breath. "But he was a great dad to me, so I . . . I struggle to see him the way William does. And it was okay because William knew I had his back. He knew I didn't think of him the way our dad does. But now . . . " He rubbed his hands over his face and shook his head. "Like you said, groveling. I'm groveling and doing everything he asks of me."

"What's he asked for?"

Shaun opened his mouth and shut it before shaking his head. "Uh, nothing, never mind. Don't you need to get to the airport?"

I looked down at the time. Drat.

"Happy groveling," I said and turned to leave even though part of me wanted to wait there until William returned. Until he was ready to see me.

The next few items on Neema's to-do list included collecting our jewelry and shoes and fetching one of her wedding guests from the airport.

Running low on physical energy—and my emotional energy nonexistent—I arrived at the airport and took a seat while I waited for her friend's plane to land. I had no idea what she looked like, but Neema had described me to her friend—including what I was wearing—so I had no worries she'd have trouble finding me.

To pass the time, I scrolled through the gallery on my phone. Images of William filled the screen, and my stomach turned. In the last few weeks, I'd taken quite a number of photos of him.

William cooking.

William as Batman.

William on the balcony.

Silly selfies William sent to me.

William playing my game.

William. William. William.

Ugh, my phone was more obsessed than I was.

I sorted my gallery from old to new and started again.

I scrolled until I came upon childhood photos of myself and my numerous travels with my parents. Seeing their happy faces made my chest ache. I missed my mother and father so much. It was three days until the wedding, and I was so excited, not only for my best friends, but to see my parents. Especially since learning about the dynamic between William and his father, I missed mine and the relationship we shared even more.

Images of Comic-Con flooded my screen. I couldn't help smiling at a selfie I'd taken with a very realistic Edward Cullen look-alike. I'd printed that image and framed it.

I continued scrolling and found photos of the board game area where I met Gandalf before my phone died. Included was a photo I'd taken of Gandalf versus Hulk during their epic duel. I zoomed in on the poor-quality photo, and a warmth of memories washed over me.

It had been the best day. Perhaps my mom was right, and I should upload the photo on social media. I smiled, imagining Gandalf seeing it and the two of us reconnecting after so many years.

And then I'd have a third man to worry about. Great idea.

My gallery continued through my college years. Suddenly, Neema, Lincoln, and Claire's smiling faces were in every photo. And then came Patrick.

And still I felt no longing.

"There she is!" a familiar voice called out—a voice so familiar I would've known it even if it called to me from across the world, which it often did.

My mom pointed at me, and my dad followed her finger with squinted eyes. A rush of pure love flooded through me, and I burst into a smile so wide I could feel the stretch on my cheeks. They wobbled toward me with their lopsided luggage.

I ran to them and was immediately pulled into a three-way hug.

"Rosie!" my mom exclaimed. "You have grown!"

I grinned. "Still the same height, Mom."

She laughed. "No, baby. Your face."

She cupped my chin and studied me. Any other person might feel uncomfortable under such close scrutiny, but not me. This was how she evaluated my state of being.

"A lot has happened in the last few months, hasn't it?" she said.

"Yeah. This face is what happens when mothers don't warn their daughters about their ex-boyfriends planning a proposal in front of her best friends and a hundred strangers." I crossed my arms over my chest, hoping she knew how unimpressed I was.

There was a touch of resentment I needed to work on.

My mother's mouth dropped open, but my dad interrupted her and pulled me in for a squeeze. "Rosie."

"Yes, Dad?"

He squeezed me tight for the longest time. I tried to break free of his hold after a couple moments, but his grip was too strong.

"Feels nice being able to hug you again," he said.

Once the Jones family finally managed to function without holding on to one another, we headed to the car. I tossed their bruised and battered luggage, now almost beyond recognition since the last time they visited, into the trunk. I could only imagine the stories we were about to hear.

"Mom, Dad, where am I taking you? Are you staying with us?"

"Yes, if that's okay with you," Mom said. "Neema insisted. I think she wants to make sure I finish all the candles before the wedding."

"Sure. You two can take my bed, but no hanky-panky." I shot her a stern look. "I mean it."

My dad's giggles in the backseat were not reassuring.

When we reached the apartment, Neema flung open the door. "Surprise!" she shouted as we entered, though I had clearly already experienced the surprise.

My mother pulled Neema in for a hug that might've been even tighter than the one she greeted me with at the airport. "You are radiating love and happiness." She cupped Neema's face in her hands as she'd done with mine.

Neema squeezed my mother in another hug while my dad nodded and patted her on the back in the same way he always greeted my friends. She grinned and nodded back.

"Rosie says that everything for the wedding is sorted."

"Except the candles," Neema said with a nervous laugh.

"I'll start on them tonight." My mom wiggled with excitement.

"Wonderful! Do you need anything?" Neema asked.

"No. I have everything I need in my bags." My mother walked to the kitchen. "Shall I cook some dinner?"

"Mom, you've been traveling for hours," I said. "Rest. We'll get some pizza."

My mother waved her hand in the air, brushing me off while she opened a cabinet and scanned its contents. She had a talent for whipping up a delicious curry in twenty minutes, which is exactly what she did. We inhaled every bite and collapsed on the couch in a food coma.

"How come you can't cook like that?" Neema asked, rubbing her belly.

"Ask her." I pointed at my mom.

My mother laughed. She knew we didn't have time for a cooking lesson, not to mention there was never a recipe. My mother didn't use them. She tossed spices blindly into her pot and then sniffed and tossed some more. Half the time, she only had half the ingredients she wanted, but somehow the result was always delicious.

"When are you going to tell me about Patrick's proposal?" Mom glanced at my finger. "I don't see a ring, Rosie."

"Oh, there's a ring! There's an enormous ring hidden somewhere in her room." Neema hopped to her feet and hurried toward my bedroom.

My mother had my father's name tattooed across her ring finger. A large diamond wouldn't impress her.

Neema returned with the little box that triggered my racing heart. My mother opened it and then snapped it shut, her expression unreadable. "So what did you tell him?"

"I haven't given him an answer yet," I mumbled.

"Are you having doubts?" Mom asked while Dad snored beside her.

"I know exactly what I'm going to say, but he told me to take a few days. He said no good ever comes from doing something spontaneously." I smiled, knowing how much that would upset my mom.

She narrowed her eyes. "Did he really say that?"

I nodded.

"Naughty boy. He knows you very well. I'll give him that."

"Why didn't you warn me, Mom?" I looked down at my hands, avoiding her gaze. I was angry at her, but I wasn't in the mood for more fighting. "He proposed to me on the night of Neema's bachelorette—in a club full of people, including Shaun and William and everyone."

"First, I didn't know that part. He called us to ask for our blessing."

"And second?" I asked.

"Second, I didn't want you to be prepared, because the irony is I believe the best decisions *are* made spontaneously. The longer you thought about it, the more you'd try to reason it—and you can't reason love. It doesn't work that way." While my mother generally laughed easily, her expression now was solemn.

Beside her, my father released a loud snore.

She pinched his nose, waking him. "Go to bed."

Half-awake and grumbling, he stood and stomped off.

"Night, Dad. You can throw everything off the bed," I called.

He nodded, but I'm not sure he heard me since he was basically sleepwalking.

My mom turned to me. "Rosie, if you had to answer Patrick at that exact moment, right there in front of everyone, what would you have said?"

No.

"You don't have to tell me, but I know you know." She stood and stretched her arms until her back let out a loud crack. Then, leaning down, she kissed the top of my head. "Now go to sleep. I love you forever and wherever, and I never want you to doubt that."

Round 37

I stayed up all night—not because of the conversation with my mother, but because the couch was lumpy and soft in all the wrong places.

Okay, it had *something* to do with the conversation with my mother.

Deciding there was no use tossing and turning on the uncomfortable couch, I got up early with the intention of finishing up a load of candles before lunchtime.

And I did. Far before lunchtime.

And that is how I found myself outside Patrick's office at exactly midday after texting him to let him know I was coming.

The doorman greeted me when I entered, and I had a visceral reaction as I remembered the last time I'd seen him. While I regretted every bit of that night that took place in this office . . . I didn't regret a moment after.

I caught a glimpse of Patrick out of the corner of my eye. He waved and called out to me.

"I'm glad you came," he said.

I nodded, squeezing my fist around the ring box in my pocket and swallowing the ring box–sized lump in my throat.

He held up brown paper bags and the scent of the butter chicken and ramen combination wafted toward me. "Lunch on the roof?"

One last time.

I nodded and followed him to the elevator. He looked me up and down after we stepped inside. "Casual Monday?"

I resisted the urge to roll my eyes.

Of course Patrick was wearing a beautifully ironed white shirt with a pair of beige chinos. Every strand of hair was in place, and he already looked every bit the COO he would end up being. I shrugged, clicking my red sneakers together and wishing I could go home.

We sat on a bench with a great view overlooking the city and the office block where I used to work.

He smiled and handed me the container of ramen and the cutlery. "I haven't been up here in ages. I forgot I could see your building from here."

"Not my building anymore," I blurted, then shoved a forkful of ramen into my mouth before I could say anything further.

Patrick froze. "What?"

I finished chewing and then swallowed before answering. "I resigned."

"I figured. I'm just confused. Why?"

"I didn't want to work there anymore."

His nose crinkled, and he gave me his most unimpressed expression. "Well, obviously. But I meant, why? Why don't you want to work there? It's a great company, plus you're definitely going to get that promotion as soon as you finish your MBA."

I nodded and then changed direction by shaking my head. "Yeah, uhm . . . I hated it. I *really* hated it, but you already know that. So, uh . . . I don't care that it's a good company, and

I care even less about being promoted." I slurped up more ramen, and it dripped down my chin. I grabbed a napkin and wiped it.

My mind jumped to the day I had sat on the couch eating ramen with William. The way he'd placed my aching ankle on his lap—it was the first time he'd ever really touched me, and the first time I'd ever really seen him. Had it only been a few months ago?

Patrick shook his head. "Well, okay. Where are you moving to?"

I smiled, preparing him for my next answer. "Nowhere."

"What do you mean? Are you leaving without having anything lined up? Tell me you have a few interviews, at least." His cheeks puffed up, and his eyebrows folded into a frown. "What about your Life Goals?"

"I know what I don't want, and I didn't want that."

He swallowed his last bite and placed the empty container back into the brown paper bag. "Why do I get the feeling you're not only talking about M&G?" His voice softened, and a broken smile flashed across his face. "You've been awfully quiet since Friday."

My throat tightened. "I don't want to marry you. I'm so sorry."

He nodded, his eyes turning shiny. "Can I ask you something?"

"Yeah, anything."

"If I'd done it differently—if I'd come to more game nights or if I'd pulled you into my office that night and locked the door—if I'd made you a priority back then, would it have changed things?"

Gazing off in the general direction of my old office building, I shook my head. "No, it wouldn't have." I glanced back at

Patrick, knowing he needed the truth but not wanting to hurt him—which was exactly why I hadn't answered his proposal sooner. "I think it would have delayed the inevitable. We weren't meant for each other."

My heart beat in time with the words flowing through my mind: *I was meant for another.*

Standing, Patrick rubbed his hands over his face and composed himself.

I continued. "Soon, you'll meet someone who excites you as much as your work, and you won't need to try to remember her. She'll be there on your mind all the time, and she'll be lucky to have you."

I meant every word because I finally knew what that feeling was like—and it wasn't this.

Digging into my pocket, I retrieved the ring box and handed it to him. "Thank you for everything, but I should go." I stood and made my way toward the exit.

"Rose," he called.

I paused.

"Did you ever make that spreadsheet?"

"Of course I did."

"I had that many cons?" He brought his hand up and placed it over his heart, feigning hurt.

"Just one." I sighed, surprising myself with the words I was about to say. "Excel can't solve everything."

He bowed his head as I left.

I hurried out of his building, preparing myself for an onslaught of regret.

But it never came.

The birds were still chirping, and the person struggling to parallel park was still struggling.

And I was still undeniably in love with William Ashdern.

And I wouldn't survive a minute longer without telling him this.

I rushed over to William's apartment and knocked on the door, but no one answered. I tried calling, but his phone was off. Eventually, I called Shaun, who was still at work.

"I'm looking for William. Can you tell me where he is?"

"Oh . . . Uh, I can't," Shaun replied.

"Help me," I said, pulling out the last syllable. "You owe me."

"I owe him too," Shaun grumbled.

"What's that supposed to mean?"

"He's at work. He's working on something really urgent and struggling to meet a super-important deadline." Shaun sounded almost proud of his brother.

"William?"

"Uh-huh."

"I don't think you understand," I said into the phone as I walked back down to the car. "I need to see him. When is the earliest I can see him?"

"Sit tight. I'll pass on your message, but just go home and . . . wait. Just a bit longer."

I ended the call and went straight to my apartment, where everyone was still huddled around the candles.

My mind was clearer than it had been in ages.

I gobbled down half a pizza while wearing a blanket as a cape after my mother helped me pin it on. I was not far from twenty-seven years old, with no money and no prospects, and I was not frightened. Not in the least. For the first time in my life, I knew exactly what I wanted.

I wanted William Ashdern. All of him. Every last bit of him.

And I hoped he wanted me too.

"Rosie," my mom called, "if we're going to finish the last of these candles, I'll need more of your help. Remember when we made candles together when you were nine or ten?"

"I was five, but yes." I joined her at the kitchen counter. "Don't these usually go faster?"

"Mm-hmm, but I've decided to write 'Shaun & Neema' and their wedding date on each jar."

"Mom," I whined, "that's going to take forever."

"Well, I already started on the jars, so I have to follow through." She smiled down at her own work. "Look at my darling calligraphy."

I opened the scented oils, breathing in the familiar scent of pine and lavender. It reminded me not only of my childhood but also of William. It was as if I'd walked straight into William's familiar arms.

"Mom, this smell, it's amazing. I want a few candles for myself, please." I pictured William as I spoke, thinking about the way I felt around him. Not only the way he made my body feel, but how happy I'd been. How *me* I'd been. It blew my mind how William had etched himself into my every fiber in such a short space of time.

My mother narrowed her eyes. "You're a clown, you know that?"

"It's a compliment, Mom. I like this smell. Is it pine and . . . lavender?"

"Wrong. Rosemary and lavender. It's your signature scent, Rosie. There's a subtle difference, but I thought you'd know it. We had rosemary-and-lavender-scented everything when you were growing up."

I didn't hear anything else she said because all I could think about was that William smelled of rosemary and lavender.

"How's work been, sugar?" my dad asked while scrolling through the daily news. "I'm glad you're using your vacation days."

Neema burst out laughing.

I grinned. "I forgot to tell you that I resigned, and my last day was Friday. So I'm actually unemployed."

My mother wrapped her arms around me as though I'd announced I'd been promoted. "Oh, Rosie! I'm so pleased and proud of you—for doing what's right by you."

"Mom, you don't know the half of it."

If my sweet-natured mother ever found out about Mr. Markham, I was fairly certain he would mysteriously disappear.

"I also rejected Patrick's proposal today," I added.

My mom pulled me in for another hug, tighter than the last.

"I knew you would," Neema said.

"How?" I fiddled with the wick of the candle in my hand.

"You may be able to fool yourself, but you can't fool me." She beamed.

"I knew too." My mom nodded. "Patrick wasn't the one."

"How'd he take it?" Neema asked.

"It was pleasant and weirdly sad, but better than the initial breakup."

"You see?" Neema spread her arms wide. "Even Patrick expected it."

"Do you love him, Rosie?" my mother asked, her hand firmly on my slouched back.

I straightened. "I just told you I rejected him."

"Do you love William, Shaun's *mean* brother?" My mother smiled her soft and calming smile. "Neema filled me in while you were out."

I glared at Neema.

"What?" Neema held up both hands in surrender. "She guessed it. I confirmed it."

"So you do love him." My mom nodded.

"With every part of me," I said without hesitation after having kept those words inside my chest for the longest time. "I love him more than I knew possible, and I don't know what to do with all of it. He asked me to wait, and I want to respect that, but I also want to rush into his arms and never let go because it's kind of hard to breathe without him." I fidgeted with a loose thread on my skirt. A tear rolled down my cheek and dropped onto my hand. "I feel like I've known him forever, like I was made to know him. What am I meant to do?"

"I think you know."

"I'm terrified. What if he doesn't love me back?" My heart cracked at the mere thought of it.

"Zero chance of that," Neema said, pinching me. "I've read his wedding speech, and it was pretty much an ode to you, as if Shaun and I aren't the ones getting married. I mean"—she giggled—"he did call you a little hobbit cheerleader or something, but mostly it was clear as day that he thinks you're perfect and he thinks of you all the time."

Noise filled my ears.

The rest of Neema's words disappeared as something pinged against the side of my brain.

Waves of memories flowed inside my mind. Back and forth. Coming closer until I could almost taste the thought before it washed away. Back. And forth.

Hobbit. Cheerleader.

Cheerleader. Hobbit.

William.

Hobbit.

It couldn't be.

Could it?

Gooseflesh tickled across my skin. Gandalf. William. It could be a coincidence.

But somehow, I knew it wasn't.

It didn't matter that the probability of William being Gandalf was frighteningly low. It didn't matter because the probability of me finding someone who matched me in every beat was even lower. And yet, somehow, I found him.

I found him twice.

And I could find him again. As many times as he needed me to.

Round 38

I was going to tell William I loved him.

And I believed he loved me too. But I remembered the fear in his eyes, the hesitation, and I understood it now. Loving someone is terrifying, and I think perhaps William had loved me for a long, long time.

"His phone is dead, and he's not at his apartment. I checked," I admitted, releasing the makeshift blanket-cape to replace it with another. A cape I hadn't used in ages.

I rushed off to my bedroom, and Neema followed.

"I can't wait," I said, rummaging through my closet, looking for the one thing he'd never be able to ignore me in. "I'm going to his office. Now."

My mother clapped her hands together, and Neema shrieked.

"Let me fix *this*." Neema gestured to my outfit.

"Hold that look of disgust until you see what I have planned." I threw more articles of clothing on the floor until I found my original hobbit costume, which was still my favorite after all these years. "If he needs even more time, he's going to have to turn me away in *this*."

My mother squealed, and I shooed them out of my bedroom and changed, finding the costume much tighter than I remembered. Nevertheless, it was too late to back out now. Swinging open the door, I came face-to-face with Neema, my mother, and my father, who had started slow clapping.

"Oh, this is going to kill him." Neema howled with laughter. "I didn't think it would be this provocative." She pulled me into her room and plugged in her curling iron.

Fifteen minutes later—a record short time for Neema—my curls were coily enough to challenge Frodo.

She stood back and wiped her brow. "My work here is done."

I turned to my mom. "Any last words of advice or encouragement?"

"Rosie, you don't need it. You got here all by yourself. Now go get him, tiger."

Even after turning off Neema's car, my heart hummed with nervous energy. I had googled the address for Thunderstruck's offices and hoped there was only one in town. I opened the center console and retrieved my phone. I dialed William's number but reached his voicemail.

It was for the better.

I needed to see him, and I needed him to see me. He could turn me away, but I needed him to know how I felt. How I've always felt.

I needed to see his face when he saw me in this costume.

It was my turn. My move.

But I still hadn't figured out what I would say. Shrugging to myself, I decided I'd wing it and speak from the heart. How bad could it be?

Walking along the sidewalk in my hobbit socks, I reached the main door and rang the bell.

The last time I'd surprised a man in his office, it didn't turn out too well for me, and this time I was wearing something far less appealing.

"Uh, hello?" A young man peeked at me through the glass doors.

"Hi, could you let me in? I'm here for the . . . uh . . . LAN." I probably should have brought a laptop with me.

His eyebrows drew close as he scrutinized my costume.

I blew out a breath. "I'm a friend of William's. William Ashdern?" I glanced down, reconsidering my outfit choice and location of confession.

"Follow me, Ms. Hobbit." He grinned, clearly amused.

He led me to what I assumed was the cafeteria. Desks were spread around the room, and every surface was covered in laptops, desktop PCs, and cables. Movement to my left caught my eye, and I gazed upon one of the gamers' livestreams projected against the wall.

"William!" the man called. "Can someone tell William there's a sexy hobbit here to see him?"

My cheeks burned hot, and my heart raced in my chest.

A number of people looked up, gawking. A quiet hum of whispers spread through the room until those who hadn't bothered looking up a moment before were soon eyeing me with the same stunned expression.

My insides were on fire. I thought I might be running a fever.

A red-haired man with black-rimmed glasses stood. "William's not here. He left about fifteen minutes ago."

"Where did he go?" I chewed on my lip in discomfort.

He shrugged. "Something about seeing a girl."

Oh.

"Are you Rose?"

I nodded, and the man grinned, his cheeks reddening. "He left to see you."

"Me? Are you sure?" My voice caught, and I curled my socked toes into their office rug.

He and a few others exchanged looks. "You're all we've heard about for the last few months."

Stunned and a little confused, I thanked the group of gamers and snuck out of the building, trying to keep myself together. Marching back to the car in a daze, I climbed in and reached for my phone.

A single text awaited me:

Neema: Come home. Now. He's here.

My heart pounded in my chest as though it might break through to get home sooner. I put the car in gear and drove home.

To William.

When I reached my apartment, it was quieter than I'd imagined it would be. I expected the same madness of activity the apartment had seen the last few days. I'd anticipated the glitter. I'd prepared for ribbons.

But there was no part of me that had predicted I'd find William sitting alone on my couch with a laptop.

I stepped inside the apartment, and he jumped to his feet. Tossing the laptop aside, he straightened his black jeans, and I couldn't help but notice the elvish scribble across his black T-shirt.

And there wasn't a part of me that doubted it anymore. William was Gandalf. What felt like a lifetime had passed, but as I stood there in the same outfit, I could see him. I could see his dark eyes, his playful smile. I could feel the tether between us. Then and now.

A wide and slightly confused grin appeared on his face as he took in my clothing.

"I remember," I choked out, frozen in the open doorway. "I remember."

William's mouth parted, and he took three quick steps, closing the space between us. His hand slipped under my chin and tilted it upward to meet his gaze. His breath came out in quick rasps. "Can I kiss you?"

My face barely broke into a smile before his mouth crashed into mine and I melted against him. His hands slid around my waist with ease, lifting me up off the ground and pulling me into his chest, where I could feel his heart raging against mine.

"Rose," he choked out as he broke the kiss.

Hearing him say my name breathed life into me. One syllable. A common name. But on his lips, it was magic.

"William, I remember, I remember." I kept repeating it over and over as though his roaming hands weren't letting me know that he'd heard. Now I remembered everything. "That's why you called me 'hobbit' when we first met," I said, inhaling and allowing oxygen to compete with the fluttering in my chest. "Why didn't you tell me?"

Releasing me, he blew out a breath before spinning around and sliding his hand into his pocket. Straightening his shoulders, he turned back toward me clutching a small transparent bag in his fist.

Discomfort and uncertainty stretched over his features. "I wanted to tell you. There were so many times I wanted to tell you, but I'd waited so long I didn't know how, and it became this big thing that I panicked about all the time ..."

I clawed open his fingers and removed the little bag, glancing at the thing inside.

My heart stopped and then raced in my chest, knocking the air out of me.

Every part of me recognized the thing I now held in my palm.

A heart marker. My heart marker.

The very same one Gandalf stole so many years ago at Comic-Con.

William took a deep breath. "You made a joke about how rude I was for calling you a hobbit, and I realized you didn't recognize me—or you didn't want to, because Patrick was right there. But I figured it was the latter because you never called after Comic-Con."

Vulnerability crept into William's voice, onto his handsome features and into his soft, inviting posture. "I waited. I waited for this girl I fell in love with in the space of a few hours. This girl that exuded everything I needed, all packaged in a tiny hobbit costume." He ran a hand through his hair and turned away from me. "I waited for you to call, and you never did. So I thought I'd spare us the embarrassment." Turning to face me now, he chewed on his bottom lip. "You also had a boyfriend ... and then when you didn't, Shaun told me to stay away from you."

I turned the heart over in my hand, unable to process any of this. "I lost Gandalf's ... your ... number before I got home."

William fell onto the couch.

"It was gone," I stammered. "I searched every pocket in my bag, but your number was gone."

Leaning forward, he grabbed my wrist and guided me toward him. "But you wanted to call me?" His voice was almost inaudible.

I nodded. "I made my mom drive back. I made her help me search the parking lot because the venue was closed. The pamphlet you'd written it on was gone. I must have accidentally thrown it into the trash or it fell out of my bag. I don't know. It disappeared." I turned the heart around in my hand. Then, stepping between his knees, I held it out to him.

"Why are you giving this to me?"

I laughed as the words poured out of me. "Because you've had my heart all along."

"That's really cheesy." He smiled and took the marker, slipping it back into his pocket. "But I'll take it."

"I'm sorry I couldn't come up with anything better." I narrowed my eyes. "I'm busy processing all of this."

He pulled me onto his lap and kissed me, his hand gripping the back of my neck, deepening the kiss in a way that made my entire body clench and flutter. The memory of Gandalf—of William—kissing me while I wore this exact hobbit costume sent me into a state of euphoria.

"I can't believe you never realized," he whispered, his eyes holding mine.

I couldn't understand either. I wrapped my arms around his neck and studied his features—his nose, his lips, his eyes—while I pictured my Gandalf.

"You wore a wig and a beard!" I teased. "And you never gave me your name."

"I wanted to plant intrigue. I thought I was very cool at that age." His dimple emerged, deep and on show just for me.

"I can't believe this," I said, giggling and thinking I may never stop.

"And I can't believe you're wearing this." He kissed the tip of my nose.

"I also can't believe I went to your office wearing a hobbit costume that barely fits."

"Seriously?" William laughed, his chest vibrating against me, and I pushed closer. "Why did you come looking for me?"

"Why did you come looking for me?" I asked.

"I came begging. Don't marry Patrick." His voice was low and traveled to my very core. His dark eyes met mine as he repeated himself, this time enunciating each word. "Please don't marry Patrick."

"I already said no," I whispered.

"He's not perfect." William lifted a shaky hand to my chin and tilted my face until I had no choice but to look at him. "You're perfect, Rose. You're the only one who's perfect, and he doesn't deserve you."

"And you do?" My heart beat hard in my chest.

Please say yes.

William shook his head. "No."

My stomach twisted. If William hadn't been holding me firmly, I'd have turned away.

"No, I'm far from perfect. But, if you let me, I'll try." He leaned down, his nose brushing against mine. "I've been trying, and I wanted to make sure that I could be everything you wanted and deserved." His breath shook against my skin. "But I needed the time. And I wanted to prove to you, to me, to Shaun, that I am worthy of you and your love, Rose."

Unable to resist him any longer, I tilted my head up and captured his mouth with my own.

Sparks flew through me as our lips met, our souls reconnecting.

Something I'd dreamed of.

"Of course you're worthy." My breath was shaking, making it hard to talk, so I kissed him instead.

"I planned a whole presentation," he said, breaking away from the kiss. "But now you're dressed as the sexiest hobbit, and I'll admit, I'm a bit distracted by it."

"What do you mean? This is how I usually dress." I lifted my hands over my hot cheeks and giggled.

William laughed. Oh goodness—that laugh. I'd missed it so much.

"Your turn. Why'd you go looking for me tonight? Is it because you remembered?" He bit on his bottom lip. "Or . . . ?"

"I came begging too."

"Begging?" His lips pressed against my cheek and then slowly traveled along my jaw, pausing on the tiny mole before finding the lobe of my ear.

"I can't think clearly when your lips are touching me." I gasped as he nibbled at my ear.

Smiling against my skin, he slid his mouth back to mine. His voice thick and low against my lips, he said, "I need to know why you're in this costume, Rose."

I giggled, and he let out a frustrated groan.

All the blood rushed to my face as the next words fell out of me with ease, without fear, without wondering whether I was making a mistake. "I wanted to beg you to love me, William. Love me like I know I love you."

He leaned his forehead against mine, taking a moment before speaking. "You love me?"

I nodded. "I love you," I said and then said it again, enjoying how his face relaxed. "I love you so much, William. I have no doubt that you are my one chance at true love. Tell me you love me too?"

"Obviously, I love you. I have been loving you . . ." He lifted his mouth and kissed my forehead before pulling away a few inches and staring down at me. "Rose, I haven't stopped loving you, and I never will."

Round 39

William loved me.

And with that thought playing over and over in my mind, I wrapped myself around him, as tightly as physics would allow, before dipping my tongue into the divot of that dimple and exploring the deep groove. I gasped as he scooped me into his arms as though I weighed nothing at all.

"Where are we going?" I asked, and finally took in the empty apartment, the abandoned candles on the counter. "Where is everyone?"

"Not here. I don't know where they've gone, and to be honest, I don't care." He walked us to my bedroom. "I think we're ready for the next round." He shot me a sexy grin.

"We are?" I curled my arms around his neck and licked whatever part of him was closest. "What's the next round? Sex? Marriage? Are we having a baby?" I teased.

This elicited a low chuckle, his chest vibrating around me as he gently set me on the bed. "If I could marry you tonight, I would, but I can't. Do you know what I am very capable of doing with you right now?"

I bit down on my lip, buzzing with excitement. "What changed? What makes us ready?" I grabbed a handful of his shirt, pulling his lips to mine.

William climbed on top of me. A small moan escaped me as I spiraled in delight under his weight, his body pressed against mine.

"So much . . ." He lifted his head and gazed into my eyes. "But mostly, I wanted you to know the truth. It started feeling like a lie. This isn't just some fling for me . . . I wanted you to be sure of me, of us."

Reaching out, I stroked his strong jaw. "Beyond any doubt."

His mouth dropped to my neck, lighting me up everywhere he touched. "Why do hobbits wear so much clothing?" he growled.

I giggled, helping him unwrap and unbutton every item. He moved backward to stare at me, that smile bringing me more joy than anything. "You are so beautiful," he said, before pulling off his shirt in one quick motion.

Moving toward me, his gaze intent on my lips, he froze and pushed my hair away from my face. "Rose, I just . . . I want you to know it's been months since I've been with anyone in any way. I swear. Since the second we kissed. Before then, actually. Since the second I realized I may have a shot with you."

"Not even Stacey?"

He pulled a face of disgust that had me bursting into a fit of giggles.

"I'm sorry for doubting you. Shaun mentioned she came over, and I was . . . scared," I admitted. "Being loved by you, exclusively, seems too good to be true."

"Don't be sorry." He kissed my nose. "I'll be sure to love you in a way that'll leave no room for doubt."

"I love you too," I said, my hands finding the button on his jeans.

Now it was my turn to stare. I'd seen him bare-chested once before, but having his body so close, knowing it was mine to touch, left me breathless.

I gasped as he lifted me and flipped me onto my back before proving that no dream I've had of him would ever live up to the real thing.

"William," I breathed out his name until I completely unraveled. The light blurred above me, and my limbs became weightless.

Not finished with me yet, William kissed his way across my body before eventually moving back to my mouth. He kissed every part of me and made sure that I knew, beyond any doubt, that he loved all of it.

And then I was lost in the high of what lovemaking should feel like, of being loved by William. My hands pressing into his strong back, his hot mouth on my neck, his fingers finding mine and holding on as though letting go meant losing me.

In that moment, I knew, again and again and again, that I would love this man forever. And he would love me. And eventually, we collapsed in a tangle of limbs, damp with sweat and excitement.

"Rose." His breath was hot against my neck. "I can't believe you chose me."

I turned, weakness overwhelming my senses, and kissed one corner of his mouth. "Of course I did." I left another kiss on the opposite corner. "And I'll choose you every time." I pressed my full mouth against his.

He smiled against my lips, and I had a feeling he was resisting making a Pokémon joke.

I closed my eyes, enjoying the way my body felt, the looseness of my muscles, the heat between us. "If you'd told me you were my Gandalf, we could have saved a lot of time."

His pouty lips landed on mine once again. "I'm not the same person I was back then . . . I wanted you to love me as I am now."

"I do."

"Finally."

I turned onto my side and faced him, laying my hand on the back of his neck and playing with the dark hair at the nape. "What made you come here tonight? Why not last night? Why the wait?"

He hesitated before answering. "I've had to stop myself every day for the last few days. Every night. Every time I picked up my phone. But I wanted to have all the tools I needed for this round because, if you didn't love me, I was going to fight for you—beg for you. Rose, I needed to prove to you that I never meant to mess things up for you, and I didn't want to arrive with empty promises." His large hands traced my curves with such intent it made me blush.

"I resigned," I blurted out. "It wasn't because of what you did. I hated it there. You didn't cost me my job. Shaun had it mixed up."

William smiled, his expression loving, and I couldn't get enough of it. If I could bottle his smile, I would be able to solve all the world's problems.

"Why do you keep saying you'll ruin everything?" I asked.

"You'll meet the guy who can explain that to you at the wedding." He blew out a breath. "I'm the product of one of my dad's affairs. His punishment for committing adultery. At least that's what he says." William's voice softened. "He said my presence ruined things—everything."

The tremble of his mouth had my heart aching, and I wished I could take away some of his pain. I ran the back of my hand over his cheek. "Your dad sounds awful."

Taking my hand in his, he kissed my fingertips. "Depends on who you ask, I guess."

"I'm gonna trip him tomorrow."

William grinned.

"He's tall like you and Shaun, I suppose?"

He nodded.

"Good. The taller they are, the harder they fall. He won't even see me coming."

William laughed and pulled me close, and I curled into the shape of him.

"Maybe I should come to the wedding, even if it's only to see that."

I met his gaze once more, wanting him to look at me and believe me. "Before the game presentation, you also said you weren't good enough, and when you said it, I almost laughed at how ridiculous and incorrect it was. Because, William, you are the absolute best thing that has ever happened to me."

A soft breath escaped him and he leaned forward and kissed me. "Seeing as how I've ended up with you, I have to believe I'm worth something."

I melted against his lips. "Shaun would love for you to come. He hasn't filled the role of best man, either." I pulled away from the kiss and met his gaze with my own. "I'm not trying to pressure you."

"I want to be there for Shaun, and Neema. I want to see you in that dress." William sighed. It was as though I could see the gears turning in his mind. "I can't hide from him forever, I guess. I'll come on one condition."

"What?"

He kissed my nose. "That we do this again and again and again, and the morning before the wedding for some extra courage."

"I'm ready as soon as you are." I curled toward him.

William tugged the blanket up, covering us before wrapping an arm around my waist as if he were an extension of me. It felt that way. It felt like . . .

Home—something I'd never had.

Round 40

My phone blared from somewhere inside the apartment. Opening my eyes, I moved to answer it but found myself weighted down by a warm, heavy leg draped across my hips. I wiggled under William until I faced him and then kissed him until he stirred.

He cracked his eyes open partway, a smile already on his face. "Mmm. Now this is how I like to be woken up." Propping himself on one elbow, he furrowed his brows. "What's that sound?"

"My alarm. I forgot to turn it off now that I'm unemployed and all."

His frown gathered, and I smoothed it out with a kiss. He tilted his head and caught my lips with his.

When I eventually peeled myself away, I threw on the T-shirt he'd been wearing, enjoying his lingering scent as if I hadn't inhaled him all night long.

I ran to the living room, where I found my phone. I turned the alarm off, and my attention caught on his laptop. It was still open and laying sideways on the couch where he'd tossed it. I lifted it, thinking I'd take it to him, and the screen lit up with a spreadsheet titled Life Goals. My heart stilled.

It wasn't *my* Life Goals.

"I forgot about that." William towered behind me, pressing his bare chest against me while peeking over my shoulder.

My body fluttered at his nearness. "Will you tell me about this?"

"I was serious when I said that I want to be good enough for you." He lifted my chin and gazed down into my eyes. "I want to think about my future with you in it. I want Life Goals with you. I'm stepping up at work and have employed some of the other developers to help me with a game I've been working on for ages, and especially over the last few days." He swallowed, and his already flushed cheeks darkened. "Remember I said I had a presentation?"

I nodded, my focus turning to the spreadsheet. He'd created goals for himself, for me, and for *us*.

"I told you." Moving my dark hair to one side, he kissed my neck. "I'm going to be the best for you, because you are the best thing that has ever happened to me."

Taking the laptop, he dragged me back to bed, grabbing his mouse on the way. I snuggled as close to him as possible, dipping one of my hands in between his thighs to continue feeling his skin, his heat, and knowing I could do this because he wanted me to.

My cheek pressed against his side, I could feel his racing heart as he clicked through a file called Overpower. Confusion stirred within me as the program loaded.

It took a few minutes to start up, and William looked down at me with dark, furrowed brows. "It's not done. This is the most basic idea of it, but I wanted to show you first and get your input because . . . if you don't like it, then it won't make sense. It won't exist." His words left him in short, jagged bursts.

The screen lit up with the word "Overpower," and my breathing became very, very shallow.

William stared at me as I watched the game start. The opening screen showed the instructions, which were almost identical to the rule sheet we'd come up with. The next screen allowed us to choose a character.

"It's single player or multiplayer," he said, his voice thick. "Online or off-line." He cleared his throat as the game began, and I couldn't do anything except watch it unfold.

"We can change an-any-anything," he rambled. "I kinda ran with it because I was inspired." He caught my eyes with his own. "Rose, I love Overpower. I wasn't just saying that to impress you or whatever. I loved it when we first met all those years ago, and I love it even more now."

He wet his lips and focused his eyes on the screen as he played through some of the game with speech bubbles popping up to guide the character he'd chosen. "Stacey dropped off some demos I'd left at her place. I needed to reference one of them for the character design—which, you know, we never covered. I tried going from the things I knew you loved, so the enchanter is Gandalf-inspired, but not exactly—obviously. It also allows for original character creation, like in *The Sims*, which I know you stress-play at least once a year."

Lines crept onto his forehead as he focused on the screen. "It's got elements to maintain the board game feel, but I wanted it to be accessible as a video game, especially for gamers who don't have access to a rowdy group of friends who come by weekly."

I bit down on my lip, allowing my silent tears to fall. I didn't want to interrupt him. I didn't want him to stop playing. I saw elements that looked like they were inspired by *Lady of War* and even Haunted Thrones.

"I hope you don't mind—and I'm not trying to toot my own horn here—but I used some things from *Walk of Death* because you said it's one of your favorites."

"It is my absolute favorite," I squeaked out, my voice cracking.

William's gaze snapped down, and his hand flew up to wipe the wetness from my cheeks. He placed his lips at the corner of each eye, kissing away my tears. "Like I said, if you never want it to see the light of day, that's okay. I didn't make this with the intention of selling it. I made it for you. So that you could play your game whenever you wanted, wherever you wanted, and with whoever you wanted . . . or even on your own."

The pressure inside my chest grew with love, threatening to tear me apart. "William, I love it. I love *you*." Sniffling, I wiped away the fresh tears. "I want to play it with you. I want to play my entire life with you, but for now"—I swallowed the lump stuck in my throat—"will you play this for a while longer?"

"Do you want to try?"

I shook my head. "I like watching you play." I giggled. "Which is kind of how we got into this in the first place."

His frown fell away as he burst out laughing with a depth that both shook me and warmed me up. "You really like it? It's not very good right now. I know."

I pressed against him harder, and he swung one arm around me.

"I really like it," I assured him. "Do you?"

"I can't get enough of it. I've had to remind myself to pause and think and eat and like . . . text you."

I giggled. I'd accept his awful texting habits for this. "And . . . do you think other people would?" I let my hands trail across his chest, memorizing every part of him.

"Because I promised myself I would never disappoint you again, I've already spoken to the CEO of Thunderstruck. He said they'd be happy to produce it and keep me as the main developer, and you and I would have complete creative control—provided we give them a cut of the profits."

A jolt of electricity struck through me, and I sat upright. "Are you serious?"

"Rarely, but in this case, I am." He turned to face me, setting the laptop aside, and I wanted to reach for it. I wasn't done watching him play. "Rose, again, I don't want to pressure you into this. I don't want any financial gain from this."

His dark brows hugged, and I reached across him and grabbed the laptop. I wiggled into his arms and opened his Life Goals spreadsheet before adding another entry:

```
Rose and William develop the video game for
Overpower together.
```

"I want Overpower to be played. I want it to be enjoyed. I spent a lifetime creating these characters, their goals, and this world." I handed the laptop back to him. "I guess video games win after all."

"Hold on, I'm not done with my presentation."

"There's more?"

"With Thunderstruck's interest, Fun&Games said they would be willing to invest in the production of a board game after the release of the video game. But they want to meet with you."

My mouth fell open. "When did you get time to do all this?"

"When I asked you for it." He kissed me. "Did you honestly think there was anything else in the world that would keep me from telling you that I love you, Rose? I loved you back then, and I love you now. I loved you when you weren't mine to love."

I slid my hand behind his head and into his hair, tugging him down to my mouth.

"I was always yours to love."

Round 41

My phone buzzed with a text message, and I glanced at it quickly before turning back to William.

"Neema is on her way back," I whispered to him.

"I should go see my brother about a wedding happening tomorrow." William climbed out of bed and waited beside the edge until I crawled straight into his embrace.

My arms tight around his neck, he lifted me, and I unashamedly wrapped my legs around his waist, squeezing and enjoying the little breath that escaped him.

"But I should shower before I see Shaun, and you should probably shower before you see Neema." He ran his tongue over his bottom lip, his eyes devouring me like a starved man.

"Maybe we should shower together, for time efficiency?"

He nodded, his expression serious. "It's water-wise too."

I giggled, and his lips landed on mine, sealing our mouths together in a scorching kiss. He walked us into the bathroom and, without setting me down, turned on the water.

His lips slid along my jaw, tasting as he went.

My eyes met his as I lifted off my shirt and tossed it to the floor a second before he stepped under the running water. Our breaths mingled with the hot steam as he kissed me, waking up every cell in my body. He glanced down at me, his eyes glimmering, and that smile I craved flashed across his handsome face.

"If I can dedicate the rest of my life to making you happy, then I'd have won," he whispered.

I knew one thing for sure: If loving were a game, William was the best at it.

After a million goodbye kisses, William dragged himself out of my apartment. Racing to my bedroom, I rushed to get ready before Neema arrived. After our shower, I'd opened my texts and found another message from her letting me know she and my parents had spent the night at a fancy hotel, courtesy of William's credit card, and they would arrive any moment.

The front door flew open, revealing an excited Neema.

"You're getting married!" I exclaimed.

"And you and William finally hooked up!" she squealed back.

My jaw dropped in horror.

She laughed. "Don't worry, your parents are downstairs."

"I'm so sorry it's all happening so close to the wedding." I covered my face with both hands. "I should have timed it better."

Before Neema could answer, my phone buzzed.

And then it buzzed a second time.

And again.

Neema grabbed it and glanced at the screen. "Oh my goodness! It's William, and he's being romantic!"

I clawed my phone from her fingers, my heart swelling as I read the messages.

William: I love you.

William: And I already miss you.

William: Last night was the best night of my life.

William: And this morning was the best morning of my life.

"You have to tell me everything in the next three seconds before your mom and her seven hundred bags make it up here."

"He's coming to the wedding." I smiled, not sure if I was smiling to myself or at her. I only knew I was smiling and may never stop.

"Oh, damn! So, you have that magic going on where, after sex, you can convince men to do whatever you want them to?"

I punched her lightly on the arm.

"I can't believe you're in love with my almost brother-in-law," she said. "We'll be sisters someday."

My mother arrived at that moment and squeezed the air out of me. "Hello, baby. Please thank William for a wonderful night with a private room so your father and I didn't have to worry about your no-hanky-panky rule."

I shut my eyes and groaned.

My mom took her seat at the table and continued with the candles. Eventually, my dad joined. I bit back a grin at the number of bags he carried. So. Many. Bags. No one ever knew why my mother packed so much, and I wondered why she'd needed all of them for one night at the hotel.

I pulled Neema into my bedroom and spent our last day in our apartment together talking about the things and people we loved, in far more detail than anyone else would be willing to listen to.

The following morning, the sky was bluer than usual—as blue as Shaun's eyes—and my heart melted knowing my best friends would have the perfect wedding day. Then it melted again, knowing I would see William, and not any William, but William in that suit. The William who loved me while wearing that suit.

My William.

After we arrived at the venue and my parents and Neema went inside, I stayed behind and unpacked the car with the help of a few waitstaff who carried it up to Neema's "get ready room."

A strong pair of arms wrapped around my waist. Dropping his lips against my neck, William left tiny kisses on my skin.

"You should know, I'm not hiding this from anyone ever again," he whispered.

I spun around and pulled his head to mine, our lips meeting as if it was the most natural thing in the world. As if we'd been doing it for years.

"Ah, William!" my mother called out.

I jumped away so quickly I fell into the trunk of the car. William shifted and offered me an arm as my mom approached.

"Hi, Mrs. Jones." William smiled, but his voice was laced with nervousness. "I'm William Ashdern, yes. It's nice to meet you in person."

"Mom." I ran to her and whispered in her ear, "He's Gandalf! He's actually Gandalf. My Gandalf."

Her eyes flashed with excitement, and she pulled him in for a tight hug. "I knew you two would find each other again."

I grinned and left William still wrapped in my mother's hug, knowing that if I waited for her to release him, I might miss the entire wedding.

Reaching the get ready room, I opened the door and let out a gasp of excitement upon seeing Neema. Two women were simultaneously working on her hair and makeup.

The woman applying Neema's makeup looked up at me. "Are you the maid of honor?"

I nodded, still unable to find my words.

"Sit. We're doing you next, and you have a lot of hair to work with." They bounced from Neema to me.

Claire burst through the door, slightly disheveled but beautiful in a navy-blue wrap dress. She threw her arms around Neema in a tight hug but was shooed away by the makeup and hair duo as she approached me.

"I'm starting to feel nervous about everything going according to plan." Neema paced the length of the room. "Tell me more about William—it's the perfect distraction."

"William?" Claire said with a little hop.

"William." I sighed his name and blushed.

"She slept with William!" Neema yelled.

"Shh!" My face flamed. "Not so loud. The wedding guests will hear you."

"When?" Claire eyed me, her jaw dropping wide. She whacked me on the knee. "And why didn't you tell me?"

I laughed.

The makeup artist huffed.

Neema snorted.

"I'll tell you everything another time." I widened my eyes in a way I hoped said, *Not now!* I was already on the makeup artist's last nerve.

Neema took my hand and gave it a gentle squeeze. "I'm so happy for you—and for me. This definitely means we'll see you all the time."

Claire and Neema went behind one of the dressing screens, and as soon as my hair and makeup were complete, I took the other. I slipped on my coral dress and ran my hands over the fabric as I glanced at my reflection in the mirror. To my surprise, I loved the way the color highlighted my black hair and how the high neckline covered enough skin while accentuating my generous curves, leaving me not at all self-conscious. I extended my leg and admired the slit traveling all the way to my thigh. It showed off my best assets while hiding areas I was less comfortable exposing. It was perfect, but my best friend chose it for me. I should have known.

I stepped out from behind the screen, and my breath hitched upon seeing Neema in her wedding gown. She was stunning and radiated so much joy that I understood why she'd wanted none of us to see her dress before this day. The white-beaded lace decorated her dark brown skin, contrasting beautifully against her complexion as though it belonged there. The entire effect was too gorgeous for words.

At that same moment, a light knock sounded at the door, and William entered. My heart spiraled into joy as though dancing for his attention.

"Hey, gorgeous." He smiled at me, and I suffered under his compliment, trying to keep my face still, but it was impossible.

He turned his attention to Neema. "You look lovely, sis. And uhm . . . Shaun's ready whenever you are."

"I'm ready," she replied with a sureness I now fully understood.

As if reading my mind, William winked at me. "See you in a minute."

My heart went into a full-on flutter as he left the room. I grinned, remembering that flutter would be dealt with later.

Round 42

We readied ourselves at the back of the aisle in preparation for the wedding ceremony. William stood at my side and offered me his arm. I took it, and using every piece of concentration in my brain, managed to walk down the aisle without tripping, without looking up at those dark eyes, and without melting at the thought of the last couple days and the rest of forever.

We reached the front, where Shaun stood ready to receive his bride, his expression soft and nervous but full of love. He beamed at William as he took his position beside him.

The music stopped, and the classic piano piece Neema had chosen played the opening chords. The guests twisted in their seats, each hoping to catch the first glimpse of the bride. Seconds later, she stepped into view. A collective gasp echoed through the room as she walked down the aisle, her ivory gown shimmering in the sunlight, and it was clear that her happiness captured the hearts of everyone, leaving us all awed at her beauty and grace.

Watching my two best friends declare their love for each other was something I would never forget.

Following the ceremony, we sat down for dinner, and I couldn't stop myself from searching the crowd for the man who supposedly looked like an older Shaun. I found him— staring at me. Or not directly at me, but in my direction at the person beside me. William.

William followed my gaze, and his eyes met his father's. His breath hitched, and his body stiffened. When the older man gave him a pained expression, I stood and pulled William away and out of the line of fire.

While I avoided conflict, a heat in my chest sprung to defend the man I loved.

"I'm a big boy," William said, his tone bitter as he gently released my hand, which was clutching onto his jacket sleeve. "I can handle myself."

"No doubt you can. But you're going to have to get used to me loving you, which means you'll never have to handle yourself."

William shot me a provocative look, pulling his bottom lip between his teeth. "Oh yeah?"

My hands shot up to my warm face. "That sounded a lot more suggestive than I had planned."

He smiled at me, but there was a sadness lingering in the soft lines on his face.

"It's not fair." I ground my teeth in frustration. "You didn't choose to be conceived. There were two consenting parties, and you weren't one of them."

"He used to say, when he looked at me, all he saw was his mistake; and his wife only saw his infidelity. As did everyone else, including his patients, their family, and their friends." A shadow moved behind his eyes, weighing down his features. "When my mom died and my gran couldn't take care of me anymore, she sent me to him. I nearly ruined his life, his reputation, and his marriage."

I blinked back tears and placed my palm on his cheek. "It's not your fault."

His expression relaxed under my touch before hardening once again. Turning around, my body straightened with anger as Shaun approached with their father following closely behind.

Face flushed, Shaun raised a warning eyebrow at his father. "Tell William what you told me."

The older man—exactly the same height as Shaun but shorter than William—cleared his throat before lowering his gaze to his feet. "William, I've been meaning to talk to you—to apologize."

William barely breathed.

"I . . . I went out of my way to be here, not only to see Shaun get married, but because I assumed it would be the only place I could see you." He gazed at William through the same dark eyes I'd grown to love.

"You didn't deserve my anger . . . or the way I treated you. It wasn't fair," he continued. "But your arrival threw my life upside down. Belinda wanted to leave, and Shaun suddenly had a brother he wanted to get to know. And everyone—every person who met you—knew I'd cheated on my wife." He inhaled a deep breath. "It was easier to send you away, to blame you. When you weren't around, we could pretend I hadn't messed up, and I wasn't the one at fault. But I was at fault—entirely. I couldn't even blame your mother." He tugged at his collar and breathed quickly. "She had no idea I was married."

The Adam's apple in William's throat jumped.

Shaun jabbed his father with his elbow, his expression hard. "And?"

William's father blew out another breath. "And I'm so sorry for all the awful things I made you believe about yourself. You don't ruin things. You don't spread misery—I did all that on my own. And judging by how close you and Shaun are, despite my efforts to keep the two of you apart, I realize I've missed out on years of joy we could have shared."

Shaun crossed his arms over his chest, his eyes darting between his brother and their father.

"I don't expect you to forgive me today, or ever," their father continued. "But I wanted to tell you I've been in therapy, and Belinda and I have worked through a lot of this. But you. I have so many regrets when it comes to the way I treated you. William, you are more of a man than I will ever be, and I am so sorry that I made you feel like you weren't good enough."

Having said his piece, he turned to leave but stopped as William spoke in the quietest voice.

"Thank you," William whispered.

I wasn't sure if his words were meant for his father or his brother, but William's father took them for himself.

Turning back toward William, he took a step forward and placed a hand on his shoulder, giving it a gentle pat.

A smile spread across Shaun's face, and he pulled his father and brother into his embrace.

After a moment, Shaun pulled away and swiped at his wet cheeks. "William, Rose: in you get. It's almost time for your speeches."

With a subtle nod at his father and brother, William weaved our fingers together and pulled me with him. As we walked away, I looked up at him, and he smiled down at me, his eyes shiny and red-rimmed. Pulling him to a stop, I stood on tip-toes and kissed him on the cheek.

"I love you," I whispered. "You okay?"

He grinned. "True love's kiss really works."

I bit my bottom lip. "You do the opposite of causing me misery."

"Oh, I am well aware." His sexy dimple popped in his cheek.

I threw a gentle punch, but he caught me and pulled me into an embrace.

Safe in the warmth of his arms and secure in his love for me, I looked up at him. "Dudley from Fun&Games called to set up a meeting for next week."

"Seriously?"

I nodded. "Because of all the lovely things you said about me when you met with them."

William blushed. He was cute when he blushed. "All true. What else did he say?"

"Not much, but it felt suspiciously like it would be an interview. They asked when I'd be receiving my MBA and admitted that they had stalked me on LinkedIn and were kind of impressed with what they found."

"Because you're very impressive."

"Stop it."

"You are." He pinched my chin between his thumb and forefinger. "You're brave and smart and funny, and somehow, you find the time to help everyone. You're there for anyone who needs you. You're incredible."

If he wasn't holding me up, I'd melt away.

His lips pressed against my forehead. "You'd be a perfect fit there."

"I don't want to get ahead of myself. I'll start the job hunt next week too. Once I can survive without being glued to your hip."

He laughed and then pulled me against his chest. My heart felt as though it doubled in size.

Lifting my hands to his lips, he kissed the backs of my knuckles. "Now come on, we have speeches to prepare for."

William took the mic at the podium and cleared his throat. "Hello. For those of you who don't know, I'm William." He paused, his gaze going to his father, who was seated near the front.

The older man smiled at him.

"William Ashdern." He cleared his throat. "I, uh . . . I wrote a really long and heartfelt speech, but I recently found out Shaun and Neema read it when I wasn't looking. So I won't be delivering it."

He winked at Shaun, who moaned and covered his face guiltily.

William continued. "What I will say is this: Shaun and Neema were made for each other, and I have no doubt they'll have a long and happy marriage." His hand tightened around mine as he pulled me closer and gazed down at me. "And there's nothing I can say that she can't say better. So let me introduce you to my favorite person in the entire universe, our very own, beautiful, hobbit cheerleader, Rose."

He handed the mic to me, and my heart shook. I'd prepared for this, but I hadn't prepared for William to introduce me like that. I was enjoying the lightness in his eyes and his big smile.

"Thank you, William." I turned to the guests. "Hi, yes . . . I'm Rose, the maid of honor, and I'm pleased to be celebrating this day with all of you. When your best friend gets married, it kind of feels like your own wedding. When your best friend is marrying your other best friend, it means you don't sleep from the moment they get engaged until right about now. So, if you find me asleep in the corner after this, don't be alarmed. But please remember to use your inside voice."

A few people in the audience chuckled.

"Jokes aside, look at them. Like, really look. How beautiful are they? Shaun and Neema are two of the most wonderful people I have ever met, and I wish them nothing but the best."

Neema reached up and squeezed my hand.

The next few words weren't planned, but they poured out of me anyway.

"Not too long ago, I resigned from a job that didn't suit me. But it was also a job that brought Shaun into my life, and more importantly, it brought these two together. Knowing this, I'd go through that struggle over and over again if I knew it would end where we are today, with the two of them falling in love." I looked down at my two best friends. "I love you both."

"We love you," they shouted in unison.

Shaun stood, kissed me on the cheek, and whispered in my ear, "Mind if I say a few words?"

I passed him the mic.

Shaun smiled out at his guests. "Thank you all for coming to celebrate with us. I'm the luckiest man in the world. I married the girl of my dreams, but I also have the best brother and friend to thank for pulling this all together." He smiled at William and me. "So, how about a round of applause for these two, who spent hours upon hours on our balcony, coming up with ways to perfect our wedding day."

Blood rushed to my cheeks as William doubled over with laughter. Neema couldn't help herself, either, and burst into giggles.

He wasn't wrong. It was perfect.

Epilogue

What are you still doing here?" Dudley asked, feigning anger as he walked into my office. "You put in leave for half a day. Go home."

I looked up from my laptop. "I'll be out in a minute. I want to finish this report and type up next week's newsletter."

It was a little bit ironic that I now compiled newsletters as part of my job after finally clearing out my inbox.

He shook his head. "No, it's after five. Go home. You've been here for a month, and you've already accumulated more overtime than the rest of us. This isn't M&G."

I clicked the save icon a few times. "I know. That's why I'm still here."

He offered me a warm smile and turned on his heel. "See you on Monday."

I packed up my things from my new desk in my small, but private, office. A pack of basic medical supplies from Claire and Dean sat on the corner. A Bulma figurine from Lincoln stood beside it. Neema and Shaun framed a photo of the seven of us at their wedding, and next to my screen, where I could glance at it all day, was the heart marker stuck against a photo of William.

William.

Even after all these months, the mere thought of him had me smiling. I took out my phone and typed a text to him.

Rose: Be home soon. Love you, x.

He replied with a kissing emoji. He still wasn't particularly good at texting, but he was getting better.

After rushing home, I opened the door and found William at his PC, clicking furiously. He cursed, completely unaware I'd entered.

I dropped my bag on the floor and walked up behind his wide back, wrapping my arms around his neck and kissing his cheek. "Hey."

He grunted and triple-clicked the close icon before twisting around and giving me one of his spine-tingling kisses. All the anger he'd exhibited toward the game disappeared from his gorgeous face.

"How was work?" he asked.

"Fun, as usual. How was it for you?"

He nodded. "I worked on Overpower more than anything else. I made some progress, wanna see?"

I sat on his lap, and he spun us around to face his screen. "Okay . . ." He opened the game that got better every time I left him alone with it.

I had thought it was impossible to have levels of love, yet the feeling I had for William grew every day. I may explode.

When he finished his demonstration, William grinned up at me. "That's all we've got so far, but we're scheduled for a release about a year from now, almost to the day."

My bones tickled with excitement. "And Fun&Games are on board."

He laughed. "Nice pun."

I shook my head with a giggle and slid off his lap before pulling him to his feet. "We're going to be late for game night. Let's go!"

He stood and made his way to the bathroom. "I need to shower and pack."

"William! I've already made us late. We don't have time."

He popped his head out of the bathroom. "I know, I'm teasing. Bags are on the couch. I just needed my shampoo. Catch!"

I caught the shampoo, and my senses filled with the scent of rosemary and lavender.

"Hey, my love?" I called.

He lifted the bags and swung them over one shoulder. "Yeah?"

"Do you know your hair smells like rosemary? It's my signature scent," I teased.

He shook his head at me and laughed. "No, don't even start."

"Is it because you were pining for me?" I asked, following him to his car.

"Complete coincidence. I'm not that creepy." He tossed our bags into the trunk. "I only kept a plastic heart for years and hoped I'd find the perfect moment to confess my love to the girl of my dreams, but that's all."

"Oh, yeah. No big deal."

I leaned in for a kiss, which he happily received. Was it normal to feel so content?

Climbing into his car together, we drove to the place where it all began.

"It will never not be weird knocking at this door," William said before pounding his fist against Shaun and Neema's door.

Neema answered and threw her arms around me. "You made it."

"Of course. I wouldn't miss game night." I sauntered in as if I lived there, even though I never had.

Shaun came around the corner and pulled me into a hug. "Hey, you. How's work? Do you have a new work best friend yet?"

"No. Still you."

"Good." He released me from the hug, and we made our way to the couch. "So, I wanted to tell you, Markham's gone."

A sigh of relief escaped me. I thought being away from him would take him off my mind, but he was still there, and as Shaun's words sunk in, I finally kicked him out.

"And I got promoted," he announced.

"Way to go!" I cheered.

"I mean, it's because you're not there." He shrugged. "But still."

"You deserve it. You love it there."

"So how is work?" Shaun asked.

William threw himself onto the couch. It was almost as if he'd never left this place.

My face broke into a smile. "Work is great."

"Great is an understatement." William smiled at me. "She literally talks about it in her sleep."

"Okay, fine. I love it. And they give me all these free games. I have a surprise for game night." I rushed over to my overnight bag and dug out a game box, holding it up. "Kaleidoscope!"

Shaun laughed. "Oh my. No, it feels wrong. We shouldn't be supporting it."

"That's what I said." William scowled.

"Oh, come on! It won, and it's my turn to pick a game, so deal with it." I moved over to where William was already sitting.

He draped his arm across my shoulders. "Who else is joining?"

"Claire and Lincoln, and get this," Neema said to William and then turned toward me. "Dean."

We all made "ooooh" sounds, having not had Dean over for game night in years.

"It does mean Hannah is coming along, but that's okay with us, you?" Neema asked, and William and I shrugged.

I leaned closer to William. "Do you want kids?"

"Of course," he whispered. "But no more than seven—or six if you want to play along. My Xbox only takes eight controllers."

He laughed, and his warm breath tickled my ear. He pulled me up and out to the balcony where it had all begun. In less than a second, he had me sandwiched against the railing, kissing me until I couldn't see straight.

"Remember this?" he whispered when he finally let me take a breath.

Wrapping my arms around his neck, I stood on tiptoes to kiss him but giggled instead.

"What?" he asked, amused by my laughter.

"I'm so happy we ended up here."

"On this balcony?"

"Together."

He smiled wider and then pressed his lips against my cheek before moving them over my mouth, down my neck, across my chest, and finally to my stomach as he lowered himself toward the floor.

I tugged on him, trying to pull him back up. He didn't budge. Instead, he remained where he was, kneeling in front of me.

"What are you doing?" I asked.

He laughed that laugh—that damned laugh that made my chest swell with love again, before his expression changed to soft adoration. "What do you think?"

My heart pounded as I admired his dark eyes looking up at me, his perfect nose. I pushed his hair back.

He leaned into it, like a cat, before slipping his hand into his pocket and removing a ring box. "I've been carrying this around with me, waiting for the perfect moment."

My knees went weak, and I slid to the ground, collapsing onto him.

"Let me finish," he said, stroking my back.

But I was already curling into his chest, my body saying yes to a question that hadn't been asked.

"I know we haven't been officially dating for a long time, but I have no doubt that I am meant to spend my life with you."

I nuzzled even closer. If I looked into those eyes, I might not find my voice to yell the answer I had planned. "William," I managed.

"Rose, the absolute love of my life, will you marry me?"

I burst into a fit of giggles. "I had it scheduled for three months from now. I was going to start hinting next week." My eyes welled with tears.

"I know. I wanted to beat you to it. I know how excited it makes you to tick something off early." He pressed his mouth against mine and nibbled at my lips.

My heart felt like it would take flight.

"So, will you make me the ultimate winner by saying yes and marrying me?"

I nodded, unable to find the right word. Something bigger than *yes*. Something bigger than forever.

Even if life was a game, with the right person, it was worth playing.

Acknowledgments

I would like to start off by thanking my parents for always supporting my writing even though neither of them read the genres I write in (which might be a good thing in this case!). They are always in my corner. They knew I was a geek and obsessed with all these silly things they didn't understand, but that never stopped them from letting me enjoy what I wanted. And of course, with my family, comes my sisters, who believe I can do anything. (They're wrong, so wrong, but it's nice knowing they think so.)

Next, to my husband: I wouldn't be able to write romance if I didn't know what loving and being loved felt like.

To my beautiful daughter, I just love you so much. I will love you forever and wherever.

Cathie, my agent, thank you for believing in this story when I was on the brink of giving up on it. Thank you for your feedback, for your enthusiasm, and for loving Rose and William as much as I do. I could literally never have done this without you.

Alex, thank you for seeing the spark in this and for being such a wonderful editor. And to the rest of the team at Forever, I will always be grateful that you've given me and my stories a chance.

Yumna, my number one since day one. Thank you for introducing me to rom-coms when my life felt like it was falling apart. They inspired me to read more and write, and this was the idea that came to mind, and you were all too happy to support it.

Nuhaa. Whew. Where do I start with you? You were one of the first people to read what was called *Let's Play* at the time. Your love for William, your fan-casting, your vision boards, and your solid belief that this needed to be in the world is the reason it is. This book should be dedicated to you.

Kelly, when I sent you this manuscript, you disappeared for about nine hours and then sent me the longest texts, and we immediately became friends. No backsies.

Zoë, my gorgeous girl, we knew that we were meant to be friends.

Rushdiyah and Zaid, the power couple whom I adore. Thank you for the motivation and for reassuring me that it's work people need to see.

Shadley, Kervyn, and Darryn, thank you for explaining games and game development to me. I really do love *The Sims* and *Stardew Valley*, but that's as far as it goes.

Katie Erin and Katie Rose (Erin Rose) and Soniya: Your feedback made my writing so much stronger. Thank you.

Amanda and Kauthar, your comments gave me life. They're here! They're finally here!

Ray, you are so incredibly talented, and the character art you gave me is perfection. My first piece of Rolliam fanart.

I'd hate to forget anyone. If I do, I am so sorry. Off the top of my head, these are the names that come to mind: Jamy, Tams, Rebecca, Samantha, Zayaan, Jamie, Raff, Aaqilah, Nadine, Keisha, Tanith, Simone, Musa, Andrea, Cassey, Bhavna, Chante, Emily, Fatima, Jenni, Kate, Linnea, Michelle,

Missa, Jacqui, Zarmeen, Muneera, Munira, Naeema, Robyn, Sara, Tanveer, Wesley, Zaakira, Zana, Jahni, Juwie, Lana, Ilhaam, FZ, Suvania, Juan, Craig, Khalida, Fahmida, and so many more. If I missed you, please tell me, and I'll definitely remember for the next one.

Thank you to all my family, cousins, and friends, for the constant love and encouragement.

Weird as it might be, I also want to acknowledge myself. Some days were harder than others. This book was born during a difficult time, and it kept me going.

By the blessings of the Almighty, I've done it.

I hope this book is a comfort to you, the readers, as it was for me. And as with anything I write: Don't try this at home ☺.

About the Author

Shameez Patel was born and raised in Cape Town, South Africa. She lives there with her husband, child, and two cats named Turbo and Charger. During the day, she juggles her time between parenting her daughter and working as an engineer, but at night, she escapes to new worlds that always have someone to fall in love with. Shameez became obsessed with fiction, especially fantasy fiction, at a young age. Her parents fondly recall receiving her first handwritten story before the age of ten, titled "The Treasures of Zombie Island," which surprisingly featured no zombies at all. She has been writing ever since.